CRUSHER

niall leonard

CRUSHER

doubleday canada

Doubleday Canada and colophon are registered trademarks.

Library and Archives of Canada Cataloguing in Publication is available upon request.

ISBN: 978-0-385-67928-2

Permissions are pending for "Pegasus" by Patrick Kavanagh
and "Sweet Thames Flows Softly" by Ewan MacColl.

Crusher is a work of fiction. Names, characters, places and incidents are products
of the author's imagination or are used fictitiously. Any resemblance to actual events
or locales or persons, living or dead, is entirely coincidental.

Printed and bound in the USA

Published in Canada by Doubleday Canada,
a division of Random House of Canada Limited

Visit Random House of Canada Limited's website: www.randomhouse.ca

10 9 8 7 6 5 4 3 2 1

For Erika

I have spread my dreams under your feet

one

It was a bit early for someone to be banging on the front door. I hurried down the stairs, hair still dripping from the shower, and turned the latch.

"Sorry, son, locked myself out," said Dad, shivering as he stepped in. He'd been out in his slippers, I noticed. I wondered why, until I saw the TV trade mag folded in his hand, and my heart sank.

Dad looked pretty rough. His pale blue eyes were red-rimmed and his fair hair was standing up in spikes that weren't dishevelled or trendy, but made him look like he'd slept in a doorway. I'd heard him come home late last night and stumble around trying not to make a noise, crashing into the furniture and cursing under his breath. But he'd got up the same time he always did, while I was out running, and the breakfast he'd made was still warm on the table: old eggs, thin salty bacon and instant coffee, white. I'd nab a glass of orange juice when I got to work, though the most orange thing about the stuff we sold was its colour.

"Bollocks," said my dad, squinting through his crooked glasses at the magazine's first inside page. That hadn't taken long.

"What's up?"

"Bill Winchester's got a second series of that time-travelling cop show. Jammy sod."

"*Future Perfect*?"

My dad gave a look as if I was being disloyal.

"Never seen it." I shrugged. "I've heard of it, that's all."

"Me and Bill worked together years ago, on *Henby General*."

"Yeah, you said." But he didn't say it very often.

Dad had been big in the early nineties. For a while he was everyone's favourite twinkly-eyed Irish actor— he'd even won an award for *Best Newcomer*. The bronze statuette still stood on the mantelpiece, gathering ironic dust. From then on it had all been downhill. He didn't keep the statuette on display out of nostalgia or vanity— it was there to fuel his envy. Envy keeps you hungry, Dad would say, which I'd never understood, because I was hungry all the time and I'd never got to like it. But all Dad's old acting mates were doing better than him. If it had been true that every time a friend succeeds a little part of you dies, by now my dad would have been a really ripe zombie.

He saw himself as a passionate, committed and challenging performer. Directors soon got to see him as temperamental, pig-headed and impossible to work with. The jobs had already started to dry up when he met my mother, and his last role had been years ago, eating imaginary pizza on a desert island in a commercial, for insurance, I think . . . it might have been for pizzas, or desert islands. He never officially retired, but he grew a beard and stopped going to auditions and quit pestering his agent for work.

He wasn't going to wait for the phone to ring, he said. He was going to make his own luck. He was going to write a TV epic so gripping and authentic that producers would be ripping each other's throats out to make it, and he'd write a really good part for himself, so they'd have to cast him. Not the lead, of course—he had to be realistic, he said. The lead could go to one of his more famous old mates, to help get the show commissioned. He had it all worked out. He'd had it all worked out for years now, and it never seemed to happen.

"Don't sweat it, Dad. You always say success is the best revenge."

"Yeah, but I might be wrong," said Dad. "Maybe the

best revenge is cutting someone's head off with a rusty saw. Maybe I should try that instead."

I carried our empty plates out to the kitchen to wash up.

"So what are you doing today?" I said, more out of politeness than interest.

"Working," he said.

Dad used the term loosely. A lot of his work seemed to consist of staring out the window. He had read every book on writing screenplays the local library could scrape together, and he was always quoting aphorisms and mottos about inspiration and perspiration and pants being applied to the seat of a chair, and he always wrote ten pages a day. The only problem was, next day he'd tear up nine of them. Some days he'd go traipsing round London doing "research," and the notes and jottings and cuttings would pile up on the dining table beside his laptop, and over dinner he'd try to tell me about his latest story idea, but I'd stopped listening long ago.

"You wouldn't believe the stuff I heard last night," said Dad. "London gangland is like the court of Caligula—they're all stabbing each other in the back. That's the real drama, and it's right under our noses, and nobody ever wants to hear about it." Then why the hell are you writing about it? I thought. But I didn't say it. The best thing about Dad was his eternal optimism. Someday, with a lot of effort and a little luck, he'd be rich and famous, and we wouldn't have to scrape by on his shrinking royalty payments and my minimum wage from Max Snax.

"You want me to bring something back for dinner?" I said.

"Nah," said Dad. "I'll probably go down the shops later." He wouldn't go into the shops, I knew, until he'd checked the skips outside for ready meals chucked out after their sell-by date. He'd serve them up with a sermon about the evils of the consumer society and the wastage it produced. I used to think, if wastage keeps us in dinners, I'm all for it.

"You know where the spare keys are?" asked Dad as I laced up my trainers.

"Hanging up," I said. "Rough night?"

"Never mind," said Dad. "Mine will turn up."

"I'll see you later, yeah?" I rose to go, expecting his routine grunted goodbye, but he put the magazine down and looked at me.

"Finn?" he said. "We're all right, aren't we? You and me?"

All right? How were we all right? I was an illiterate dropout with no GCSEs stuck in a dead-end job, and he was an ex-nobody who spent his days writing a script that would never be finished and that no one would ever want to read anyway.

"Yeah, Dad, sure. I have to go."

"See ya," said Dad.

I pulled the door shut behind me, jogged a short distance to warm up, then started to run.

"Yeah, I want the Texas Chicken Special, no salad, no sauce, none of that."

"What, just chicken and bread?"

"Yeah."

He was about five foot tall and five foot round the middle, and I could see why. I always used to wonder how guys like Mr. Spherical kept their trousers up—were their belts stapled to their stomachs? Anyway, without the sauce it wasn't a Texas Chicken Special, it was just fried chicken in pappy white bread, but I wasn't there to quibble with the customers about what the stuff was called, I was there to sell it to them. And smile. And say thank you. "Smiles and thanks—money in the bank!" Andy used to recite that at our weekly pep talks. He was fond of morale-boosting slogans, and thought he had a knack for coining them, but his own were even crappier than the ones on the Max Snax staff training videos.

I punched the order into the programmed till and

handed Mr. Spherical his change. Jerry in the kitchen slid the foil-wrapped package into the chute while I filled a litre beaker with half a litre of ice followed by half a litre of fizzy aerated syrup, wondering for the thousandth time how anyone could consider this chemically reconstituted muck to be food, and how I'd ended up selling it. I pushed the thoughts aside for the thousandth time, but they kept flopping back into my mind, like an annoying greasy fringe you can't cut off getting into your eyes. And it was only bloody Monday.

Hands on automatic, mind anywhere else but here, bish, bosh, sandwich, regulation single paper napkin, drink, tray, deep breath, stab at a smile, recite the fast-food blessing: "Thank you, sir, and enjoy—have a great day." The tubby punter grunted, turned and waddled off to the door, turned round again and bumped out backwards, into the bright April morning that I was pissing away behind this overheated counter in this sweaty polyester shirt.

"Yo, Maguire!" hissed Jerry from the kitchen. "Thanking time is wanking time!" Not quite the approved formula, but he had the Max Snax high-pitched, hysterical delivery down pat. I didn't mind Jerry. He was almost bearable, as long as you didn't try having an actual conversation with him. You couldn't look him in the eye, anyway—either he had curvature of the spine or he spent too much time bent over computer porn, jerking off. Andy wouldn't let him serve the customers, insisting that I gave a better impression of Max Snax. If I did, it was because I ran ten kilometres a day and never ate anything we sold, but I didn't say that to Andy. I flicked Jerry a cheery middle finger. He sniggered and ducked back towards the fryers, while I cursed myself.

How could I have forgotten about the CCTV? Andy had cameras all over the joint, concealed under little black plastic domes, most of them pointed at the staff rather than the punters. I used to wonder why Andy had gone into catering, when he didn't like people. He disliked the punters on a casual basis, but he made a full-time job of despising the staff. That was why he stayed in his office all day, watching us all through CCTV monitors. He wanted to check we weren't stealing the fries or sneaking off to the bogs to smoke a spliff, but he wouldn't join us on the floor to do that. Instead, he would sit poised in front of his six fuzzy monitors, waiting until he spotted an infraction of one of the hundreds of "suggestions" that made up the Max Snax Code of Conduct. Then his office door would silently open, and Andy would emerge like a nervous hermit crab scavenging the ocean floor for whatever it is hermit crabs eat. And now, as I had dreaded, his door was opening. I was about to get a three-minute lecture on proper behaviour for customer-facing operatives, which did not include obscene hand gestures to the kitchen staff.

Andy extruded himself from his office. He was in his mid-thirties, I guessed, and always wore the shirt and tie he considered appropriate to a management position. I was always morbidly fascinated by Andy's hairstyle— he had a decent head of hair, but by carefully calcu- lated use of a comb-over, he managed to make himself look like a balding fifty-year-old. His complexion was blotchy and pale, and he compensated for this with a fake tan—not from an expensive sun bed, but from a bottle. Closer inspection, which I usually tended to avoid, confirmed it. Sun beds generally don't leave pale streaks on your orange forehead or a faint tangerine tinge on the collar of your shirt.

"Finn . . ." Andy bobbed and weaved and avoided my eye. He'd missed my finger to Jerry, I thought. This is something else. Probably a shit job he doesn't have the inclination to do himself—that's what he was paying us the statutory minimum wage for. "We have a clientele turnover issue." I stared at him, doing my best to look mystified. I knew what he was saying, but I wanted to see if he could express it in English. "Over there." He nodded as discreetly as he could towards the table in the corner of the restaurant furthest from the counter.

She'd arrived mid-morning, ordered hot chocolate, and sat there sipping it for the next forty-five minutes. She was about my age, in the brown uniform of Kew School for Girls, although I doubted the stud in her nose was an approved part of the outfit. Her tangled black hair fell across her face and she was wearing too much eyeliner, but it failed to hide the fact that she had clear, pale skin, fine bone structure, and curves even the frumpy uniform couldn't straighten out. Not as curvy as she could have been, for all that: at a guess she was about five kilos under her healthy weight. That was one reason she stood out in here. The other was that she was the only customer. It was too late in the morning even for the student crowd, and too early for the weekday lunch crowd.

"What's the problem?"

"She's blocking our prime seating."

I glanced over. I wasn't aware we had any prime seating. All of them were bright green plastic around bright yellow tables, and all of them had the same thrilling view of our car park, if you didn't allow for the vast window stickers that advertised Max Snax's latest blend of herbs, spices, salt, more salt and chemical gloop that coated our pinky-grey mechanically-recovered-chicken-product.

"But there's no one else here," I pointed out.

"Because she's blocking our prime seating!" hissed Andy. "And her attitude . . . it doesn't fit with our corporate image."

The first few weeks after I started work here I had found Andy's bullshit funny. I used to relay his latest examples of ridiculous corporate gobbledegook to my dad, and we'd both have a go at talking like that— "Could you transfer the sodium condiment across the consumption platform?" Then, after three or four months of it, I'd realized I might be working in Max Snax for years, soaking up the smell of stale fat, rolling myself in Max's special chemical mix until I was permanently coated in it, and the joke was on me, and it wasn't funny any more.

"Tell her she has to order something or re-allocate her custom."

"Re-allocate her . . . ?"

"Now, please, Finn."

He darted back towards his office. For a moment his little crab antennae waved, sniffing the greasy air, then he slipped inside and the door clicked shut. I could visualize him settling back into his vinyl leather-look executive armchair, watching the monitor, waiting for me to redeploy unwelcome clientele. Timing me, probably. I sighed and made my way over.

"Hi there."

She had been staring at the traffic turning the corner at the junction outside, as if waiting for a car crash to break up the empty monotony of her morning. She turned to me. Her eyes were bright green, almost too large for her heart-shaped face. I found myself wondering what colour her hair really was under the jet-black dye.

"Can I get you anything?"

"Didn't know they had waiter service here." Her tone was off-hand, a little amused, as if she was flirting, but not really. Her heart wasn't in it.

"We don't."

"Then why are you asking?"

"The manager wants you to buy something."

"I did buy something."

The amusement had evaporated. She knew what I had come over to say, and was going to argue about it. It was pointless, and her morning was spoiled before we'd even started, but a row would do as well as a car crash. I hadn't felt sorry for her till then.

"Let me get you another not-chocolate," I offered. She missed the pun, and I was glad. It sounded ingratiating and pathetic.

"Forget it. It tastes like piss mixed with soap."

"Really? I wouldn't know."

Her nostrils flared angrily. I was angry too, wondering why I'd got myself into a playground spat on

Andy's orders. And wondering whether she'd put stuff on her lips to make them that shape and colour.

"So I have to order something, or you'll throw me out?"

"No, you don't. I'll buy it, and you won't even have to drink it. But that way you can sit here as long as you like."

She sighed, glanced out across the car park again, then flashed me a huge smile. "Actually, Finn, could you do me a Max Snack? One of those big triple-deckers?"

Of course she knew my name. It was printed in big happy Max Snax font on the little badge pinned just over my left tit. Punters always ignored it until they wanted to complain.

"With everything?"

"Yeah, extra barbecue sauce, pickles, the works."

"Sure." I didn't move.

"And a giant cola."

"OK."

"And could you put it all on a tray? With lots of napkins?"

"Sure."

"And then could you shove it up your arse?"

I nodded. "You want fries with that?"

"Oh, just piss off."

She stood up forcefully, as if she expected the chair or

the table to go flying, or both, preferably. But of course they were screwed to the floor and she just winced as she bounced between them. I made sure she noticed me notice.

"Thanks for coming to Max Snax. Have a great day." I heard myself deliver the line with exactly the amount of patronizing insincerity, and a processed-cheese grin of exactly the width that the Max Snax staff training videos specified. She looked at me with even more contempt than I felt for myself at that moment, glanced down at my beige polyester shirt with its fetching perspiration stains under the armpits and down the sternum, and walked out. Even as I watched her go, my skin prickling with embarrassment and humiliation, I wanted to follow her. She had that sort of walk.

And then the place was empty again. An empty plastic cell. Even with me standing there, stinking of sweat and stale fat, the place was empty. Just the little black plastic dome of Andy's CCTV camera watching me. I couldn't even give it the thumbs-up and flash it a mock-triumphant grin; I'd had enough irony for one day.

I went back behind the counter, grabbed a damp cloth and started wiping down the counters, the cash register, the menus, everything in sight. Trying to keep busy so the urge would subside and pass—the urge to rip off this stiff nylon blouse and these shapeless, pocketless trousers and run home in nothing but my tatty briefs. Leaning time is cleaning time. Thanking time is wanking time. Frying time is dying time . . .

Andy was back. He was wearing his blazer, the one with the brass buttons and the shiny elbows. He wore it at the Friday morning Max Snax staff training sessions, or when he announced the month's sales figures, or whenever he gave someone a new pip on their plastic name badge.

He was offering me one now.

"That was exemplary, Finn. Really well-handled."

"It's OK, Andy. Don't bother." He wanted to reward me for getting rid of customers?

"Come on. Three more of these and you're a Max Snax Star. That's a six per cent pay rise."

If I turned it down he'd know I hated Max Snax, and him, and the uniform, and the job, and he'd hire some other school dropout. But I needed the money. I couldn't drive, and I could barely read. What else was I going to do?

"Thanks, Andy."

I took it off him. The first hole on my name badge already had a golden stud—you got that on your first day at work, just for turning up. I snapped the new one into the second little hole, and it didn't hurt much more than punching it into my forehead.

"Keep this up, you'll have a branch of your own someday."

The rest of my shift was a deep-fried blur, and as usual I showered and changed before I left. The workplace shower was another reason I stuck the job. Our shower at home was like being peed on by an old bloke with a prostrate problem, but this one at work fired out scalding hot water that came down like a tropical storm. I was the only one who ever used it, and it felt like the one time and space in the world that I ever had to myself.

I stooped in front of the washroom mirror—it wasn't quite high enough for someone as tall as me—combing my mousy-brown hair with my fingers. I generally kept my hair short, or it would spring up in spikes I could never control. The rest of my reflection I tried not to look at. It wasn't that I minded how I looked; apart from the kink in my nose where a sparring partner had broken it, it wasn't such a bad face, according to my dad—triangular, with a big chin that currently needed a shave and a kind of girly mouth. My teeth were pretty straight and even, and my pale skin was clear (this week anyway). But I could never meet those washed-out blue eyes because they always seemed to ask how they'd got here, and whether they'd spend the next twenty years looking out from behind the counter at Max Snax, and I never had the heart to answer.

I stuffed my uniform into my backpack—planning to wash it at home—laced up my running shoes and headed out across the car park, dodging pedestrians as I built up speed. Pushing my pulse to 140, I pounded along the backstreet pavements, heading home.

The street lights were flickering on as I pulled up, panting, outside the house. I stretched as I got my breath back, glad to see I was still supple enough to touch my knees with my forehead. But as my pulse slowed and my breathing found its resting rhythm I realized something was bugging me. The house was dark, as if Dad had gone out. But he usually worked on his writing till I came in from work—my coming back in was his excuse to knock off for the day.

The curtains were already closed. Had they ever been opened? I fished my keys from my backpack and opened the door. As I reached for the light switch I registered something about the silence.

"Dad?"

It was too deep, as if the house was empty; but it didn't feel empty.

Our house was small—the door opened straight into the living room. The light came on dimly, brightening as it warmed up. Dad disliked the overhead light, and only switched it on when he had one of his fits of tidying-up. Now it flooded the room in the way he disliked, cold and harsh, and fell on him where he sat at the table. Not sat, so much as slumped, the way I'd seen him once or twice when he'd been to the pub and somebody else was buying.

I paused in the doorway, certain something was wrong, trying to figure out what exactly. "Dad?" It was too cold in the room. He couldn't hear me—he still had his earphones in.

I'd found him like that before a few times, early in the morning. He'd be resting his head on his folded arms. Now his arms were pinned underneath him, at an odd angle, and he wasn't breathing. I knew that, even before I consciously worked it out, even before I registered properly that the crown of his head was a sticky mass of blood, and something heavy and bulky lay on the floor by his chair, itself stained with red, with bloody hairs sticking to it.

My dad was dead. He had been sitting at his desk, plugged into his music, and someone had crept up behind him holding his award for *Best Newcomer 1992*, and hit him over the head with it, and kept hitting him until he died. His eyes were open and his glasses had fallen off. There was blood coming from his mouth and clotting in his beard, and pooling on the table, and he was dead. And the house was empty and silent.

two

The wall of the interview room was a regulation blue-grey, but I wasn't really aware of that, although I'd been staring at it for what seemed to be hours. I was running through everything that had happened since I walked into the house; how the cold silence had been broken by sirens, faint at first but gradually growing louder and louder, one becoming two and then three, their shrieks overlapping into a cacophony. I was still standing there, mobile phone in hand, when blue lights started flickering through cracks in the closed curtains, illuminating the room in flashes like LEDs on a Christmas tree. Someone, probably me, had responded to the insistent rapping at the front door, and opened it. Two enormous coppers, stab vests over their jackets and peaked caps pulled down over their eyes, asked me to identify myself.

Our narrow street was one-way, but when I was

eventually led outside by a female copper I found police vehicles had come in from both directions and jammed the street solid. There were so many flashing lights it was like a rock concert, and the air buzzed and crackled with radioed conversations. Underneath it all, like the murmur of the sea, were the hushed conversations of neighbours craning their necks to see past the barricades of police vehicles and speculating about what had happened at our house, holding up phones to snap pictures of the chaos to stick on their Facebook pages. I knew most of them by sight, and they knew me, I presumed, but none of them were friends. Dad and I hadn't had that many proper friends. Just each other.

Hours passed in the police station as I sipped endless plastic cups of oily tea, made a statement, then went over the statement again. All the time experiencing the same weird calm sense of detachment, as if the most important thing was to be clear and cold and logical, and to remember every detail, without putting them together to look at what they meant, or to figure out how I should feel about it. I had entered a house and found a man at a table with his head bashed in. The coppers, uniformed and plain-clothes, had come and gone, polite, soft-voiced, solicitous, sympathetic . . .

Footsteps had paused in the corridor outside. I

blinked back into the present, turned my face away from the wall and watched the door open. Two plain-clothes officers entered, one well-fed and heavyset, the other lithe and wiry. They were followed by a uniformed PC, possibly one of the uniforms who had turned up on my doorstep earlier, but the stab vests and crew cuts made them all look alike. The older, beefier detective was white, in his mid-fifties I guessed, with craggy features and thinning brown hair going grey at the temples. His suit had a slightly rumpled air, like it had once been classy and sharp but had been worn too often. The younger one was black, with skin so dark it shone. He could not have been much older than thirty, and his head was shaved bald. He carried himself like an athlete and his suit was impeccable, his tie crisp and neat and symmetrical. If it wasn't for his deadly serious expression you'd think he'd fallen out of an expensive menswear catalogue.

"Mr. Maguire," said the older one, "I'm DI Prender-gast, and this is DS Amobi. Are you up to answering a few questions? We'll try to keep it short."

"Yeah, sure."

"We just want to go over your statement again. Would you like something to eat, or a drink?" Amobi's caring tone was convincing. His voice was deep, with a faint African twang—Nigerian, maybe. I shook my head as they pulled the chairs out from under the table and settled down opposite me.

"Are you warm enough?" asked Amobi, glancing at my paper boiler suit. My clothes had been taken away for forensic testing as soon as I'd arrived at the station.

"I'm fine," I said.

The room was too warm, in fact, and it was stuffy. There had probably been a succession of suspects and victims in here throughout the day, stumbling or sobbing through their stories. And now me. There were no windows in the room and the door gave onto an internal corridor; there was a ventilator in the ceiling, probably part of an air-conditioning system, but I guessed it was switched off in the evenings to save money.

Prendergast ignored my response to Amobi's question and waded straight in. "You found the victim's body when you came in from work, and dialled nine-nine-nine on your mobile, yeah?"

"Yeah."

Prendergast glanced briefly at the clipboard on his lap. I presumed it held a copy of my statement. "The victim was your father?"

"My stepfather. He married my mother when I was three."

"What about your real father, your natural father?" asked Prendergast. "Where's he?"

"No idea," I said. "I've never met him. My dad was my dad."

Prendergast chewed his lip and rolled his pen between his fingers. "And your mother, where's she?"

"In the States somewhere. She left us, about five years ago."

"So it was just you and your stepfather who lived in the house?"

"Me and my dad. Yeah."

"Anyone else have keys, anyone else have access?"

"No. He said something about losing his keys. Last night."

"Right," said Prendergast, as if this didn't really interest him. "Were you aware before you entered the house that there might be something wrong? Any sign that someone had broken in, anything out of place?"

"I noticed the curtains were closed. Dad liked the curtains open, for the light."

"Were they open when you left this morning?"

"Yeah. He opened them while I was in the shower." Prendergast made a silent, brief note; Amobi glanced at him, his expression composed and neutral, but I sensed he thought Prendergast already had a theory he wasn't sharing.

"Take us through this morning, from when you got up till you left for work."

I talked about that morning, again. It didn't take long. But I noticed Prendergast was writing nothing down, and trying not to smirk. I began to see where this was going, but got to the end of the story before my anger bubbled up to the surface. Amobi sat there, relaxed and attentive; he hadn't made up his mind about anything from what I could see. When I finished speaking, Prendergast let a few seconds tick by. Eventually Amobi leaned forward.

"Finn—did you notice anything missing? Had anything been taken?"

"Dad's laptop."

"Any idea of the make?"

"A MacBook, about six years old." Amobi slowly took a note. Dad had bought it from a bloke in a pub a few years before. Maybe it had been nicked, I never asked. It was already pretty clapped-out when he got it, but it was reliable, and it did enough of what he wanted: browsing the Net for research, soaking up the endless writes and rewrites and edits and rewrites.

"He must have been using it when . . . when he was attacked. Listening to music. He did that while he worked. He wouldn't have heard a thing."

Prendergast nodded as if this all made sense. Amobi noticed me frown.

"What?" said Amobi.

"His notes were gone too," I said. "He used to write stuff longhand before he put it onto the computer. He had loads of printouts and cuttings and background stuff. Whoever killed him must have taken them."

"We found another laptop upstairs," said Prendergast.

"If it's an old Dell, it's mine."

"Why do you think this intruder left that behind?"

This intruder. I shrugged. "Because it's a piece of crap?"

"Was there any money in the house? Anything valuable?" Amobi was taking notes of his own. Slowly, not in shorthand. I caught a glimpse of his handwriting; beautiful copperplate.

"No. Nothing. We're not exactly loaded."

"Was there anything that might have attracted the attention of a burglar?" asked Prendergast.

"Like what?" I asked.

"Drugs," said Prendergast. He had sat back in his chair with his hands crossed on his belly, like a bloke listen-ing to a story he's heard a hundred times before but is too bored to interrupt. His fake-relaxed pose conveyed its own sense of menace, as theatrical as cracking his knuckles.

"No."

"Would this intruder have had any reason to think there might be drugs in the house?"

"Why don't you find him and ask him?"

"Maybe we already have." Prendergast's smirk had vanished, and in its place was anger and indignation, as if someone had murdered *his* father and was giving him the runaround.

Amobi cleared his throat and cut in, "Perhaps we should take a break. You're sure you don't want anything to eat, Finn?"

"I'm OK, thanks," I said, still staring at Prendergast. His smirk was back. Amobi stood up and pulled back his chair, and eventually Prendergast lumbered to his feet. He was overweight and out of condition, and the way he kept finding things to do with his hands suggested they weren't happy unless they were holding a cigarette. But he was a big man and I could sense a deep dangerous current of bitterness and anger surging underneath that soft muscle.

Prendergast and Amobi left. The uniformed PC stayed in the room, but took a seat, saying nothing. I wasn't in the mood for conversation anyway. I was still trying to figure out what it meant, the scene in our downstairs room, my dad slumped over the table, his headphones plugged into nothing, his laptop gone, his notes gone. The laptop was an ancient piece of crap, but some smackhead might have thought it worth something. But how would a smackhead have got into the house and crept up on my dad without him noticing, even with earphones in? And what would a smackhead have wanted with all those pages of scribble and ancient dog-eared photocopies of news cuttings?

My dad once mentioned a writer he'd known from Northern Ireland whose gritty tales of Protestant extremists got him bullets in the post and death threats over the phone. He'd fled to England, to an undisclosed address. "I'm pathetic," Dad had said. "For a minute I actually envied the poor bastard. Someone gave a shit about what he wrote."

Is that what my dad had done? Pissed someone off with his script? Was that why all the notes were taken, and his laptop? I didn't even know what the story was about—he'd changed it so often I'd stopped listening. It started off being about a guy under witness protection, then it had turned into a cop drama, then been about bent bankers and politics . . .

With the laptop gone, how was I going to find out? He'd backed up the stuff onto a memory stick, yeah, but last time I'd noticed, it was still plugged into the laptop, and now it was gone too.

The door burst open again, and Prendergast entered, a manila folder in his hand. He stood there staring at me, then jerked his thumb at the PC. "Coffee, milk, no sugar. You want anything?" This last to me. I shook my head.

The PC hesitated, and Prendergast glared at him. "And take your time, all right?"

Reluctantly the PC left the room, and Prendergast shut the door behind him. He sighed as he slipped off his jacket, draped it over the back of one of the chairs and sat down heavily opposite me. His grey-green eyes were red-rimmed; they looked as if they'd had a sense of humour once, but had become pickled in cynicism.

"So, what was it about?"

"What was what about?"

"This bust-up you had with your stepfather."

"We didn't have a bust-up."

"Pull the other one. You're a bloody teenager. They argue about bloody everything. Drugs, was it? You were dealing again, and he found out?"

"I don't deal in drugs."

"Come on, Finn. Three months' youth custody, expelled from school, it's all in your record." He tapped the folder. "Weren't doing very well there anyway, from what I've read. Failed every exam you ever took. Not surprised you turned to dealing, it's the only way you'll ever make a decent living."

I said nothing. There was nothing to say. Prendergast opened the folder and pretended to read it.

"Diagnosed as suffering from dyslexia. From the Greek, meaning thick as shit."

Did he think he was being original? I'd heard that same pig-ignorant gag a million times.

"I have a job. I work at Max Snax on Ealing Road."

"Yeah, yeah, selling chicken-burgers—that's just a cover, isn't it? The punters come in, you slip them something under the counter, another twenty quid and sir can go super-large?"

I let him talk. He was smirking again.

"There was no *intruder*, was there? Your stepfather lays it down—quit dealing or get out of his house. You sleep on it, you think, his house? This could be my house. Why don't I just get rid of him? And you take his bowling trophy or whatever it was and you clout him over the head a few times and you leave him there, bleeding his brains out, and you jog to your dealership job and serve deep-fried crap with crack all day like nothing's happened. End of your shift, you jog home, come in, get your mobile out and you say *'Someone's killed my dad.'"* Prendergast put on a little-boy-lost voice. "But I've listened to the call you made. You're all calm and collected. You're not upset, you're not surprised. Because you don't give a shit. You just won the raffle."

The worst thing was, he was right about the last bit. It was like I'd felt . . . nothing. Maybe I'd been in shock, maybe I still was, maybe it just hadn't hit home yet but someone had killed my dad, and I just felt . . . curious?

More bothered by the hows and whys than the fact my dad was dead. Until now, that is. When I looked at Prendergast I felt plenty. It was all coming back, the anger, the impotence, the feeling I was talking underwater, drowning where no one could hear me. And sheer bloody frustration that everything was stacked against me and the police didn't give a shit about the truth— they just wanted to boost their clear-up figures.

It had been years ago, when Dad and I had been really skint. I'd started walking the streets all night and hanging out with half a dozen dead-end no-hopers just like me. We'd go looking for trouble and if we couldn't find any we'd make some, and one night we found someone's stash of ketamine and coke abandoned in a park, and like a stupid fourteen-year-old punk I'd taken some to school and tried flogging it. And a kid in the year above who had once tried to bully me and got my fist in his mouth reported me and the cops came and some smug fat bastard just like Prendergast had decided I would make a great example to other lippy brats who stepped out of line.

The school didn't hesitate—I was already on their shitlist. The conviction for dealing had screwed what little future I'd had left. My last year of education was in a shithole with metal detectors at every doorway, a hot-line to the local nick and a nursery for the babies of the girls in Years Ten and Eleven. The kind of place where barely being able to read was par for the course. I left well before my seventeenth birthday and no one came after me to change my mind.

"Ninety per cent of the time the person who reports finding a dead body is the murderer," said Prendergast. "You might as well have written a confession in your stepfather's blood. We're going to get to the truth eventually. Save us all the sob stories and the pissing about, all right?"

"You got it all wrong," I said. "We didn't argue. I just killed him because I was fed up looking at him. I wore two sets of gloves and a mask so you wouldn't find any fresh DNA on the murder weapon. I changed my clothes afterwards, put the stuff with all the blood-stains in a plastic carrier bag with a brick and chucked the lot into the river on my way to work. You won't find it. You won't find any evidence, and in an hour or two you're going to let me go home, because everything I just told you is inadmissible. You never cautioned me, you haven't offered me a brief, you're interviewing me with no other officer or adult friend or social worker present. Maybe when they do turn up I'll tell them you stuck your hand down my trousers. Yeah, I'm dyslexic, but I'm not the one who's thick as shit."

Prendergast was trying to smirk again, but underneath

those cracked capillaries in his cheeks his jaw was clenched. He had hoped this would be open-and-shut, that he could hector and bully me into a quick confession, because he had other things on his mind. He was too angry to be doing this job, it seemed to me. I half expected him to kick the chair back and have a swing at me; he was an old-fashioned copper. Let him, I thought, I could use the practice. I could take a punch, and at the very least I'd leave him with his nose in need of straightening.

One or both of us were saved by the door opening, and Amobi standing there looking tense. "Sir," he said. Prendergast ignored him, glowering at me. "DI Prendergast, sir," said Amobi. "I need to speak to you a moment?"

Prendergast snorted, pushed back his chair and stood up. The uniformed PC returned—no sign of any coffee—and sat back in his corner seat, not meeting my eye. There was an urgent, hushed conversation on the other side of the door. I couldn't hear what they were saying, but I got the gist: Amobi, the uptight, fastidious junior detective, was trying to stay deferential while he laid into a senior officer for ignoring every rule of procedure and possibly jeopardizing a murder enquiry, and Prendergast's voice was coming back, loud, brusque, short on words and very much to the point.

Amobi didn't come back in straightaway. I sat there while the clock ticked, thinking about my dad, wondering why he'd been killed, wondering if I'd ever know. Something told me this wouldn't be a police priority. Yeah, they didn't like unsolved murders, but unless there was a PR angle, or the victim was a child or a pretty girl, they'd leave the file open until it was buried deeply enough under other cases to be officially written off. Maybe I was the prime suspect, but the evidence was pretty thin, and now Prendergast had managed to screw up the case before the investigation proper had even started. The cops upstairs in the neat uniforms with the gold braid would be desperate to kick this into the long grass.

Amobi entered again, doing a very good impression of casual and relaxed, as if he hadn't just witnessed his boss having a dump in the swimming pool.

"Finn, we have no more questions for now. Is there anyone you can stay with tonight—a relative, a family friend?"

I shook my head. "No, there isn't. Can't I go home?"

"It's still a crime scene," said Amobi. "But I can ask. Wait here, please."

He left again. I suddenly realized my head was swimming. I was tired, really tired. I was sweating and chilled in this stupid paper suit, and I felt hungry and sick at the same time. I didn't know whether it was day or night outside. I just wanted to go home and go to bed.

Amobi returned. "If you really want to go home, that won't be a problem," he said. "The Scene of Crime people are all done, and the clean-up crew. Two of our uniformed officers will give you a lift."

"Thanks," I said.

Amobi stroked his nose between two fingers, contemplating how he was going to say what he was dying to say. "Finn, DI Prendergast said you made certain statements when you were alone with him? Regarding the incident?"

"I didn't murder my dad," I said. "It was a wind-up."

"OK," said Amobi. "But bear in mind, DI Prendergast doesn't have a great sense of humour. You need to be—"

"Can I go home now, please?"

It was still night, as it turned out. The small hours of the morning. It had been raining, and the yellow of the street lights gleamed and bounced and glared from tarmac and sleeping cars and shuttered shop fronts. I sat in the back of a patrol car, pushing down the associations that brought up, trying not to look at the close-cropped necks of the uniformed officers in front. They sat silent, not bothering with small talk. Were they tired as well, I wondered? Were they being considerate to the child of a murder victim? Or did they just not want to have a late-night casual chat with a punk who had brained his dad and walked out of the nick a few hours afterwards? I was curious, but too shattered to care.

They watched me walk to the door and open it with the key that had been retrieved from my jeans, which were still with forensics. When I shut the door behind me and stood in the darkened hall I heard the engine rev and speed away, tyres hissing on the tarmac and shashing through distant puddles. Silence. I reached out and flicked on the light like I had a few hours earlier. No body at the table this time. There was a faint smell of disinfectant, but otherwise the only sign that strangers had been in here were the ruts in the dust where stuff had been shifted as the room was searched. And when I looked closely, the furniture was at odd angles, as if someone was trying to recreate the way it had looked a long time ago, in the days before my dad had been killed. But I was too tired to look. Leaving the light on I stomped wearily up the stairs, my stupid paper suit rustling. My bedroom had been searched, I could tell—it was way too tidy. I shuffled out of the tired grey trainers the cops had lent me, pulled the paper suit off and left it crumpled on the floor, collapsed onto my bed and shut my eyes.

* * *

If I had any dreams, I didn't remember them when I woke mid-morning, the pale cool sun shining on my face. My first thought was that I was late for work—really late for work—and that my alarm clock must not have gone off. Then I remembered it had, and I had switched it off and gone back to sleep without ever waking up. Then I remembered everything else. I lay there staring at the grey cracked ceiling, trying to feel something. Did the part of me that should feel the right sort of sorrow, did that part of me not believe he was dead? The rest of me believed it. So many thoughts were crowding into my mind I couldn't begin to put them in any order.

Should I go to work? The police still had the clothes I'd been wearing yesterday, and the uniforms I had brought home to wash. Andy kept spares in the office, but gave them out grudgingly and docked your pay so that effectively you bought them—he'd never let you wash and return them . . .

To hell with it, I wasn't going in to work. Someone murdered my dad yesterday, in this house. At the same time a tiny voice in my head said, "So what? You're not dead." I let it talk. Maybe it had something useful to say. "You're lying in bed, you feel fine, you're calm, you're not in shock. You're actually a bit hungry, you should fix yourself some breakfast. What's the big deal about weeping and wailing? It doesn't get you anywhere. It's

just feeling sorry for yourself, and you don't do that."
Yeah, that's right, I remembered. I don't do self-pity; I'd
never feel anything else if I did.

"Should I call work?" I asked the voice.

"Sod that. What are you going to tell that twat
Andy—*Someone murdered my dad so I'm taking the day off?*
Call him later, maybe. Right now there's other stuff to
think about."

It was true: as I lay there the thoughts and worries in
my head were still jostling and milling about aimlessly,
like tube passengers on a station platform when all the
trains have been cancelled. Where's my dad's body?
When do I get it back? Who sorts out the funeral? Who
do I tell?

Who the fuck killed him, and why? It must have
had something to do with that script, or whoever did it
wouldn't have taken the laptop. What the hell had my
dad found out? Who had he talked to? He'd come in a
bit pissed on Sunday night, and happy, the way he was
when he'd had a chance to talk about himself and how
he nearly had a career—he used to flaunt his failure like
a badge of integrity, or make a comedy routine out of it,
and often enough it got him a few free pints. But where
had he been drinking? There were a dozen pubs within
fifteen minutes' walk of our house, and he didn't mind
catching a bus if he'd worn out his welcome locally.

Maybe it wasn't that complicated after all. Maybe it really was just some smackhead who'd heard that I used to deal, and thought he'd chance his arm and see what he could find. Maybe I hadn't closed the door properly when I left that morning, and he'd sneaked in.

Wait, no. I swung my legs out of bed and sat there on the edge of the mattress, frowning, trying to focus. Dad had lost his keys, and the next morning he was killed, by someone who'd come into the house while he was working. Did he really lose those keys, or were they lifted from his pocket?

What was in that script of his? I needed to read it, the latest draft anyway. The cops hadn't been interested in that angle. If they'd asked, I would have told them that Dad used to back everything up, religiously. He'd written half a novel once, years ago, and lost all of it when the hard disk crashed. Since then he used an external drive, and then memory sticks, when they got cheap enough. The memory stick had gone, yeah, but he backed up his stuff into AnyDocs as well, the free email and web space provider. I knew his username; but I'd never asked him his password. I'd never needed it, never even been curious.

Shit. I knew it wouldn't be anything stupid like "password" or "1234." Dad was too paranoid about other writers stealing his ideas. He never wrote his password down, either—he said the only asset he had left from his acting days was a good memory. I'd never guess it, not in a million years.

I knelt on the floor and peered under the bed.

My laptop was gone too. Mains unit and all. Of course—the cops said they'd found it. They must have taken it away to check the hard drive for evidence. Prendergast was probably going through it now, looking for my VAT receipts for coke and skunk, or maybe my blog entry on how to kill your dad and get away with it.

The doorbell rang. Or rather it buzzed. It was so old and clapped-out it mostly functioned by rattling against the wall. I dug out another pair of jeans and stepped into them, grabbed a relatively clean T-shirt and stumped down the stairs to answer the door. I guessed it was either Prendergast, or a neighbour, or the postman with something to be signed for.

But I was wrong. It was a redhead, in her late thirties, I would guess. Pretty enough, with fine even teeth, but with a slightly tense expression, as if she expected trouble. Her clothes were more smart than pretty—a sensible if shapeless raincoat, green jumper, grey slacks, minimal jewellery, and rather than a handbag a briefcase on a shoulder strap. As she turned to me I saw her don a practised smile. She held up an ID card with a prominent heading: "Social Services." Her mugshot made her look scared of the camera, but in the flesh she seemed cool and competent.

"Mr. Maguire, I'm Elsa Kendrick, Social Services? We've been told about what happened yesterday, and wanted to make sure you were all right. Is this a good time for us to talk?"

I shrugged and stepped back, opening the door for her. "Sure. Come in."

She stepped inside, glancing around the ground floor with a professional eye. She tinged her smile with a hint of sadness and sympathy. She was good at her job—it was pretty convincing.

"Can I just say how very sorry I am? It's such a terrible thing to happen. How are you feeling?"

"OK, I suppose. Sorry, can I get you anything?"

"Not unless you're getting something for yourself."

"I was just going to make some coffee..." I supposed it was a formula she had to follow, consoling a grieving relative; let them be busy if they want to, let them lose themselves in distracting daily routines. I put the kettle on, got out two mugs. Everything was clean; Dad had liked a tidy kitchen, even if his desk was a disaster area.

"You seem to be coping well, anyway," she observed. I looked at her, wondering if she was making conversation or a professional judgement. She seemed to guess

40

what I was thinking. "You're seventeen, am I right? And I understand your father had no regular work?"

"Yeah," I said. "I mean, no. He was an actor." As if that said it all. But she seemed to accept it as an answer, and nodded, her eyes cast down.

"How will you manage? Living alone, I mean?"

"I don't know. I'll manage, I suppose."

"Do *you* have a job?"

"I work at Max Snax, on Ealing Road."

"Management, or behind the counter?"

I laughed. "Yeah, right, management. I work behind the counter. I should be there now." I poured the hot water onto the coffee granules, stirred the drinks noisily.

"I'm sure they'll understand. What with you losing your father."

"I haven't told them yet."

She nodded again. Somehow I expected her to offer to call them, but she didn't. I felt vaguely irritated; was she actually going to do anything useful, or was she just here to look sad and make noises and drink my coffee? She wasn't even writing any of this down.

"What about your dad's family? Have you told them?"

"He didn't have much of a family. A brother out in China or Thailand, I think. His parents died in a car crash seven years ago." I held the mug of coffee out to her.

41

"Thanks. What about your mother? His ex-wife, I mean?"

"What about her?"

"Have you told her? Has she . . . have you been in touch? You have contact details for her, don't you?"

"No, actually, I don't."

"I see." She frowned as she sipped at the coffee, though it was still way too hot to drink. We moved back into the living room.

"My mother left years ago. We haven't heard from her since. She didn't care then and she's not going to care now. Dad and I always looked after each other and we managed fine." This wasn't quite true: the last few years, I'd mostly looked after him.

"Right, I see." She slipped abruptly from caring-sympathetic mode to brisk and business-like, plonking the mug of coffee down on a work surface and turning to the briefcase she had left on one of the armchairs by the TV.

"I have some information and leaflets you might find useful. Trauma counsellors, victim support. Also we have a special unit for carers. Not that you're caring for anyone, I mean"—she stumbled over that, and blushed, but blundered on—"but it has details of benefits you can claim, and contact numbers for Social Security."

The pamphlets she offered me seemed second-hand and a little dog-eared. It was a big briefcase to be lugging around, considering how little she had in it. I glanced through them, and the letters of the words danced that tired old tango. I'd decipher them later.

"What about if I need to get in touch with you? Are you my caseworker now, I mean?"

"Oh no, I'm only here to make an informal assessment—to see if further intervention was necessary. And you seem to be coping fine, just like you said. Thanks for the coffee." She grabbed her coat and bag, as if eager to get away. "I have other clients to visit. Any questions or anything you need, just call Social Services."

"And ask for you? Elsa Kendrick?"

"I'm usually out and about, but you can leave a message." I followed her to the front door. She fumbled with the latch, and flashed me a bright, tight smile as she finally managed to open the door.

"All the best. And sorry again about your dad. He was a good man, I heard."

She slipped out, shutting the door quietly behind her. Her footsteps clacked away rapidly. I went back to the kitchen, dug out two pieces of bread, checked them for mould, bunged them in the toaster and set it going.

That had been short and sweet. I'd had social workers before; I'd given up trying to remember their names because it was never the same person twice in a row, it seemed to me. All of them were overworked and barely organized, constantly referring to case folders, getting my name mixed up with some other delinquent two streets away. Kendrick hadn't taken any notes, but she'd known about what had happened—all about me, about my dad, about our circumstances—without even looking at a file. She turned up the day after my dad was murdered—the other social workers I had met were always about six months behind with their cases. Maybe she was that mythical beast, a social worker who actually managed to be good at their job and stay on top of their casework. I'd never believed they'd existed. But that ID was kosher—I was dyslexic, not blind.

Except . . . she hadn't actually been that helpful. She'd asked more questions than she'd answered, and left in a rush. The leaflets she'd given me—would they tell me what to do about the household bills? Those were still in my dad's name, but maybe that wouldn't matter, as long as I made sure they got paid. But what about the benefits Dad had been getting? Weren't they what paid the mortgage? The mortgage . . . who did the house belong to now? Me, or the bank? I wasn't even sure which bank Dad had used.

The toast had popped up while I wasn't looking, and was sitting there growing cold and stale. I decided to leave it for now. I had to clear my head somehow, figure out what I was going to do.

* * *

The late-morning air was damp and fresh in my mouth, and before long I could feel the familiar burn in the bottom of my lungs. I was heading up the Thames towpath at eighty per cent of my top speed. My favourite time to run was about four or five in the morning, when I could really let rip without any fear of colliding with dog walkers or joggers, but right now the towpath was quiet, apart from the odd cyclist. The ones coming towards me I dodged, the ones heading my way I liked to keep up with and overtake, partly for the challenge and partly because it really wound them up.

At first the running had just been part of my fitness training for the boxing club that Dad took me to, then it became an end in itself. I liked boxing and I was good at it. Some wag nicknamed me Crusher Maguire, and after a year or so a lot of fighters in my weight range were starting to avoid me. Then Delroy got sick and the club closed temporarily and never reopened and I had to train by myself. Running was my favourite routine. Just me and the wind in my face and the burn in my chest and my breath in my ears. My dad had tried running with me for a while—he never asked me to do anything he wasn't willing to try himself, he said—but before long he packed it in. He couldn't keep up, and I didn't want him to. I needed to push myself to the limit.

It was the boxing club that straightened me out. The clarity of it, the focus. Being right in the moment. The tiniest lapse in concentration and you got clobbered. And you soon learned that no matter how big or hard you were there was always someone bigger and harder, and that taught you to think as well as fight. Taking me there was the brightest idea my dad had ever had.

I came to the next bridge, wheeled round and headed back the way I came. A glance at my watch told me I was fifteen seconds outside my best time. I pushed myself harder.

Dad had done all the courses he could afford and read every book in the library about firm parenting and tough love and all that fatuous horseshit. He knew I was angry, and knew I was off the rails, and he knew why, and he wanted to help. But he couldn't help the way I felt any more than I could. I'd put him through purgatory—the fights in school, the truancy, the petty crime, the pathetic attempt at dealing. He'd always stuck by me, come to court, tried to persuade anyone who'd listen I was a good kid, in spite of all evidence to the contrary. Somehow he'd always been on my side, even when I really was guilty as hell. He'd never blamed me. He'd never even blamed my mother for leaving either, though you didn't have to be Freud to work out that's when I started going wrong. The heart wants what the heart wants, he'd say, then snort. He never said, her heart hadn't wanted him any more. Or me.

Back to Kew Bridge, twenty seconds under. That was better. I stayed on the towpath till it petered out at the new riverside redevelopment, then headed back up across the High Road, heading for my street, trying to keep the pace up right until the last minute to override the pain from the build-up of lactic acid in my calf muscles.

Dad tried to get me not to hate Mum, and he failed. I wanted him to hate her as much as I did, and I failed. He always loved her, even after she left us. I remembered hiding behind their bedroom door once, meaning to jump out and say "boo," and I'd heard them together, heard him sing their favourite song, "Sweet Thames Flows Softly," about two lovers whose affair flowers and fades on the river. I'd heard the joy and affection in his voice, and I'd snuck out without them seeing, and never let on I'd been listening. It must have reminded him of how he'd lost her, but Dad would still sing that song; he hummed it every time he switched on his laptop.

Into my street. Still some energy left. Top speed, right down the middle of the road.

A thickset man in a rumpled suit was leaning on a car opposite our house, staring at it as he pulled on a cigarette. Prendergast.

He looked up, surprised and slightly alarmed, as I approached. Recognizing me, he relaxed again, tossed his cigarette down on the road and screwed it into the tarmac with his shoe. I pulled up, gasping for breath, glanced at him, went straight into my stretches while my pulse slowed. My sweat dripped onto the kerb in grey spots.

"Business as usual, that it?" said Prendergast. I frowned at him. "Most relatives of murder victims wander round in a daze for days, weeks sometimes. Sit staring into space, forget to wash, forget to eat, can't sleep if they tried. You don't seem that bothered."

"I'm not most people," I said. Keeping my sentences short while I got my breath back. I didn't want to waste my breath on Prendergast anyway.

"You'll be pleased to know our investigations are making progress," he said. "Tracing your dad's last known movements. And yours. Your manager down at Max Snax, he's wondering where you are, by the way. I apprised him of your circumstances." This with a sour grin. Prendergast talking police-jargon to Andy . . . that must have been a meeting of tiny minds.

"Any suspects yet?" I hunkered down, stretching each leg in turn, bending to hit my knee with my forehead.

"Your dad spent his last night drinking in the

CRUSHER

Weaver's Arms, over on the Griffin Estate," said Prendergast. "He left at closing time, alone. Witness saw him
turn into this street, singing to himself. After that . . . the
last person to see him alive was you."

"Someone came in the next morning, after I left," I
said. "Using the keys he'd lost. Or had lifted."

"No DNA, no fingerprints except your dad's, and
yours," Prendergast said.

"I live there," I said. "Of course you're going to find
my fingerprints and DNA."

"Nobody was seen, coming or going. Except you, the
next morning. Running from the house."

"I always run," I said.

Prendergast grinned. "Funny," he said. "A lot of
punks these days watch a few TV shows about forensics
and think they know it all. But real life doesn't work like
that. It's messier, less dramatic, more predictable. Eventually the kid who did this will get drunk or stoned and
shoot his mouth off, from guilt or the need to big himself
up. And whoever he tells will tell someone else, and
in time we'll get to hear about it, and then we'll move
in and nick him. Sometimes it doesn't even take that
long—they come in and confess. The ones who don't
have any real friends, or anyone they can trust. Eventually the truth always comes out."

"Since when do you lot give a shit about the truth?"

49

I said. "You just decide what happened, then select the evidence to fit. Whatever takes the least amount of effort."

"Oh yeah," said Prendergast. "You've got a criminal record, haven't you?"

I'd had enough of his smirk. "When do I get my dad back? I'd like to bury him."

"The coroner will want a postmortem," said Prendergast. "Then he'll open the inquest. Tomorrow or the day after. He'll decide when to release the body."

"Do I go to the inquest?"

"An officer will contact you with the details. All part of the service." Prendergast smirked again and pulled a few folded sheets of paper out of his inside pocket. "Sign this," he said. He handed me the sheets, pulled out a cheap retractable ballpoint and clicked it.

I unfolded the papers, looked at them. Prendergast sighed, looked away in exasperation.

"Go ahead, read it through first. I've got all day."

"What is it?" I said.

"A list of the items removed from your house as part of our investigation," said Prendergast. "We need your signature acknowledging their safe return." He opened the rear passenger door. There was a cardboard box on the back seat, crammed with stuff from my house wrapped in tough plastic bags. I could see my laptop near the bottom. I checked the pages again. Yeah, it was definitely a list. I saw the logo for "Dell." They'd copied the hard drive, I supposed, so they could take their time checking for hidden files without me getting nervous.

I leaned the papers on the top of Prendergast's car and scribbled my signature. From his grimace I guessed he was worried about his paintwork, and I wished I'd leaned harder on the pen. I gave him back the papers and the ballpoint and lifted the cardboard box out of the back seat of the car. My dad's wallet was in there too, I noticed, along with the spare house-keys.

"We'll be in touch, Mr. Maguire," said Prendergast. He climbed back into his car. I headed for my front door while he bumped down from the kerb and drove off, too fast for such a narrow street.

I kicked the door shut behind me and dumped the box on the table, across from where Dad had been sitting when he was killed. It was absurd, I thought, tiptoeing around as if he was still there, sleeping on his folded arms. He was gone, and I had to get used to it.

I took out my laptop and laid it down where Dad used to work. The power brick was in a separate bag with the mains lead. The battery didn't hold a charge any more—without being plugged into the mains the machine would barely boot up before it died again.

I plugged the mains lead into the wall socket and the

power lead into the laptop, then pressed the "on" button. It sighed and buzzed and wheezed into life like an old dog being dragged out for a walk.

I wondered what the cops had thought of the stuff they'd found on it. They would have looked at all my social sites first—that wouldn't have taken them long. It wasn't the dyslexia that put me off posting stuff about my life. It was just that I didn't have much I wanted to say. And whenever I looked at other people's pages they never seemed to have much to say either, though admittedly that didn't stop them saying it. I did try to join in for a while, and after a lot of effort realized it was just more of the noises kids made at the back of the school bus, only written down.

Of course, it made a lot of difference if you had a lot of friends. And I didn't. I knew what the cops would make of that . . . anti-social loner. Even assholes get to be right once in a while.

I put in my password and the laptop grunted and groaned some more. The cops hadn't asked for my password, though they were legally entitled to. Obviously they'd managed to bypass it somehow. If I ever did have anything worth hiding on a PC, I needed to come up with better security.

The desktop appeared. I fired up the browser and navigated to the AnyDocs website. Up in the top right-hand corner were the log-in and password fields. *NoelPMaguire*, I put for the username. My dad used that label for everything online. Then the password. It had come to me when I was running, what it might be, and then I'd seen Prendergast, and for a moment it had slipped from my mind.

As I carefully typed the password I could feel my tongue poking out the corner of my mouth, the way it had done since I was a kid, trying hard to get the letters in the right order. I pulled it back in and clamped my mouth shut.

I typed, *sweetthamesflowsoftly*. Hit "Enter."

On the screen a little circle chased its tail while the system pondered. The screen flickered.

A long list of documents appeared. The topmost one was called, *The Boss—Episode One—Fifth Draft*. Last modified two days ago. The day before my dad was murdered.

I double-clicked on the title, and eventually a page appeared. It looked like most movie scripts I'd seen: a block of text, a space, a name in the centre of the page, another block of text with narrower margins. That would be the dialogue. I checked the foot of the page. 1 of 120. Christ Almighty.

I took a deep breath, concentrated, and started to read.

three

It was dark by the time I'd finished and my head was aching. I hated having to read in front of people; by myself I could work at my own speed, though so slowly it infuriated even me. I didn't think it was only my dyslexia that made my dad's script so hard to read. Everyone in it talked too much and never got to the point, or they got to the point really quick and then spent ages repeating it and talking round and round it. There were loads of twists and turns and double-crosses that made the story really hard to follow, and the characters did things that made no sense and just made life harder for themselves for no real reason that I could see.

But then I didn't suppose whoever killed Dad was a drama critic.

My stomach had been rumbling for the last hour, so I dug out a bag of pasta and put the kettle on to boil.

I had what was left in the bag; better tell Dad to get some more, I thought without thinking. Then that hit me too—Dad had gone, and all the things he'd done that I used to take for granted wouldn't get done any more, unless I did them. He wouldn't come home from a Monday morning shop with a sack of dried pasta past its sell-by date. He wouldn't leave half-full mugs of tea to go cold on the floor when he fell asleep in front of the TV. He wouldn't leave unflushed turds in the bog. He wouldn't sing while he cooked . . . I stood there for a while, thinking about what all that would mean, trying to get my head round it, wondering when it would start to hurt. The kettle clicked off, and I poured water into a pan, added salt, lit the gas and waited for it to boil up again.

Dad's script was about an ageing London gangster called Grosvenor—rich, successful, feared and respected in the underworld. He had a faithful lieutenant called Dunbar, an Irishman with some sort of dodgy terrorist history who took care of Grosvenor's dirty work. That was obviously the part my dad had written for himself. In the script this Grosvenor had a nephew—young, hungry and ruthless—who wanted to make a name for himself even if it meant starting a gang war, and Dunbar was caught in the middle.

The script featured a raid on a van transporting

bullion for Heathrow airport. That bit had sounded familiar; a raid like that had really happened, six months ago. A security guard had been shot and killed, and no one knew for sure how much gold had been nicked. The cops hadn't made any arrests or any progress. There were rumours it was pulled off by professionals, big-time organized criminals, but the witnesses were too scared to testify.

I drained the pasta, stirred in some pesto from a jar and grated some stale Cheddar into it.

The thing was, I could guess who Dad had based his story on. During my brief and undistinguished career as a criminal I'd heard one name spoken with fear, awe and reverence: Joseph McGovern, the Guvnor. The hardest nut in London, the gangster the cops had never been able to touch. Grosvenor, McGovern—Dad had barely bothered to change his name. Not that it would have fooled anyone if he had.

Dad used to say that the best stories came from the horse's mouth. As an actor, if he wanted to research a part, he didn't read about it or take the writer's word for it. He went out and found a real person who did what his character did, and learned from them, and watched what they did, and listened to their stories. He had driven a few writers and directors mad, I remembered, insisting he knew more about his character than they did. As a writer he would have done the same. He would have gone out looking for guys involved in organized crime and asked them lots of questions. And now he was dead. I couldn't help smiling—I could just picture Dad saying, *I must have been asking the right questions.*

I chased the last smear of pesto around the dish with the last spiral of pasta, pushed the dish away. I knew what I was going to do. My dad had been murdered, and even if there was something wrong with me, even if I couldn't mourn him or weep for him, I could try to find out who killed him, and why. I had no idea what I'd do when—if—I did find out; I'd burn that bridge when I came to it. But I wasn't going to carry on with my shit life as if nothing had happened and none of it mattered, and I wasn't about to sit on my hands while Prendergast and his crew farted around trying to pin Dad's murder on me.

I knew where I was going to start. Prendergast had told me.

The Weaver's Arms was fifteen minutes' walk from our house, a little mock-Tudor building that had once been a neighbourhood pub among London terraces crowded back to back. When the back to backs were demolished and replaced by high-rise flats the pub had been left, sitting alone in its little scruffy concrete beer garden in a rolling sea of landscaped council lawn dotted with litter and dog shit. At this time of night it looked warm and welcoming from the outside, the yellow glow through its frosted windows making it look like a cosy English pub. All it needed was a few feet of snow to cover up the cracked stained pavement out front, and it would have looked like a Christmas card.

I pushed the door open and was immediately hit by a stink of sweat and stale spilt beer, and the racket of voices raised over a jukebox pounding out thirty-year-old music. The place was doing good business for a Tuesday night—half a dozen blokes my dad's age were leaning on the bar, snorting and barking at each other, cackling at each other's gags. Dotted around were knots of drinkers murmuring over halves of lager, and an enormously tall and skinny bloke in the corner was feeding coins continuously into a slot machine—the sort that would silently eat a tenner in change, but make an enormous noisy fuss when it paid out fifty pence.

Nobody looked at me twice as I approached the bar. I was underage, but with my height and build I could easily pass for eighteen. The problem was, I didn't know the form. I rarely went into pubs—training was cheaper than drinking—and now I was here I didn't know where to start. Which of these guys had been drinking with

Dad a few nights ago? I cursed myself—I hadn't even brought his photo with me. I had one on my mobile phone, but it was ancient, and the screen on my phone was crap.

"You're Finn, aren't you? Noel's boy. I'm very sorry for your trouble." The guy talking to me was Indian or Pakistani, a head shorter than me, incongruously dressed in a blue nylon quilted coat and fingerless gloves. I recognized him; he ran a newsagent's on the Griffin Estate. He was clutching a pint glass half-full of lager and he was swaying slightly. That's why all these old blokes were leaning on the bar—by this time of night they could barely stand up.

"Thanks," I said. "Can I get you another?"

"No, let me," said the newsagent. "A pint? Maureen, a pint of best for Noel's son, here."

Two old blokes nearest my end of the bar looked up, and I noticed their faces registered not just curiosity, but pleasure, like I had turned up to stand in for my dad.

"You're Finn? The boxer? Your dad told us all about you," said one, extending a bony hand. He was about sixty, I guessed, smartly dressed in a crisp shirt and freshly pressed trousers, like he'd just come off a golf course. The man beside him was ten years older, dressed in jeans and sweatshirt, looking like a student who'd been seriously overdoing the fags and booze.

"Very sorry about your dad. He was a good lad," said Scruffy.

"It was awful, what happened," said Smart Shirt. They each shook my hand in turn, and there was genuine compassion on their faces. "I'm Jack," said the smartly-dressed one. "This is Phil"—pointing to the scruffy bloke—"and you've met Sunil."

Sunil the newsagent passed me a pint. "Here—to your dad. A good friend, a great talker, and an amazing drinker."

"Cheers," I said.

We drank.

I was glad I'd eaten that pasta. As far as drinking was concerned I was a lightweight, and after my second pint I could feel my concentration wandering, and I cursed myself inwardly. I'd meant to drink slowly, nursing a half of lager and asking lots of questions, but Dad's old drinking buddies kept buying me beer as if getting shitfaced was some form of therapy, which I suppose it is. They were falling over themselves to tell me what a great geezer my dad was, as if I'd never met him.

But in a way, I never really did know the Dad who went drinking. Right now, Sunil was telling some story I'd guessed he often told before, of how Dad had once hidden under a pub table from some huge bloke with Maori tattoos who claimed Dad had been knocking off his wife. While he told the story the other two butted in with what they thought were hilarious details. I'd been trying to be subtle, but I thought if I didn't get to the point soon I'd end up with my arms round these guys singing along to Frank Sinatra on the jukebox, like those ancient old girls in the far corner, screeching like foxes fighting over bin bags.

"Wasn't my dad here a few nights ago?"

"Which night was that?" They frowned at each other and scratched their heads as if I was asking them to re-call their earliest memory. "Friday?" said Jack. "I wasn't here, the wife was coming out of hospital—"

"The night before last," I said. "Sunday."

"That German bloke," said Phil. "You were there, Jack, he bought you that cigar."

"Oh right—Hans," said Jack, brightening.

"Hans?" I asked.

"A journalist," said Sunil. "From *Suddeutsche Zeitung*."

"Why was a German journalist talking to Dad?"

"He was doing a story on the Guvnor. Noel said he was too, and they were sort of comparing notes," said Phil.

"What did this guy Hans look like? What age was he?"

"Forties?" shrugged Phil.

"Bit under your height, pretty fit as far as I could tell," said Jack.

"Generous," said Phil. "He bought drinks all night."

"Blond hair," said Jack. "Great English."

"And he could hold his drink," said Sunil. "He must have had, what, twelve vodka and oranges? You'd never have known."

That rang a bell. Oh yeah, Delroy, who ran the boxing club. He didn't like booze that much, but if he had to fit in and look like he was getting pissed, he would let everyone think he was drinking vodka and orange. But it was just orange juice. Unless you taste it, you can't tell there's no vodka in it.

"Did you tell the police about this guy Hans? When they came asking about Dad?"

"They didn't seem to think it had much to do with anything," shrugged Jack. "Here, finish that pint and we'll have another."

"What about the Guvnor? What did Dad tell Hans about the Guvnor?"

There was a tiny hiccup in the flow of conversation. Phil pulled his nose. Sunil sipped his pint.

"He told him not to ask questions," said Jack at last.

"Why not?" I said.

"Because you never know who's listening," said Sunil.

"You don't mess with the Guvnor, that's all," said Jack. "We told your dad that, he didn't care."

"What do you mean, you don't know who's listening?"

"McGovern owns businesses all over West London," said Sunil. "Strip joints, casinos, restaurants, even dry cleaners. For all we know, he might even own this place."

"And the less said about it the better," said Jack firmly. He pointed at my glass. "What's that, bitter?"

"My dad was writing something about McGovern," I said. "I was wondering if that was why he was killed."

Jack sighed, looked away. Phil leaned forward. He hadn't shaved in a few days and his stubble glinted grey.

"Finn," said Phil, "If your dad pissed off the Guvnor, and he sent someone to sort your dad out, no one will ever be able to prove it. Doesn't matter in the end if he did or he didn't. You go around telling people the Guvnor had your dad killed..." He plonked down his glass, as if he'd gone off beer suddenly, and rose unsteadily to his feet. "I'm starving. I'm off to find a kebab."

"Missus will be expecting me, and all," said Jack. He gulped down the last of his pint.

"I have to be up at six," said Sunil. "It was good to meet you, Finn. Take care, yeah?"

"Yeah, take care," said Phil, as he pulled on a greasy Army greatcoat.

"See you around," said Jack, slipping into a smart blazer. He clapped my shoulder, waved to the barmaid and headed for the door. The other two did the same.

I let them go.

When I shut my front door the sound echoed through the house like I'd slammed it. It was colder inside than out; we had central heating, but Dad hated switching it on. "Put a bloody jumper on, if you're cold," he'd grunt. Actually he felt the cold worse than me, and would sometimes sit watching the telly in a greasy old sleeping bag with a woolly hat on his head, like a dosser in his own living room. I certainly couldn't switch the heating on now; I'd never even opened a utility bill, I didn't know how much we used to pay, or how we paid it. I pulled out my wallet. One twenty-quid note left. How long would that last? I knew Dad's wallet was in that box of effects Prendergast had brought back, and I knew the PIN for his bank card, but I had no idea how much money was in Dad's account—not much more than a hundred quid, I guessed. And wouldn't his account be frozen, now that he was dead? Or would the bank even know he was dead, unless I told them? I didn't think they'd do me for fraud for spending my dad's money. But most of that money was Government benefits. If nobody told the DSS Dad was dead they'd keep paying out, but as soon as they learned the truth, they'd ask for their money back. And unless they were feeling generous, or they lost track of the paperwork, they'd quite likely demand interest or prosecute me. Or both.

I had about a hundred and fifty quid saved up from my job, stashed away in a Post Office account Dad had opened for me years ago. When he was alive, that had seemed like a lot, but now . . . I'd call that social worker, Kendrick, in the morning, I decided. At the very least she'd be able to tell me what I should be doing next, as far as finances were concerned—every day there seemed to be more things to worry about. I thought I'd been the practical one, looking after my dad. I'd never been aware of all the boring grown-up shit he'd handled, and never discussed.

I put the kettle on. It was too late for tea and coffee but there was some just-add-hot-water powdered soup in the cupboard that Dad used to buy because it was cheap. I'd turned my nose up at it whenever he'd offered to make me some, but now I thought it would warm me up, at least.

I wrapped my hands round the hot steaming cup while my laptop wheezed into life, its little hard drive rattling away like a matchbox full of ants. Eventually the desktop appeared with a tinny fanfare. I'd never bothered with a password, because I'd never had anything I was that desperate to hide, and anyway I found it a huge pain in the arse to enter one. All that appeared on the screen was a row of dots, and I could never tell which character I'd gotten wrong or how I'd screwed up.

Now I opened a browser and carefully typed "McGovern, organized crime" into the search engine box. My finger hovered briefly above the Enter key. I found myself thinking, what if the Guvnor sees me Googling him? Then I felt stupid, as paranoid as those old pissheads in the Weaver's Arms. As if McGovern didn't have better things to do than watching all of the Internet to see if his name came up. I stabbed the Enter key.

Lots of hits, pages and pages. The ones at the top were newspaper articles. I sighed; this was going to take me for ever. But I started clicking.

It was weird. McGovern's name, and his nickname, seemed to crop up in loads of newspaper stories, with lots of waffle about his underworld connections and his property empire, but it was hard to find any clear details. Once McGovern had even been summoned to appear in court, charged with tax evasion, but all the charges had been dropped when paperwork had mysteriously gone missing. If McGovern had nobbled the case somehow, nobody dared to suggest it. Maybe the newspapers were scared of being sued for libel, or maybe the Guvnor had other ways of handling unfavourable publicity.

I'd only managed to read three articles and my eyes were hurting with the effort. I thought I'd try one more click, and landed on a blog calling itself The Inside Duff, claiming it had all the "gen" on the London underworld. According to this blogger, McGovern was involved in every major crime from the Great Train Robbery to 9/11, and anyone that had ever crossed him had ended up buried under major architectural landmarks in London, because McGovern owned most of them.

The blogger tried to sound outraged and disgusted, but even I could tell he secretly admired McGovern. Born to working-class Irish parents in Northolt, the Guvnor was a diamond geezer and family man who—according to this blog—never hurt anyone but other criminals, gave shitloads to charity and never boasted about it, and was too smart and too ruthless to ever get caught. There was even a blurry picture of his house in north-west London—a huge tacky palace that made the average Premiership footballer's mansion look like a garden shed.

The story my dad had been writing didn't flatter McGovern this way. In his script The Boss was a thug who had risen to the top of the shit heap by being more vicious than any of his rivals. The script wandered around the point, yeah, but Dad's version of McGovern seemed a lot more convincing than anything I had read on the Net.

I realized I hadn't closed the curtains. When I came in I'd turned on the lamp in the corner, but apart from that the only light in the room came from the screen of my laptop. When I looked out the darkened window my reflection was brighter than anything outside; my bulk hunched over my laptop, squinting at the words. I blushed, wondering if any passers-by had noticed my lips moving as I read. Or whether anyone was watching me from the inky shadows outside. I got up and tugged the curtains shut, then headed for the front door and locked it too. The back door I had locked and bolted before I left for the pub. Of course, I realized, my dad's keys were still missing. OK, no one could come in while I was here, but I couldn't bolt the front door—there was a big bolt fitted to it, but the door itself had warped so the bolt didn't line up with the doorframe any more.

In fact, I realized, there could be someone in the

house right now, someone who'd come in while I had been down the pub. Someone who could have crept up behind me while I sat at the table reading. I stood still and listened. Not just listened; I tried to feel if there was anyone else present. But I didn't hear anyone, and I didn't sense anything. The house was empty apart from me, and I was alone. I suddenly felt a twinge of self-pity, and just as quickly stifled it, mentally screwing it into the carpet with my heel like a cockroach. None of that shit—not now, not ever.

I climbed the stairs, cleaned my teeth without looking at my reflection, left my clothes in a heap on my bedroom chair and crawled under the covers.

four

"Social Services."

"Hi there . . . um . . . I'm looking for someone—Elsa Kendrick?"

"What's this regarding?"

"My father died recently, and I'm seventeen." I winced. I wasn't making any sense—I sounded like a five-year-old who had dialled 999. "Um—I need some advice on managing money and that sort of thing, and she said I should call her, if I—"

"Hold, please."

Thirty seconds of electronic tinkling followed. I glugged the last of my instant coffee. It had a sour tang—that milk was definitely on its way out. I'd have to go shopping. I hated shopping.

"Social Services." A different voice, another woman—this one in her twenties, I guessed. It was only 9:20 in the morning but already she sounded harassed and tense.

"Hi, I wanted to speak to Elsa Kendrick?" I didn't want to have to start explaining myself all over again.

"Elsa's on leave at the moment, can I help?"

"Oh, right . . ." Bollocks, I thought. Here we go again on that bloody merry-go-round, a different face every day.

"Um . . . any idea when she'll be back?"

"I'm afraid not. She's away indefinitely." What the hell happened to her? I thought.

"Sorry, when did she go on leave? I spoke to her yesterday. I thought—"

"Yesterday? Elsa was sus— I mean, she went on sick leave two months ago."

"Wait, did you say she was suspended?"

"I'm sorry, was there something you wanted? Maybe I can help."

"Red hair, mid-thirties, right?"

"Sorry, who am I talking to?"

"Where does she live, do you know?"

"I can't give out that sort of information. Look, if there's something you need, tell me what it is and I'll see if I can help. Otherwise I'm sorry, we're very busy."

"It's fine. It doesn't matter."

"Can I take a name and number? Someone will call you back."

"No. Forget about it. Thanks."

I hung up. They wouldn't have called back anyway, they never did. I stared at my mobile as if it might flash up an icon telling me my call had got me nowhere. If Elsa Kendrick was on sick leave, why did she come round here with a bunch of Social Services leaflets? Asking questions about Dad, and about where my mother was? Maybe she was in the phone book . . . ? Unlikely. A social worker wouldn't let her home number be listed, or she'd be pestered all day and night by cranks and drunks and weirdoes and the plain desperate. If I wanted to find Elsa Kendrick I'd have to think of some other way.

When the phone rang in my hand I nearly dropped it. The word WORK flashed up on the screen as the handset vibrated. Shit—Andy.

"Andy, hey."

"Finn, good morning, how are you?"

"I'm fine, thanks, all things considered."

"That's good, that's good. We heard about what happened. That's really terrible, we're really sorry."

I was impressed. He sounded almost human. Damn it, I thought, I should have called him about taking some time off, let him know . . .

"Andy, I'm sorry I haven't been in to work, everything's kind of screwed up, I don't know if I'm coming or going."

"That's OK, that's OK, that's why we're ringing up—we wanted you to know you shouldn't worry about it."

Why did he keep saying *we*, I wondered? Were there two of him or something?

"Thanks, Andy, I really appreciate it. I'll try to be back as soon as I can. I don't even know when the funeral's going to be."

"We don't want you worrying about that sort of thing, Finn. That's why it's been decided we should really re-examine our options vis-à-vis your position."

"What?"

"We've been reviewing the staffing levels and rotas anyhow, and we need to make some efficiency adjustments."

"Hold on—say that again?"

"We really appreciate all your hard work and we wish you all the best in the future," Andy recited.

"You mean you're firing me?"

"We need to redeploy our resources externally," said Andy. Was this bullshit intended for his benefit or mine? Or was the guy really incapable of human speech? Either way I wasn't surprised he was doing this over the phone. If we'd been in the same room I'd have decked him.

"Which means you're firing me."

"The fact is, we have to be strict about the image our

staff projects, on and off duty. We can't afford to have anyone on the team in trouble with the police."

"Andy, I'm not in trouble with the police. My dad was murdered."

"But they're not looking for any other suspects at the moment, as I understand it."

"Who the hell told you that?"

"I'm afraid I cannot discuss references we may or may not have received. Your outstanding wages will be paid as usual—"

"Was it a copper called Prendergast?"

"Like we said, we wish you all the best in the future. And if you're ever in this neck of the woods again, do call in, and remember to ask for your special Max Snax Veteran's Discount."

"This neck of the woods? I fucking live here, you prick!"

"Sorry, Finn, but we have to go. Have a really great day."

And he went. Before I even had a chance to tell both of him where he could stick his Max Snax Veteran's Discount.

My knuckles were white on the handset, as if I was gripping Andy's windpipe. He'd fired me? Fired me! Two days after I'd won my second golden stud? Thank Christ I'm through with that place, piped up the voice in my head. Screw Max Snax, and Andy, and that shit job.

Yes, it was a shit job, I thought, but it was a job, and now I didn't have one. How long would the money I had last? I should find out which bank Dad used, call their customer services, tell them what'd happened.

To hell with that—the first thing they'd do would be to freeze the account. Leave it for now. There was someone I needed to talk to, somehow.

McGovern's house looked even bigger than in the photographs. Not that I could really tell from where I was standing—across the street, surveying the place from behind a tree surgeon's lorry bumped up on the verge. The perimeter wall was pretty forbidding—four metres high, smooth rendered brick painted white. Every seven metres or so stood a pillar crowned with a cluster of video cameras. The entrance gates were only about three metres high but they were plated in sheet steel, also painted white; unremarkable, anonymous, and impenetrable. All this security wasn't unusual in the neighbourhood—there were other sprawling millionaire mansions, and one or two Middle Eastern embassies. But there the high walls and cameras were intended to keep thugs and criminals out . . . in McGovern's case, it was the other way round.

Now I'd found the house—the name of the street had been mentioned in that Inside Duff underworld blog—I had no idea what to do next. It occurred to me vaguely I could wait till dark, dress like a ninja and throw a grappling hook over the wall. There were a few mature trees whose branches were blocking the cameras' view, I noticed. But I didn't have any black clothes with me. In fact, I didn't even own any black clothes—they showed up my dandruff. On the other hand, I didn't feel like walking up to that front gate and pressing the entry buzzer either. *Hi, my name's Maguire, I think Mr. McGovern may have had my dad murdered?* Either they'd tell me to piss off, or they'd let me in and I'd never be seen again. Not that many people would be looking.

It had taken me an hour to get here, and I didn't feel like going home just yet. It was mid-morning and the street was deserted, though not exactly quiet. The tree surgeon was up a plane tree nearby with a chainsaw, lopping off the spring growth and letting the green branches fall onto a cordoned-off section of pavement. His mate, in hi-viz jacket and ear protectors, was at the tailgate of the truck, feeding the branches into a shredder. The blades of the machine kept up a constant deafening whine that every minute or so rose to a crescendo as a branch was fed in, ground up and sprayed in fragments onto the growing heap in the back of the truck. I noticed another lorry just like the tree surgeon's coming down the street, indicating left . . . McGovern's mansion was on its left. This other truck was towing a shredder, rather shinier and newer than the one beside me. The lorry slowed, turned in, bumped up over the lowered kerb and stopped with its nose against McGovern's white steel gates. It was painted in a classy pastel green, with a business name in dark-green lettering I didn't quite catch. The driver rolled his window down, poked the entryphone button with a gloved hand and shouted something into the mike. It gave me more time to read the name on the side of the van: "Daisy Cutters Garden Services."

I couldn't hear what the driver was saying, and it seemed that neither could the person controlling the gates—the driver had to repeat himself a few times to be heard over the roar of the shredder. But eventually the gates jerked and rolled open with a whine, slowly revealing a fake-cobblestone drive curving up to the white painted portico of McGovern's house, where steps led up to a solid wood door. I just had time to register that the house resembled one of those shiny plastic Hollywood mansions you see on US TV soaps featuring shiny plastic Hollywood starlets when the gates started to hum shut again. Dammit, I thought, if I'd been quicker, I could have sneaked in behind the lorry before the gates closed . . . Except, of course, I would have been spotted by the CCTV. The security staff probably would have set dogs on me, and waited a good while before calling them off. All the same, it gave me an idea. I hesitated . . . Was I really going to do this? If I was, I had better do it right now.

Screw it. I stepped back behind the tree surgeon's truck, pulled off my hooded sweatshirt and my T-shirt and tied them round my waist.

The shredder in the street was still grinding and spewing when I pushed the button on the entryphone a few minutes later. I heard it crackle into life and a voice squawk out of it, but I couldn't make out what it said. I stood well back from the microphone and shouted, "I'm with Daisy Cutter," but I was pretty sure whoever was listening and watching couldn't make out a word. The voice over the intercom squawked some more, and I stared up at the TV camera and nodded at the gate. I was shirtless, wearing jeans and carrying more leafy green branches in my arms than I could manage. On my face I wore the bored, harassed expression I thought a gardener's gopher might have if he'd been sent to go pick up the trimmed branches that had fallen outside the client's wall, but I wasn't sure if whoever was controlling the gates could even see my face behind all the foliage. Nothing happened, and seemed to go on happening for a long time. Had they seen me dash across from the other side of the road? Shit—had they clocked the fact that I wasn't wearing gardening gloves? I shivered, and it wasn't the breeze that was chilling me.

The gates jerked and shuddered and slowly parted, the motors whining. I staggered forward with my armful of greenery and gave the camera a grateful smile and a nod. I had barely stepped through when they hummed shut again, coming together with a soft metallic ring. They reminded me of a dinner gong . . . and I was the starter.

I was pretty sure the security people would still be watching, so I had to go through with it. I staggered up the drive, scattering fresh green leaves in my wake, towards where the Daisy Cutter lorry was parked. The real gardening crew was nowhere to be seen, but I could hear a petrol-driven strimmer firing up on the far side of the house. From what I could see there were more than enough bushes and trees in the grounds to keep a two-man crew busy all day. I dumped my armful of branches by the shredder, pulled on my T-shirt and hoodie and headed towards the sound of the strimmer, still trying to look as if I belonged. I glanced casually around to see if anyone was about, sizing up the house itself. Close-up it still looked Hollywood somehow; everything was shiny and new, expensive and vaguely fake. Beyond the portico, by heavily draped French windows, was a sun terrace with a set of wrought-iron table and chairs that looked like they'd come from a catalogue and had never even been sat on. Leading away from the terrace and heading off nowhere in particular was a timbered framework laid out like a tunnel, for roses to climb on. A pergola, that was the word for it. I dodged into it and paused, looking around for CCTV cameras. If I could see them, they could see me. But this seemed to be a blind spot. I leaned back into a gap between rose bushes and tried to figure out what to do next. Tricking my way through the front gate had seemed like a great idea, but I would never get out the same way. In fact, I couldn't see how I was going to get out at all, and I didn't even know what I was looking for. What the hell was I doing?

I was looking for McGovern, that's what I was doing. Why not just ask him to his face if he knew about my dad and the script he'd been writing? Even if he didn't answer the question, I thought I'd be able to tell something from his reaction. Maybe he'd get some of his heavies to work me over for trespassing, but what the hell, I'd been smacked around before. When I realized I could take on anyone in the boxing club and win, I'd started boasting about it, and Delroy had arranged for a special visit from an ageing clapped-out middleweight.

He hadn't even had my reach, but he still knocked seven shades of shit out of me. What doesn't kill you makes you stronger, my dad had said, getting out a bag of frozen peas for my jaw. I thought that was bollocks at the time, and I still did. It was quite possible McGovern would just kill me, and if he only half killed me it wouldn't make me stronger.

Presuming McGovern was there. He might not be. The man had properties all over Europe, supposedly, and an island in the Caribbean. Who'd want to be in North London in April when they could be on a beach in Jamaica? Maybe this whole journey had been a waste of time. But to hell with it, I was here now, and I couldn't squat in the bushes till it got dark. I might as well look around.

Pretending to be with the gardening team had got me this far, and it might buy me some time if things went pear-shaped. I pulled a few stems off the rose bush behind me and got a few bloody scratches from my trouble. Clutching them in my hand, I walked on round the house, feeling like some village idiot carrying a bouquet of twigs and thorns for his favourite goat. The house seemed to go on for ever; I guessed it had started off with four walls and a roof, then been extended sideways and to the rear, and those extensions had sprouted more extensions, and extra floors, and carports. Between the outbuildings and extensions little sun terraces and patios and barbecue areas were dotted around, some looking vaguely Spanish, others all black and white and minimalist, as if whoever designed them couldn't make up their mind what they liked.

I heard voices; a child screaming. The screams had a ringing echo like you'd hear at a swimming pool. About ten metres away was a long, low outbuilding with a slanting glass roof. The screeching was coming from there. That's where everyone was, I thought, hanging out at the indoor pool. Mind you, what's the point of having your own pool if you can't keep screaming kids out of it? The screeching went on and on—a little girl, by the sound of it. She would pause for breath, then start again, and nobody was scolding her or trying to get her to shut up, from what I could tell.

By now I was at the corner of the pool building. The brat's echoing shrieks were so brain-piercing I had momentarily forgotten to check for CCTV. I peeked round the corner, to find that the end wall was made up of glass panels that folded back so that the pool opened straight onto a sun terrace. The middle door-panel was open, and through the plate glass I could see a girl of about five in a frilly pink swimsuit, crouching slightly, hugging herself, and screaming at the top of her voice. She was looking at the pool, where the water was splashing and slopping, stirred up by a boy of maybe six as he threshed about just below the surface. He was drowning in the deep end.

I threw the daft handful of rose stems aside and ran to the door, pulling off my hoodie, then started to undo my belt. The kid's struggles were getting weaker—how long had he been in there? I hurled myself in, jeans, trainers and all. My denim jeans immediately become waterlogged, and felt a hundred times heavier. My trainers seemed to be streamlining my feet, so no matter how hard I kicked with my legs I still sank. I wished I'd stopped to take a breath before I jumped, but it was too late now. I gave up trying to surface, straightened out and swam underwater straight for the kid, who was now slowly descending, mouthing like a fish, his blond hair hanging round his pale, scared face like a halo. I struggled towards him, felt his arm brush mine, clutched it and dragged him towards me. His body was limp, more dead weight. Not dead, not dead, I thought, please not dead. Hugging him to my chest, I aimed for the surface, kicked and kicked. My head burst clear, and I gulped down air. The kid was limp and heavy in my right arm, and my left arm swung out behind my head, trying feebly to swim half a backstroke and simultaneously feel for the end of the pool. My lungs were burning and my stroke growing weaker when my fingers brushed the end wall. I scrabbled for a handhold, scratching uselessly against the smooth, warm tiles, and I almost dislocated my arm stretching out and backwards before I grasped the hard rim of the tiles at the pool's lip. With the last of my strength I folded my body towards it, my right arm still hugging the kid. The girl had stopped screaming—now she just sobbed and gasped.

"It's OK—it's OK!" I panted. "He'll be all right. Go get help." She stared at me, and swallowed. "Go get *help*!" I barked. She turned and ran off, her little feet slapping the wet tiles. I looked around, and realized I was only three metres from a ladder. Kicking my leaden legs and hopping one hand along the edge, I managed to drag the two of us towards it. It was easy to throw the kid over my shoulder; he was as floppy and as light as a wet tea towel. I climbed up the ladder and as soon as his feet were clear of the rungs I lowered him onto the tiles, then scrambled up after him, my jeans flabbily hugging my legs.

He'd been threshing about a minute ago—with any luck I'd still have time. As I leaned over him I tried to remember everything, *anything* Delroy had taught us about first aid, and I cursed myself and the other kids in the gym for how we'd messed about, pretending to grope the practice dummy and not really listening. A few things came back to me—head back, check the airway is clear, for a child cover both the mouth and nose. I tasted a hint of snot as I put my open mouth over the lower half of his face, but to hell with hygiene, I thought, and blew, and paused, and blew. Heart massage—what was it? One hand for a kid, fifteen pushes to the sternum—

Now I could hear shouts and shrieks and arguing and blame approaching from the other side of the glass doors, but kept going. Three breaths to the mouth and nose, heel of the hand to the sternum—one, two—

The kid coughed, winced, rolled onto his left side and puked. And coughed some more, great racking wheezes, hacking water out of his lungs. I fell back, my legs folded beneath me, utterly exhausted, and realized I had an audience. The little girl, clutching the hand of a blonde in her late twenties with tumbling hair, an amazing figure and too much make-up; a younger, pinch-faced girl of about twenty with black hair scraped back in a ponytail, looking terrified, shocked and clue-less; behind the two of them, a scarred gorilla in a suit, impassive and silent. And walking round to stand in front of all of them a slim, fit, tanned bloke with silver hair and blue-grey eyes.

I'd seen photos of him on the steps of a courthouse. Then the collar of his overcoat had been turned up, his flat cap pulled down, and he'd been wearing shades, but it was the same bloke. McGovern stooped down by the little boy, who was still coughing and retching, and laid a hand on the kid's head. "You're all right, Kell. You'll be all right."

The Guvnor turned his pale grey eyes to me.

"Thanks," he said. "Now who the fuck are you?"

five

"Kell, you go over there and shake that man's hand."

The little boy, in a thick towelling robe slightly too big for him, walked over to face me, held out his hand and piped up, "Thank you."

"You're very welcome," I said. "Next time make sure there's a grown-up around before you go swimming, OK?"

"OK." He grinned at me as if he hadn't been dead a few minutes earlier.

We were all standing in the living room, or rather one of the living rooms, in the main house. On my way in I had glimpsed a warren of similar lounges leading off the hall. In this one three big sofas in white leather had been laid out in a C-shape around a glass and chrome coffee table piled with glossy style magazines. Above a vast black marble fireplace, its iron fire basket full of dusty unburnt logs, a huge flat-screen TV hung in a custom-built alcove. The wallpaper was pale gold and textured like woven silk. There were gilt and dark wood side tables scattered around the place, bearing heavy cream side-lamps with gilt trim, and yet more glossy magazines. It was all a bit fussy, more expensive than stylish, from what I knew about style . . . which admittedly was bugger all. I felt self-conscious, standing barefoot on the soft white wall-to-wall shag pile carpet, water still trickling down my legs despite the heavy towelling robe I'd been given over at the pool house.

McGovern hadn't got much further than asking who I was when the women had started fussing over the boy and arguing about taking him to hospital. It seemed the kid was McGovern's son, and the blonde with the eye-popping curves his second wife, Cherry. Kirstie—the teenage girl with the Essex facelift—was the nanny. McGovern sent me to get out of my wet clothes, and while I'd unpeeled my soaking jeans in a little changing room to the side I'd heard the voices of the two women, shrill with shock and fear, defensive and tearful, answering the questions McGovern was asking in a calm, low, steady voice. From what I could make out, through the overlapping apologies and lamentations and excuses, each woman had thought the other was keeping an eye on the kids. Cherry had been shopping online, while Kirstie had been on the phone to her boyfriend.

By the time I came out, holding my wet clothes at arm's length, Kirstie had disappeared. Presumably she'd caught the rap for what happened, though from the look on McGovern's face there was still plenty of blame to go round.

"Come in the house," he said to me, then turned and led the way. His wife followed, carrying the little boy, now recovered, in her arms while the little girl trotted after her. McGovern's minder—the gorilla with the scarred face—waited impassively for me to follow them, his hands politely folded in front of him. He shadowed me over to the house to an open French window and waited as I dropped my sodden clothes on the tiled patio before entering.

"Right," McGovern was saying to his wife, "Kelly's calmed down now. Take him back and put him straight in that pool."

"Joe . . ." she protested, but not with a lot of conviction.

"He's had a fright. Best thing is get him back on his horse. And this time you go in with him, all right?" He chucked the boy's chin. "Mum's going to give you a swimming lesson. This time, mind you stick to the shallow end."

The kid nodded. "Yes, Dad," he squeaked.

His mother glanced in my direction. For a moment I sensed she wanted to come over and hug me, but if she did she thought better of it. She probably avoided cuddling other men in front of her husband, especially total strangers who had walked in off the street, even if they had saved her son's life. She threw me a tight, timid smile instead, dazzling enough to leave me gaping like a goldfish.

"Thanks again," she said. Taking her little boy's hand she led him back out the way we had entered. The kid just had time to wave and flash me a grin before he vanished. The little girl had been sent upstairs earlier to change out of her swimsuit, so now it was just me and McGovern in the room. And his minder, of course, who stood to one side, so huge and motionless he might as well have been a wardrobe.

"I didn't catch your name earlier," said McGovern.

"Finn Maguire," I said, watching his face carefully. No reaction that I could see—the name meant nothing to him. Or it did, but he was too shrewd and self-controlled to let his true emotions show on his face.

"A Paddy, like me, yeah?" He smiled.

"A Londoner," I said. "My stepfather was Irish. I took his name."

McGovern held out his hand. I took it. It was firm and

cool and muscular, and I could feel his measuring mine the same way.

"Thanks, Finn. You saved my kid's life."

"You're welcome, Mr. McGovern," I said.

Another man entered the room, moving silently. Thirty-something, slim and lithe, the way he moved suggested he was either a fighter or a dancer, and dancer seemed unlikely. Dressed smart-casual in spotless clothes with discreet designer labels, his face was sharp, narrow and angular, with high cheekbones and a thin nose. A grin seemed to flicker constantly across his bony face like he was thinking of a really funny joke he wasn't going to tell you. Right now he carried a plastic carrier bag with the label of a South Ken fashion store. Its rustling was the only thing that betrayed his presence, but McGovern knew who he was without looking round.

"James, this here's Finn Maguire."

"I heard. The hero of the hour." His voice was soft, his tone sardonic. He offered the bag to McGovern, who opened it, took out some clothes and handed them over to me.

"Tracksuit. One of mine, you look about my size. Put it on."

"Thanks," I said. I tossed the jacket onto a sofa, shook

out the pants and pulled them up under my robe, trying not to worry about McGovern or his minder or James catching a glimpse of my knob. I shrugged off the robe, laid it over the sofa and pulled the jacket on, while McGovern took a seat on the sofa opposite, and James sat back on the one between us, relaxed and curious. There was a pair of brand-new trainers at the bottom of the bag too. I took them out and slipped them on quickly. They were a size too big, but I wasn't about to complain.

"Get you something to drink, Finn?" said McGovern. He sat forward, elbows on his knees, fingers interlinked, his pale grey eyes fixed on me. He didn't blink much, I noticed. I knew that trick as well. I could go a long time without blinking, and knew how it could rattle someone looking at you without them even being sure why. There was something down the back of my trousers, I realized, cutting into my bare arse. I pulled out the label I'd been sitting on. The tracksuit was brand-new, and the price on the tag was astronomical. I tugged it off, crumpled it up and stuffed it into my pocket, not wanting to litter the spotless chi-chi decor.

"I'm good, thanks," I replied. The small talk would end soon, I knew; I felt the same cold clarity that used to fill my head when I ducked through the ropes into the ring, the adrenaline surge that made my calf muscles twitch.

"I'm glad you were there when my boy needed you," said McGovern. "And I'm grateful. But I'd really like to know how you got in, and what you're after."

"I walked up to the front gate with an armful of branches," I said. "I was hoping the guy on the entry-phone would think I was with the gardeners. And he did."

McGovern shook his head, chuckled quietly. He turned and looked at James.

"I'll have a word," said James.

"More than a word," said McGovern. "What am I paying those pricks for?"

James said nothing.

"Anyway, Finn, you've got balls. You a boxer?" He jerked his chin at me.

"I've done a bit," I said.

"I can always tell. Any good?"

"I get by," I said.

I was trying not to babble or sound nervous, and now I worried about going too far the other way. But McGovern didn't seem displeased with my terse responses. He sat back, stretching a beefy arm across the back of his sofa.

"Let's get to the point, all right? What were you doing wandering around my house? I mean, you weren't here to rob the place. You don't look that stupid."

"I need a job."

"A job?"

For the first time McGovern looked surprised. I was kind of surprised myself. I'd had no idea what I was going to say to McGovern if I met him, but without consciously figuring it out I'd become convinced that direct questions would get me nowhere. It was a lucky break—for me—that I'd found his son drowning, and I had to press home my advantage, make the most of the favour he owed me, right now. Accusing him to his face of having my dad killed would just piss him off and squander whatever goodwill I'd earned. If I could just get on the inside, get closer to people who worked for him, maybe I could work my way towards the truth. Besides, I really did need a job, and it was tough enough to find one without being a dyslexic, freshly-fired dropout.

"Do I look like the bloody DSS? Or your parole officer?" I wasn't sure if McGovern was amused by my cheek, and I couldn't tell from looking at James, whose sneer never seemed to leave his face.

"I don't mean anything heavy, or dodgy, you know, Mr. McGovern. But I heard you owned some restaurants, nightclubs, that sort of thing, and . . . I've worked in catering."

"What, as a chef?"

"More front-of-house sort of thing."

"Where?"

My face was burning now. "Max Snax, near Kew Bridge."

"You what? Fried fucking chicken? Hear that—kid thinks I'm fucking Colonel Sanders."

This was directed at James, whose smirk had blossomed into shoulder-shaking laughter, unsuccessfully stifled by his hand over his mouth. McGovern looked amused, but vaguely insulted too.

"Mr. McGovern, I'm sorry, I'm pretty desperate. I'll do anything, wash dishes, scrub out bogs—I just need the work. My dad died . . ." Now I was blinking. Ashamed at myself for pleading with a psychopathic criminal for the privilege of cleaning out his toilets. Pleading for sympathy from the man who might well have had my father killed. Why the fuck hadn't I just asked McGovern straight out to tell me the truth? *Because he'd have lied to you,* said the voice in my head, *and then he might well have killed you too.*

"I don't have much money," I went on. "I can't read that well, and I have . . . form. For dealing." That sparked his interest, I noticed.

"Grass?"

"Cocaine." I didn't mention I'd got busted almost before I started. "Somebody— I heard you had, you know, fingers in lots of pies. I thought if I could get in to see you, face to face, you might give me some credit just for . . . having the bottle."

McGovern looked thoughtful. "When did he die? Your old man?"

I looked right at him. "Two days ago. Someone broke into our house, hit him over the head. Took his laptop, and all the notes for the story he was writing."

I looked over at James. He was looking at me, his face as neutral and unreadable as that of his boss. McGovern was rocking his jaw from side to side, thinking.

"That's a shame," said McGovern. "I'm sorry for your trouble."

"Thanks."

He looked at James. "What about the Iron Bridge?"

I'd heard of the Iron Bridge—who hadn't? A seriously upmarket restaurant in Pimlico, right on the river, facing Battersea Power Station. It had had its own cookery series on TV a few years back, and its plain-speaking Geordie chef, Chris Eccles, was still a minor celebrity. McGovern had shares in that place? But James was wrinkling his nose.

"Na," he said. "Matey likes his staff to look like supermodels."

"Give him a bell," said McGovern. James said nothing. "It's the least we can do for our boy Finn," went on

McGovern, and there was something so fake about his kindness that for the first time I felt chilled. He leaned forward again, fixed me with his blue-grey stare. "I'm a silent investor over there. I don't tell Chris Eccles how to run his kitchen, but if I ask nicely he'll find you something. Give James here your mobile number, he'll call you in a day or two, tell you where to go, who to talk to, all right?"

That was my cue. I recited my number to James, who tapped it into his phone, then I got up, clutching the plastic bag.

"Thanks, Mr. McGovern. I'm really grateful. And I'm sorry about, you know, trespassing."

"Don't let me see you round here again. And you keep this to yourself, OK? I don't want every Tom, Dick and Harry climbing over my gates looking for work."

"Won't say a word, I promise." I shot him a big cheesy grin, but McGovern didn't see it. He had taken out his wallet. Now he tugged out a few fifty-pound notes, folded them in his fingers and offered them to me.

"Please, Mr. McGovern, I can't, there's no need."

"Fuck off, you already said you're broke. This will keep you going till we sort you something out." He stuffed the notes into the right-hand pocket of the track-suit jacket.

"Thanks," I said. "And I'll bring the tracksuit back."

"Forget it, it's a gift. In fact, it looks better on you than it would have on me."

I headed for the door. "I hope little Kelly will be all right."

"He'll be fine. Can't say the same for Stephan, though."

"Stephan?"

McGovern was grinning broadly. "Security. He was doing the front gates today. James is going to send him on a . . . what do you call it? Refresher course."

I didn't want to think about the re-education Stephan had in store for him. But I figured that anyone who worked for the Guvnor would know the consequences of screwing up. And then I realized that "anyone" would soon include me.

"Terry will drive you home." The huge minder stepped forward.

"That's all right, I'll take the Tube," I said.

"Terry's my driver. He'll drop you right at your door. I insist." Of course, McGovern wanted to know where I lived. Did that mean he didn't know already? He held out his hand again. "So long, Finn, and best of luck, yeah?"

"Thanks, Guvnor."

I wasn't sure McGovern actually cared for that nickname, but maybe he didn't hear. He had already turned away to talk to James, and my view of them was blocked by the mountain that was Terry. I took the hint, gathered up my soggy clothes, stuffed them into the plastic bag and followed Terry meekly towards the carport.

Terry drove me home in one of those four-wheel-drive tanks wealthy London mums use to shuttle their kids about, protected from the riff-raff by two tonnes of steel and leather and tinted glass. The ride was so smooth and silent Terry could have run over a motorbike without my noticing, I thought. Maybe he already had. I was perched in the back while the driver's seat creaked under his massive bulk. He drove without a word, not cursing the traffic, not looking at me in the rear-view mirror, not listening to music or any radio station. I glanced at the rear of his massive shaved head, wondering how much he overheard about his boss's business. A hands-free headset plugged into his ear flashed a blue light every few seconds. I would have thought a car this flash would have a hands-free phone system built in.

Shit. My phone.

It had been in the pocket of my jeans when I jumped into the pool. Groping the plastic bag on the seat beside me I could feel that it still was, along with my wallet and my London travel card. The soaking wouldn't have affected them, but when I dug the mobile out of the pocket of my sodden jeans, it was clear dunking it in McGovern's pool had done it no good at all. It was seriously dead. It wasn't a case of bunging it in the airing cupboard and hoping for the best, either—I could see a bubble of air sliding about under the screen. It might come in handy as a spirit level, but that was about it.

"Number eighteen, yeah?" said Terry, as he turned into my road.

"Yes, thanks. Two thirds of the way down, on the left."

Our street was so narrow that delivery vans and minicabs would usually bump up on the kerb to let other traffic squeeze past, but Terry didn't bother with that. He pulled up, blocking the road, and sat with the engine running while I fumbled with the handle, heaved the door open and abseiled down to pavement level. "Thanks for the lift," I said, and was rewarded by a tiny nod. I shut the door, but he didn't drive off immediately. The front passenger windows were only lightly tinted, and I could feel him watching me as I turned away, walked up the short path, produced my keys—still cold and wet—and opened my front door. Still he didn't move. When I stepped inside and shut the door behind me I finally heard the faint smooth purr of the vehicle speeding away down the street.

The cardboard box full of the stuff Prendergast had returned was still sitting on the living-room chair, and the bowl I'd eaten breakfast out of was still sitting beside it, the cereal dried onto the sides like papier mâché. It used to drive Dad bonkers when I left my crockery sitting out, though he often did the same himself, as I liked pointing out to him.

After a little rooting around in the box I found what I was looking for—Dad's ancient mobile phone with its tiny monochrome screen. Dad had never been able to afford a modern flash one, and claimed he didn't want one anyway. He said he never could see the point of a handset that ran out of juice in one day when his old one easily lasted a week. Or did, that is, when he bothered to charge it, every month or so. He had left it charging when he went out to the pub that last night, though I'd told him often enough there was no point in having a mobile if he didn't take it with him. I quickly checked the last few numbers he'd called and that had called him, knowing the police would have done the same. Just as I expected, the last ten incoming calls were from me, some of them months ago, and all the calls he'd made were to our landline here at the house. No leads there.

When I opened the back of my dead phone, yet more water dribbled out of it. I chucked the battery, pulled out the SIM card, wiped it dry-ish on my tracksuit jacket, slid the SIM into my dad's phone and held down the "on" button. After a few seconds the handset flickered into life, farting a tinny little fanfare. It was a rubbish phone, and it wasn't going to impress any fashion victims or gadget freaks, but it would have to do for now.

As I stomped upstairs to change out of McGovern's tracksuit there was a beep-beep from the phone and the screen flashed up a voicemail icon. Someone had tried to call me earlier, presumably while I was dripping onto the Guvnor's shag pile carpet. I didn't recognize the sender's number, but it was local. I dialled my voicemail and listened.

"Mr. Maguire, this is Detective Sergeant Amobi from CID." His deep, calm voice made him sound more like a priest than a cop. "I called round to your house earlier, but you weren't in. I wanted to let you know that the inquest into your father's death will be held at Fulham Coroner's Court tomorrow morning at eleven a.m. As you were the one who found the body, you will be expected to attend and to testify.

"If you can't make it, the inquest will probably be adjourned until you can, and that might mean a delay in your father's body being released for burial. I'm sorry about the short notice, and for doing this over the phone rather than in person. I'll keep trying to reach you. If you get this message, I'd really appreciate it if you would call me back, here at the station, or on my mobile." He recited his number, and rang off.

Amobi sounded straight enough, but he wasn't running the investigation into Dad's murder—that prick Prendergast was. I would have liked to tell someone what I'd found out—about that "German journalist" at the Weaver's Arms that night, for one thing. CID had the means to contact that German newspaper—the *Zeitung* or whatever it was called—and find out if Hans was for real, and if he was, what Dad had said to him about the Guvnor. But according to Dad's drinking buddies the cops already knew about Hans and weren't interested. Maybe that was them playing their cards close to their chest, and in fact they really were looking, but I doubted it. Prendergast had already made up his mind.

Maybe I should take a lawyer along to this in-quest . . . or maybe that would suggest I had something to hide. Screw it, I thought, I wouldn't know where to find a decent lawyer at such short notice, even supposing I could afford one. I recalled the lazy, clueless jobs-worth who had pretended to defend me on the dealing charge years ago, and I figured that if it came to the

103

worst I could do a better job myself. But I was going to attend the inquest all the same. I wanted to get Dad's body back, not leave him lying naked in some industrial fridge for months. I called the number back and got put through to a bored-sounding detective who told me Amobi was out of the office and took a message.

The next morning I changed my clothes about three times, trying at first to look smart, then thinking I looked too much like The Defendant. I fretted, wondering if it even mattered how I dressed for an inquest, until I ran out of time, grabbed the blazer Dad had found for me in a charity shop last Christmas, pulled it on over a cleanish white shirt and jeans, and ran for the bus.

I arrived just in time, which spared me a wait on a plastic chair with the miserable-looking punters I glimpsed drifting around the corridors like souls in limbo. The uniformed woman on the front desk sent me straight to a shiny, over-lit room with rows of functional wooden benches facing a raised platform where the coroner sat, a silver-haired, sharp-faced woman in her fifties with half-moon glasses. The bloke in a suit sitting directly below her was the court clerk, I guessed. After standing for a quick muttered conference with the coroner he called out my dad's name.

I'd expected Prendergast to be there, but he'd sent along a bland junior detective constable called Jenkins, who took the witness stand and droned through the known facts of my dad's death like he was reading his girlfriend's shopping list. It all seemed accurate to me, except he claimed to have been one of the officers attending. I didn't remember seeing him there, but then he had the sort of face that was easy to ignore. Also he told the coroner that they were pursuing several lines of enquiry, when as far as I knew they had one prime suspect—me. But I restrained myself from jumping to my feet and shouting "objection."

After the detective left the stand my name was called, and I clambered self-consciously into the witness box, trying to push aside the bad associations. I wasn't put under oath, but simply asked questions, and answered as clearly and as dispassionately as I could. I wondered if I was being too dispassionate, but the coroner didn't seem to care. She made a few notes with her silver pen, conferred with the clerk of the court, and declared to the few people present that the victim's identity and the cause of death had been established to her satisfaction: Noel Patrick Maguire had been unlawfully killed by person or persons unknown, and she was adjourning the inquest until police had completed their enquiries.

I must have looked surprised—from what Amobi had said, I thought the inquest would be opened and closed the same day—because the coroner took her specs off and explained to me that I would be given a death certificate, and that I should take it to my local registry office to register the death. Since the police had declared they no longer needed to hold my father's body, it could be released into my care as next of kin.

I was out before noon and back on the Tube for the long schlep west to our local council offices, where births, marriages and deaths had to be reported. I'd never been there before; the offices were hemmed in by wilting willow trees, presumably intended to soften the building's brutal bulk and hard straight lines. I guessed it had been built in the seventies by an architect with shares in a concrete-pouring company. Signs in half a dozen languages pointed this way and that, to places where you could pay your council tax or complain about fly-tipping, but the location of the registry office appeared to be classified. Eventually I found a door with a glum notice sellotaped to the inside, forbidding the throwing of rice and confetti. It was oddly comforting to notice how often it had been ignored—there were lots of little pink paper horseshoes and grains of rice scattered about.

Through the door more signs led me to a small grey office where a small grey vase of plastic flowers sat on a small grey side table, and a small grey woman in a cardigan inspected my dad's death certificate. She took

me through a list of routine questions—my dad's full
name, date of birth, what he claimed to do for a living—
stamped a few bits of paper, gave one to me, handed me
back the certificate and directed me to a revolving rack
of leaflets in the corner.

What to do in the event of a death. The same leaflets
Elsa Kendrick had offered me from her big briefcase,
the morning after I came home from the nick. I looked
across at the main council building and thought about
going over, finding the Social Services office and asking after Kendrick again. Maybe I could find out why
she had gone off sick, why she'd come to visit me, and
how she'd known about Dad's death. But I knew they'd
only keep me waiting for hours before telling me they
couldn't tell me anything, and I'd had enough of strip
lights and plastic chairs and local government offices
for one day. I caught a bus back east that dropped me
outside the twenty-four-hour shop near my house, run
by two Indian blokes who, as far as I knew, never left
the premises. I grabbed a frozen steak and a pint of milk
and took them to the counter. The bloke grimaced when
I offered him the Guvnor's fifty-quid note, scribbled on
it with a security marker and held it up to the light. Then
he reluctantly punched the purchase into his bleeping
till, took the fifty and handed me my change. I was
heading home when I noticed a business I had walked

past a million times and never once been curious about. This time I paused.

The premises looked like a suburban house, separated from the street by a manicured lawn and a flowerbed dotted with anaemic daffodils. Behind the net curtains in the front window I could just make out a mahogany desk with a fancy pen mounted upright in a stand, beside a thick blue ledger lying closed on a blotter. Beyond the house was a yard surrounded by high walls, and on the wall facing the street solemn white lettering read: *Parker and Parker, Funeral Directors.*

I went up to the door, turned the handle gingerly and pushed. Somewhere a mournful little bell tinkled, and the cloying scent of lilies hit me in the face.

six

Dad woke me by plonking a glass of orange juice on my bedside table.

"Sorry, Finn," he said. "But you need the vitamins." He smiled. His hair was still sticky with blood, I noticed. His mobile phone was ringing, but he just stood there, smiling at me.

"You going to answer that?" I said.

"You answer it. Tell them I'm not at home any more."

It really was ringing, his phone—my phone—vibrating so wildly it was about to dance off my bedside table. No glass of orange juice. I picked up the phone and squinted at the screen. *Number withheld*. I pressed "answer."

"Finn Maguire," I croaked.

"Be at the Iron Bridge five p.m. Tell 'em I sent you." It took me a second to register who was calling, but then I recognized the sneer in James's voice.

"Five p.m.? Today?" Dad's body was going to be laid out in the undertaker's today. From the brief, angry pause before James replied I got the impression he didn't like having his instructions questioned.

"You want this fucking job or not?"

"Yeah. I mean, thanks," I said. "I'll be there."

He hung up.

I checked the screen for the time. It was just gone seven. I'd always supposed professional criminals slept late and did their gangstering at night. But maybe James was just going to bed. He'd done me a favour anyway; spring sunshine was streaming in the window, and my legs felt twitchy. I hadn't been running for a few days, and I needed to make up for lost time.

While I ran I thought about the arrangements I'd made for Dad's funeral. The undertaker, Mr. Stone, was a pale, podgy guy in his late twenties, with beautifully manicured hands and a practised sympathetic expression that looked even graver when I'd mentioned how skint I was. He'd asked me if I intended burial or cremation, and I'd gone for cremation. Dad had always found graveyards depressing, and I presumed he hadn't wanted to end up in one. He'd never visited the graves of his own parents, and didn't feel guilty about it—he said once that he'd done his bit while they were alive and could still appreciate it. The undertaker explained smoothly that cremation required another doctor's signature, but that he would see to all that. I guessed that service would be added to his bill as well.

One of Elsa Kendrick's leaflets had explained the government grants that people with no income could get to help with funerals. The money went direct to the undertaker, but it didn't cover everything, and I got the impression that under his sad, calm exterior Mr. Stone was taking every opportunity to bump up his bill. Of course, most people burying relatives don't want to be thought stingy, and are too embarrassed to haggle, but I didn't care what people thought. Especially when it came to my dad—finding a bargain was almost a vocation, for him. I sensed Stone the undertaker was getting a bit fed up with me insisting everything should be done on the cheap—like when I went for a Monday service because it cost less than one on a Saturday. When I asked if he was related to any of the Parkers, he explained smoothly there were no Parkers any more. The firm had been bought out years ago by a big national chain. I could see why big business had got involved: a market where the product never goes out of fashion and the clients think it's bad manners to haggle. Not that I envied Stone his steady job.

I got back home from my run forty seconds over my average time, and scolded myself mentally for slacking off. After a shower and a shave I ate my breakfast out of the bowl I'd left on the table. I rinsed it out first—I'm not a total slob.

I still wasn't sure how I was going to pay for the funeral. I had no idea what this job at the Iron Bridge restaurant would pay, presuming they gave me a job. For all my attempts to cut corners, Stone's written estimate suggested I'd end up owing him a few hundred quid. I still had most of the money McGovern had given me, but I was saving it for a piss-up for Dad's old mates at the Weaver's Arms. I was pretty sure that Dad would have preferred that to being cremated in a posher coffin.

But now the whole business of money was really starting to get to me. The bank, the benefits people, they'd have to be told. What would happen when I couldn't pay the mortgage? Would the bank take the house back? Or was it my house now? Did I inherit it from Dad when he died, or was he supposed to leave it to me in his will? I didn't even know if he'd made a will. Jesus . . . maybe it would end up belonging to my mother. Where the hell would I live then?

If Dad *had* ever made a will, I had a good idea where I might find it.

I pushed open the door of his room. The curtains were still open. Dad always made his bed right after he got up, but that was usually as neat as he got in here.

Shirts and jeans of varying degrees of dirtiness were still piled on his bedside chair. His chest of drawers was strewn with copper coins not worth the trouble of gathering up, old pens, and dried-up bottles of anti-perspirant he hadn't thrown away. The room still smelled of him, I noticed, but the scent was fading, succumbing to the smell of gathering dust. I transferred the clothes to the bed, dragged the chair over to the wardrobe, and climbed up onto it. Under a crushed, musty collection of hats was a Chinese fibre suitcase with two clasps, one busted. I grabbed the handle, dragged it down, plonked it onto the bed and flicked the good catch open.

The case was crammed with documents, some in manila folders, others in envelopes, in no particular order that I could see. The first envelope I looked into held yellowing official certificates. The topmost had the word "BIRTH" at the top. In a column on the left I made out my birth name, Finn Pearce Grey. The next document had the word "MARRIAGE" at the top. Noel Patrick Maguire, actor, to Lesley Helen Grey, actress. I put the certificates back. They were no use to me.

A second bulging manila envelope held a whole wodge of printouts, all similar. I recognized the bank logo on the top left-hand corner, but the entries and the figures and the endlessly repeated phrases merged and blurred as I stared at them. I did make out three words that kept reappearing at the head of each page: *Interest-Only Repayments*. I stuffed them back in the envelope and went on searching. After half an hour my eyes were aching and my head was pounding and I hadn't seen the word Will anywhere.

I stuffed the envelopes and folders back into the suitcase, flipped the lid shut and clicked the catch. I was going to shove the case back on top of the wardrobe, but decided not to bother; I'd probably need it again soon. I slid the case under Dad's bed, picked up his shirts and stuffed them into the laundry basket. Then I wondered why. He wasn't going to wear them, and I didn't want them. But I wasn't ready to stuff them into a bin bag and dump them in the doorway of a charity shop. I wasn't being sentimental, though part of me wished I felt that way. I just couldn't be arsed.

The Chapel of Rest was dimly-lit, slightly stuffy and windowless. For a moment it reminded me of the room in the nick where I'd been questioned, but this one was slightly larger. Its most distinguishing feature was Dad, lying in a casket resting on wooden trestles. The coffin was shiny lacquered chipboard trying to look like wood, with golden plastic handles that weren't even trying to look like brass. Presumably when you bought the cheapest possible coffin Mr. Stone made sure everyone could tell, in case any other punters got the same idea.

Dad was beyond caring, of course. He looked asleep, although his head was tilted slightly too far back, as if he was trying to keep his chin clear of his shirt, but maybe that was to conceal the damage to his skull. Stone's people had dressed him in his second-best suit. My dad only had two: this one was the dark-brown designer number he found in a second-hand shop, and it still looked pretty smart. His charcoal one would have looked even smarter, but I needed that one myself for the funeral, even if my shoulders strained the seams of the jacket and I couldn't quite button it closed. Dad's fair hair and scruffy beard—tinged with grey—had been combed, maybe even been trimmed. If they'd used any make-up, I couldn't tell. His skin was the colour it had always been; but it was too still, unnaturally still, deathly still. When I touched his forehead it was cold. I had a sudden urge to kiss it all the same, the way he used to kiss me, even when I got to be taller than him, but I held back, thinking that would look too weird and creepy.

Then I realized I didn't give a shit what it looked like, and I leaned down, and I kissed his forehead. It was like kissing a smooth round stone coated in cold wax.

Stone was standing in the corner, hands clasped over his crotch. "Thanks, Mr. Stone," I said. "He looks OK." Stone nodded. I wasn't sure if I'd said the right thing. I didn't know if there was a right thing to say. I hadn't prayed since I was a little kid at Catholic school, and I hadn't cried since Mum left. I wasn't going to start now; neither did anyone any good.

"Will you be staying to greet friends and relatives?" asked Stone, as I turned to leave.

"I haven't told any of his friends yet," I said.

"It's just we've already had a call from a lady wanting to pay her respects," said Stone. "Although I didn't get her name, I'm sorry."

"Did she say when she was coming?"

"I told her she could view the body any time after two."

"I can't stay. There's a meeting I have to go to." It sounded like a feeble excuse, but that couldn't be helped.

"Not to worry," he said. "We'll see to it."

I left, but I didn't go back home. I took a window seat in the cafe opposite instead. Originally the owner had wanted to create a chic French bistro, but the locals' constant demand for egg and chips had worn him down, and now the sad smell of stale chip fat clashed with the cheery red gingham decor. I ordered a coffee and got a big cafetière that must have held four or five cups, but I didn't neck it; I didn't want to be in the loo when this woman, whoever she was, turned up to pay her respects. I had an inkling of who she might be. I had thought the cafe would be an ideal vantage point, but I hadn't allowed for the bus stop right outside. Every ten minutes a double-decker would pull up and sit there rumbling, blocking the view. When the second one turned up I was still craning my neck to see the undertaker's front door when I realized the woman I was looking for had just climbed off the bus.

Though I was practically next to her, on the other side of the window, Elsa Kendrick the social worker seemed too preoccupied to notice me. She pulled up the collar of her coat, checked the traffic and hurried across the road towards Parker and Parker. I thought about going after her, but buttonholing her in the Chapel of Rest over my dad's body didn't seem like a good idea. Besides, she'd lied to me once, and she could just as easily lie to me again, and walk away leaving me none the wiser. I decided to take a leaf out of the Guvnor's book.

I went to the counter and paid for my coffee, keeping one eye on the door of the undertaker's premises across the road. About twenty minutes later Kendrick re-appeared, a hanky clenched in her hand, her face downcast, her eyes and nose reddened. Turning left she walked to the bus stop on the far side of the road, just

117

up from Parker and Parker, to head back the way she had come. I waited in the cafe until the north-bound double-decker appeared, counted to ten while Kendrick boarded with the other passengers, then dashed out of the cafe and across the road. The bus driver was just closing the doors when I got to the stop, but when I joined my hands in jokey supplication he opened them again. I swiped my travel card on the reader, turned and quickly surveyed the lower deck. No sign of Kendrick— she must have taken a seat upstairs. As the bus moved off I pushed my way right to the back of the lower deck, slid down into the rearmost corner seat, and waited.

It had been a bit of a gamble, but I couldn't see any other way of finding out where Kendrick lived, short of chasing the bus on foot. When she'd arrived, I'd noticed, she had come down the steps from the top deck of the bus, and I'd been hoping she'd travel back that way too. I could see why she'd prefer the top deck: the lower was always packed with enormous buggies, gloomy pensioners and school kids playing crap music through the tinny speakers on their phones. Luckily it was still too early for school kids, but there were plenty of gloomy pensioners sucking their dentures, and several mums lugged buggies and babies on and off through the course of the journey. At every stop I tensed, getting ready for Kendrick to come down, but the bus trundled on and on, further into the endless grey warren of shops and streets and traffic lights that was West London, until we were about five miles from my house. Still she did not appear. I was beginning to think I'd screwed up, and that she'd never got on the bus. Maybe she'd noticed me following and shaken off her tail . . . no, she'd have to be paranoid to think anyone was following her. Except, of course, I was.

Buses always make me doze off. They might be noisy but they're warm, and the movement rocks me to sleep. I heard raised heels clacking down the stairs, realized my eyes were closed, and opened them just in time to see Elsa Kendrick at the exit doors, ringing the bell. The bus slowed and stopped, the doors hissed open and she climbed down. Turning left she walked back the way the bus had come, and I waited till she had passed before I started to rise from my seat. The old man in the flat cap who had settled in beside me snorted and scowled, as if I was getting off just to inconvenience him, and took his time moving aside. The doors had already started to close by the time I got to them, and I had to wait agonizing seconds for the driver to open them again. I jumped out and looked around as the bus moved off, and caught a glimpse of Kendrick's red hair as she crossed the road further down at a set of lights. Crossing the road behind the bus I nearly ended up on the handlebars of a pizza delivery moped coming the other way. The rider meeped his little horn and swore at me through his helmet, but I ignored him and hurried on.

Kendrick walked with her head held high and her hands in her coat pockets. She moved quickly and with poise, quite light on her feet. She had a nice figure, I had to admit, and it wasn't hard to keep my eyes on it. When she turned left abruptly and disappeared I hurried my pace.

I was just in time. When I got to the corner she was about ten doors further up, fishing in her handbag. The terraced houses were narrow and set back from the pavement by tiny low-walled front gardens about two paces deep. If she had looked back I would have had nowhere to hide—apart from behind a lamppost— but finally she pulled a bunch of keys from her handbag, chose one, opened the door in front of her and stepped inside without a backward glance. I heard her letterbox rattle as the door shut.

I walked up and paused at her gate. The house was slightly larger than ours, but where most other houses in that street had one front door, this had two. It had clearly been converted into upstairs and downstairs flats, and I had no idea which door was hers. There were no obvious clues from where I stood. A small flower-bed had been cut into the concrete of the front yard, and a few scrawny rose bushes were poking optimistically through its sticky brown clay. Both front doors were identical mass-produced hardwood numbers, unpainted, with a few panels of yellow-tinted rippled glass to allow the sunshine in, when there was any. I saw a light go on behind the right-hand door, towards the rear of the flat—in the kitchen, I guessed. The bell pushes were identical too—black plastic numbers, each with a little clear window below for a name, neither with any name in it. What the hell, I thought, I've a fifty–fifty chance of being right. I pressed the right-hand button, heard a bell buzz, and waited. Footsteps approached and I saw Kendrick's face through one of the glass panels, checking me out, before her hand reached for the latch.

She only opened the door halfway, and when she saw my face I could see her thinking about shutting it again. I spoke before she had the chance.

"Ms. Kendrick, I'm sorry, I called Social Services, but they said you were on leave."

"This is my home. You shouldn't have come here." There was a large glass of white wine in her hand, I noticed.

"I'm sorry, I just wanted to talk to you. I know you

were a friend of my dad's." I didn't, but it seemed like a fair guess. Not many social workers cried over their dead clients. "I just wanted to talk to somebody about . . . everything that's happened. I need advice." I wasn't sure if the little-boy-lost routine was working, but she hadn't slammed the door yet.

"How did you know where I lived?"

"My dad left lots of papers behind. I'd been looking through them." It wasn't a lie. Not as such.

"He wrote something about me?" She looked worried, and at the same time intrigued. I glanced at my watch. I was going to be late for this meeting at the restaurant. Sod it, so I'd be late. "Can I come in? I promise I won't take up too much of your time. I have a job interview at five."

That at least was true, and I suppose she could tell, because she stepped back and opened the door for me to come in. I shut it behind me and followed her down the narrow hall, sealed off from the stairs by a thin partition, and into the front room. Two rooms downstairs and a kitchen at the back, I guessed. The middle door—the door to her bedroom, I supposed—was shut. The walls and carpet of the living room were in pale neutral colours, with cream-coloured throws draped over square, modern armchairs from that flat-pack Swedish store. Pale colours make a place look bigger, I knew, and this flat needed all the help it could get. The whole place was anally neat, although there was an odd sweet-sour smell underneath, like perfume that had gone off.

"Would you like a drink?" Kendrick waved her wineglass at me, then blushed. "Tea or coffee, I mean, of course."

"I'm fine, thanks," I said, perching on the edge of the sofa. I wasn't sure how I was going to play this, or where to start.

"You said you wanted advice."

"Yeah. This has all happened so fast, I don't know where to begin."

"Did you read those leaflets I left you?"

"I looked through them. The thing is, when you came round, I thought it was official business. But your office said you've been on leave for months now. You were close to my dad, weren't you?"

She looked down, embarrassed and timid now she could no longer hide behind her expired ID, and perched herself on the edge of the armchair, facing me. "I couldn't believe it, when I heard what had happened," she said. "Especially when I heard . . ."

"That the cops thought I did it?"

"I wanted to see you for myself. I'm sorry about . . . all the business with the official ID. Your dad hadn't

123

told you about us, and I was trying to respect that. But as soon as I took one look at you I knew the police had it all wrong. Noel told me so much about you—he was so proud of you. What you'd been through, and how you'd straightened yourself out, through sheer willpower."

"Yeah. But it was mostly his willpower."

"So what was it he wrote about me?"

I opened my mouth and closed it again. "I don't know," I said finally. "A lot of his papers were stolen."

She seemed amused that I'd managed to fool her by appealing to her vanity. "He didn't write anything about me, did he? And he never did tell you about us." It was her turn to sound like a sulky adolescent.

"I thought there was something going on," I said, "a few months ago. He'd got himself a decent haircut, smartened up his appearance. Bought that brown suit when he couldn't really afford it. Sometimes he'd come in really late, and creep about trying not to wake me up, but I could tell . . ."

"What?"

"That he was happier." Her face brightened. She looked wistful. "Maybe he meant to tell me. We never talked that much. Well, he did, but I never really listened. And now it's too late." That was true as well. I'd noticed the truth could be a way of disarming people.

124

Kendrick sighed and took another drink of wine. It was a big glass but it was already nearly empty.

"How did you two meet?" I asked.

"He was at the Coach and Horses—our local—doing some research. He was supposed to be meeting some architect or something, he said, and he thought I was her. Maybe that was just a line, but it worked."

"I'm sure it wasn't," I said. "He always found research easier than actually writing. What was he researching?"

"Oh, there's this local urban myth, about some gangster who buried his victims in the pillars of the flyover. Where the motorway crosses the canal."

She smiled at the absurdity of it. But having met the Guvnor it didn't sound absurd to me. Who had Dad been talking to?

"After that he was up a few times a week. Sometimes he'd spend the afternoon here, with me . . ." She looked coy. I guessed they hadn't been playing Scrabble. "He was such a sweet guy—I can't believe that mother of yours walked out on him. And her own child. What a bitch."

She said that with such bitterness it sounded as if she was the abandoned child, not me. I wanted to reassure her I'd got over it, but decided it was none of her business. Besides . . . I wasn't sure I ever had.

"I asked him to stay over a few times," she went on.

"He never did. Always had to get home to you." This with a tight smile of envy. "He was going to bring me to meet you. Soon, he said. He had to get you used to the idea first, of him having a girlfriend, after it just being the two of you for so long. And then . . ."

"He was murdered," I said.

She flinched, then smiled sadly. "Yeah."

"And you never met any of his friends?" I asked. "At the Weaver's Arms?"

Oh, crap. The Weaver's Arms—the story the old blokes told me . . . my dad hiding under a table.

Elsa saw the look on my face. "What?"

"Sorry, Elsa—but can I ask, are you married?"

"Separated." She held up her left hand, and I could just make out a fading white band on her ring finger.

"When did that happen? The separation."

"Last year. Long before I met Noel."

"What does he look like? Your husband."

"My ex, you mean? He's forty or so. Big belly. Bald on top, short white hair. And he has these tattoos all over his forearms. Fake Maori ones."

My dad hiding under the table from a huge bloke with Maori tattoos . . . Dad had been knocking off his wife.

"Why did the two of you split?" I said. "Sorry to be so nosy."

"Jonno has . . . a bit of a temper." Her voice had dropped almost to a whisper. She drained her wineglass.

"Was he ever violent towards you?"

"Now you sound like the social worker," she said, and got up. "Sure you won't have anything?" I shook my head. She went into the kitchen. I followed her and stood in the hall while she took a bottle of wine from the fridge and refilled her glass.

"What does your ex do for a living?"

"He's a lorry driver. International. He's back and forward to Germany and Holland all the time."

"You must have been lonely."

She glared at me, as if I'd been pitying or patronizing her. Maybe I had, I realized, and went on hurriedly, "Is he in the country this week?"

I was trying not to say, "Where was he the night my dad was murdered?" but she got the implication anyway and froze, her wineglass halfway to her lips.

"No." She shook her head. "He couldn't have. Not even Jonno. That's just too—"

"If I wanted to talk to him . . .?"

"You mustn't. He'll—look, he probably wasn't even here that night—"

"Fine, he can tell that to the police."

"Don't tell the police. Please, Finn. You don't know what he's like."

127

"I won't tell them I spoke to you, I promise," I said.

She turned away to sip her wine as if she was ashamed of me watching her.

"He's in the phone book," she said finally. "Under *Haulage*. Jonno Kendrick."

"OK," I said. A glance at my watch told me I had less than an hour to get to Pimlico for this job interview at the restaurant. I was on the wrong side of West London and rush hour was just starting. "I have to go," I said. I turned and headed for the door.

"Finn, wait." She plonked her wineglass down and came after me. "Promise me you won't do anything stupid."

"Thanks, Elsa. And thanks for . . . making Dad happy," I said.

"Stay a bit longer," she said. "Have a proper drink." She grinned. She had a lovely shy smile that went all the way to her eyes. "I won't tell anyone if you don't."

"Sorry, Elsa, I really do have a job interview," I said.

"Call them. Put it off. You've been through a terrible experience, Finn. We both have." She laid her hand on my arm and looked at me, and abruptly I found myself wondering what she'd done as a social worker to get herself suspended. She must have caught what I was thinking, because she pulled her hand away and started playing with her hair.

"Bye," I said, as I turned the latch.

"Take care, OK?"

She shut the door behind me and I hurried back towards the main street. That was weird, I thought. Did she really just make a pass at me? I'd started off afraid I'd never get into her house, and ended up worried I'd never get out. I wondered if Dad had felt the same way.

seven

I arrived at the Iron Bridge five minutes late and sweating. The doors were open, but it was too early for any customers. The decor was muted and classy, with discreet lighting glinting off crystal wineglasses and spotless cutlery laid out on crisp cream linen. It wasn't cutting-edge trendy or chintzy nostalgic, it was just timeless and cool. A waitress all in black apart from a white cotton apron was flitting like a hummingbird from table to table, deftly arranging tiny pots of flowers. She looked up as I entered, and I could see that the staff were chosen as carefully as the decor. Slim and curvy with perfect skin and dark brown eyes, she was Malaysian, or Chinese perhaps. She approached me with a wide, relaxed smile. If my jeans and trainers and sweatshirt made me look more like a mugger than a customer, she didn't let her opinion show.

"Hi there, can I help you?"

"I'm here to see Mr. Eccles? About a job."

She blinked. Of course, I thought, Eccles is a celebrity chef, he's on telly, he doesn't do his own hiring and firing. I should have asked for the major-domo, or whatever the manager is called in a place like this.

"I'll find out if he's available," she said at last. "Who shall I say is asking for him?"

"Maguire," I said. "Finn Maguire." I didn't mention the Guvnor and I didn't intend to. Whoever interviewed me would know who'd recommended me, I thought, and besides, I was a bit embarrassed by the association.

"Take a seat," she said, waving a graceful hand. I thanked her, but I didn't sit down. While she headed out back I tried not to fidget or put my hands in my pockets. The place intimidated me, but I didn't want to look like a total chav.

She returned a few minutes later and gave me a practised smile. "Would you come this way, please?" Standing aside, she gestured for me to precede her towards the back of the restaurant. By the swing doors leading to the kitchen was an unadorned door so discreet it was almost invisible. I stopped, unsure whether it opened with a push or lowered like a drawbridge. I may not have looked like a chav, but I may well have looked like the village idiot. The waitress stepped ahead of me, pushed the door open gently, and directed me down a dim corridor painted dark red. "Chef is in the office," she said. "First door on the left."

I knocked on the first door and waited. I wasn't sure I heard anyone tell me to come in, but I just wanted to get this ordeal over with, so I opened the door and entered.

Eccles's office was in much the same understated decor as the restaurant, but it was dominated by a sleek desk of pale wood with a computer perched on it—one of those super-slick ones with everything integrated into the massive screen. I noticed the office had its own kitchen en suite. It seemed odd, when there was a fully equipped commercial kitchen next door, but maybe Eccles liked to work up his new recipes in a private setting.

Chris Eccles himself was seated at the desk, in chef's whites, looking through a pile of receipts and scribbling figures onto a pad beside him, ignoring the computer. It figured somehow; he always made a big deal on his TV show about preparing ingredients by hand. I walked up to the desk, a little nervously, and cleared my throat. He looked up, unsmiling, and examined me over the narrow designer glasses that had become one of his trademarks.

"Hi. I'm Finn Maguire."

Eccles glanced at his watch. It was seven minutes past five. I had the impression he wanted to bollock me, but he merely jerked his chin at the chair facing his desk.

I sat down and laid my hands in my lap, wishing I'd gone home from the undertaker's to change and shower instead of chasing Elsa Kendrick across West London.

"I'm told you have kitchen experience," said Eccles. Straight in, no small talk. His tone was neutral, as if the decision had already been made and he was only going through the motions. On camera he had a twinge of Geordie to his accent; in real life it seemed he didn't bother.

"I don't, I'm sorry. Only serving at a fast-food place."

Now he looked pained. "Which one?"

"Does it matter?"

"And what sort of position did you have in mind?"

"Anything, Mr. Eccles, I'm really not fussy."

"Front of house?"

"Waiting tables, you mean?"

"Yes, waiting tables. Serving customers. Handling wine."

"I could do that, but . . . I don't think I'd do your place justice."

Now his jaw was working. It was a strong, square jaw, and he had thick black hair that rarely did what it was told. Viewers—not all of them female—used to swoon at the way he rolled up his sleeves and wrestled with his ingredients, twinkling for the camera. But he wasn't twinkling now, now he was looking really pissed off, as if some zany celeb had come in and asked him to do egg and beans on toast and serve it on a plastic tray, naked apart from his apron.

"Sorry, Mr. Maguire, but do you consider waiting on the public beneath you? Because that's what we do here."

"No, no. Look, Mr. Eccles, I think you might have got the wrong idea. I know who it was that suggested you see me"—*told you to hire me*, I guessed, but that was probably better left unsaid—"but I'm not one of his—I mean, I don't expect—"

I took a deep breath and started again. "Thing is, I really do need a job. A proper job, and I really will do anything. Cleaning toilets, washing out bins, I don't mind. I mean, if I'm good enough, and you think I could handle it, I'd love to learn to work front of house, someday. But believe me, you don't want me out there any time soon, not unless your customers like their food in their laps."

Eccles looked thoughtful, as if he wanted to believe me, but thought this might be some sort of trap.

"And what will you tell our mutual friend?"

Obviously he meant McGovern, and obviously McGovern was no friend of his.

"I won't tell him anything. Even if you don't have anything for me to do, and send me home. He owed me a favour, and meeting you was the favour. He never promised me a job. It's up to you. Honestly."

Eccles took his glasses off and tapped the arm against his teeth. It was a weird moment—I'd seen him do that on telly, in a commercial for Irish butter. "Come with me," was all he said. He stood, pushed back his chair and strode out of the room, me scampering after him like Igor after Dr. Frankenstein.

As we entered the kitchen a low hum of activity jumped in volume. There was a lot of clattering of pans and shouts of "Yes, Chef!" Clearly all the kitchen staff were terrified of Eccles and determined to look busy and efficient. He led me past one counter where a frantic girl folded and crimped tiny sculptures of pastry, and another where a chef, his hands glittering with scales, gutted and filleted a gleaming pile of fish. Right at the back of the kitchen a tall lugubrious bloke in chef's whites topped off with incongruous long black rubber gauntlets was scraping what looked like dried egg off a stainless-steel pan.

"Gordon," said Eccles. The tall chef turned and practically jumped to attention, barking, "Yes, Chef!"

"You're on fish," said Eccles. "Go help Eric. And listen very carefully to what he tells you."

Gordon beamed in delight and tugged frantically at his rubber gloves. He was being promoted, I realized.

135

How many eons had he been serving his apprenticeship here, scrubbing pots?

"Yes, Chef. Thank you, Chef," he babbled. Eccles merely jerked his head for him to get a move on. Picking up Gordon's discarded gloves, he slapped them against my chest.

"Got a dishwasher at home?"

"No."

"You know how to wash up, then."

"Yes."

"*Yes, Chef.* You want overalls?"

"I'm fine like this, Chef," I said.

"So get stuck in."

And he walked away.

Pulling on the rubber gauntlets I surveyed the teetering stack of pans to my left, encrusted with pastry, dried-on egg and what looked like fish skins burned onto stainless steel. I squirted soap into the vast shiny sink, turned the hot tap on full blast, picked up a handful of steel wool and started to whistle.

After half an hour I was wishing I had asked for overalls, because it was hot steamy work, and my T-shirt was clinging to my torso with sweat. I didn't think it was the sort of kitchen where going topless was encouraged—the kitchen staff were all in full buttoned-up uniform, though it was as hot as Hell's boiler house in there. Eccles moved among them calmly, rarely raising his voice except to be heard over the hiss and roar of the pans and burners. He saved the histrionics and drama for his TV shows, I guessed. Gordon came to see how I was getting on at one point, and I got him to show me where the overalls were. They were so big and loose they let in a cool draught, so wearing just them as a top I could toss my sweaty T-shirt to one side and keep going.

In the course of the evening the noise and activity rose to a roar, and the dirty pans piled up like shrapnel from a battlefield, but I scrubbed them down, rinsed them off, stacked them on the worktop to my right and kept going. At one point the pastry chef I'd noticed earlier dashed over, plonked down cutlery and a plate of salad with a chunk of salmon baked in pastry, and ran off again. I ate it in snatches so as not to slow down my output. It was bloody delicious. Apart from that, everyone else in the kitchen pretty much ignored my existence, which was fine by me.

I noticed the noise diminishing before I ever thought to look at the clock. It was gone half eleven, and the pile of pans had shrunk to the extent I could actually count them. By twelve I was rinsing down the sink with a cloth, unaware that Eccles had come to watch me. When

I sensed him there and looked round, he was standing with his arms folded and a vague grin on his face as if he'd won a bet.

"That'll do," he said.

"Do I get the job?"

He snorted. Reaching into the rear pocket of his chef's trousers he produced a slim wallet, opened it, deftly thumbed out five twenties and handed them to me. I stared at them.

"For seven hours' work?"

His look told me not to ask stupid questions.

"Thanks very much, Mr. Eccles." The rubber gauntlets slurped as I peeled them off.

"Your name's Finn?" he asked, as if he hadn't really been listening earlier.

"Yeah."

"Sort out your shifts with Josie, the manager, OK? And if you can't make it for any reason, call her."

"I won't," I said. "I mean, I will. I mean, I'll be here, Chef."

He nodded and walked out, to reverent murmurs of "Night, Chef." I chucked the overalls into a laundry basket, wrung out my T-shirt and tugged it back on.

On the Tube home I kept touching the notes folded in my pocket as if they might vanish like fairy gold. I'd signed up for seven nights a week, with two days off every fortnight. A hundred quid a night, seven nights a week . . . But maybe that was just a starting bonus. Maybe once Eccles put me on the books properly he'd start paying me the statutory minimum. No, I thought. He's paying me over the odds because he thinks I'm part of some protection scam, and if he doesn't stuff my pockets I'll go running to the Guvnor. But I'd told him it wasn't like that—all I'd wanted was a fair night's pay for a fair night's work. Maybe I should tell him again, I thought. A hundred pounds a night, though . . . bollocks, I'd tell him sometime soon.

Then I remembered—the money hadn't really been the point, not originally. The point had been to get inside one of the Guvnor's businesses, to see if I could dig up the truth about who killed Dad. But if Eccles's restaurant was just a cover for some criminal operation, it was a pretty elaborate and expensive one. Restaurants could launder money, I supposed—I had been paid in cash, after all—but not on the scale of a bookie's or a casino. Did the Guvnor invest in the Iron Bridge because he wanted part of a classy and upmarket establishment to complement his usual nightclubs and brothels? But if Eccles was that scared of McGovern, how the hell did he end up in business with him?

Unless he was never given an option.

I wasn't sure how much I could find out about the Guvnor by washing pans every evening, but suddenly I realized I was too knackered to think about it any more. It was nearly one when I turned into my own street, and I was so shattered I could barely lift my feet. I didn't notice the girl till I was practically beside her; she'd been hidden by a bay window of the house that poked out onto the pavement, two doors up from mine. In fact, I walked right past her, and she had to call to me from under the hood of the anorak that was hiding her face in shadow.

"Hey," she said. "Got a light?"

"Sorry," I said. "Don't smoke."

"So I can't bum a cigarette, then?"

"Why do you need a light if you don't have any cigarettes?" I said.

She pulled her hood back, shook her hair free, looked more closely at my face, and grimaced.

"Oh, shit," she said. "It's you."

Last time we'd met Andy had claimed she was hogging the best seats in Max Snax and sent me to throw her out. What she was doing in my street at one o'clock this morning I had no idea, but rather than leave her there I invited her into my house, and she shrugged as if she didn't care one way or the other. She came in all the same, though, and now she stood in the middle of my living room, hugging her parka tightly around her.

"It's colder in here than it is out there," she said.

"I know. You want a hot drink?"

"Can't you just turn the heating on?"

"Sure," I said. I went to the boiler in the kitchen, flicked the switch and listened for the *tick tick whumph*. When I came back into the living room she was flicking idly through the window envelopes on the table addressed to my dad. I was pretty sure they were bills, and they'd been piling up for the last few days, but I hadn't been able to bring myself to open them. I'd never have made head nor tail of them anyway.

"My name's Finn, by the way," I said.

"I know," she said. "I heard you might have some weed. Or some sniff."

"Who told you that?"

"So do you or don't you?"

"I have beer," I said. "That's it."

"I'll have a beer, then." Still hugging her anorak about her, she let herself fall backwards onto the sofa. The fake leather creaked and farted as she sank into the clapped-out cushions. I didn't move. She glanced up like she was wondering what was holding up her order, met my eye and looked away. "I'm Zoe," she said in a small voice.

As I fetched the second-last can of beer from the fridge

I saw that if she asked for anything to eat I was stuffed. All the fridge held was half an onion wrapped in cling film and going mouldy, and an empty margarine tub. I really would have to resign myself to going shopping.

"So how's business in the glamorous world of high-speed catering?" Zoe called from the other room. I returned and handed her the can.

"Same old. Sorry, all the glasses are dirty," I said.

"Where are your parents?" she asked as she pulled back the tab and took a slug.

"My mother left a long time ago. My dad's dead."

"Really? Wish mine was." Her childish bravado irritated me. She had no idea what it meant.

"He was murdered. A few days ago. Funeral's on Monday."

"Shit." She looked embarrassed. I suspected that didn't happen very often. "Sorry, I mean." She took another swig. Now I felt childish, as if I'd been boasting. *My dad's deader than yours.*

"I don't work at Max Snax any more," I said. "They fired me. I was actually glad, because I hated the bloody place, but I never had the bottle to quit."

"So what are you doing now?"

"Washing pans in a restaurant."

"Doesn't exactly sound like a promotion."

"Money's better," I said.

"Aren't you having one?" She held up the can.

"I'm too knackered," I said. "And I don't drink that much anyway."

"I should go," she said. But she didn't move.

"Aren't your folks wondering where you are?"

"My dad doesn't give a shit," she said. "And the feeling's mutual."

"So where does he think you are?"

"At a friend's." She shrugged again. I wondered how bad things must be at home if she'd rather be sitting in the house of a total stranger with nobody knowing where she really was.

"What were you doing in Max Snax anyway?" I said. "At that time of the morning? Have you been excluded from school or something?"

"I was just bunking off. You don't think I'd wear that shit-brown uniform if I didn't have to? Why don't you put some music on?"

"Hi-fi's knackered." I yawned.

She put the can down, as if she really meant to leave, but still didn't get up off the sofa.

"Thanks for this," she said. "I really should go."

"Want me to call you a taxi?"

"No thanks. Don't have enough money anyway."

"What were you going to use to buy drugs from me?"

"Why do you have to ask so many bloody questions?"

143

"It's my house," I said.

"Use your fucking imagination," she said. But she couldn't meet my eye. She had the shameless slapper act off pat, but it was still an act.

"In that case, I'm really sorry I don't have any weed," I said. "What do I get for the beer?"

"Sparkling conversation."

I laughed, and she joined in, and we sat there giggling like kids for a moment.

"Where are you planning to go?" I asked. "If you turn up at home this time of night, it'll just make your dad more suspicious."

The giggling evaporated. "What do you care?" she said. The tone of her voice made it sound like she said that a lot.

"You can crash here if you want," I said. "On the sofa. I can leave the heating on for tonight, down low. There's a spare quilt upstairs." It was on Dad's bed, but I wasn't going to offer her his bed. I didn't want her in his room, though I didn't mind her downstairs. In fact, I had to admit, I quite liked her being there. I didn't want to say so, though. I thought it'd sound lonely or lecherous or creepy, or all three, and I wasn't any of those. Was I?

"No thanks," she said, testing the sofa with her shoulder blades. "This thing's all lumps. What's it stuffed with, newspaper?"

"Suit yourself," I said.

"Can't I sleep in a bed?" She looked directly at me, with her head tilted slightly to one side. I was pretty sure she didn't mean my dad's bed. I was tempted, of course; you couldn't make out much of her shape under that big parka and those jeans, but I remembered those legs from last week. Even the way she swigged beer from a can was distracting, and she had the face of a sulky, scolded angel. But I felt I was being taken for granted, and I didn't like that. I could feel a serious objection building in the region of my crotch, but I overruled it.

"Take it or leave it," I said.

"OK," she said meekly. I wasn't sure if she was relieved or offended.

"You want the quilt?" I said.

"Yes please."

"What about a toothbrush?"

"Do I get a bedtime story as well?"

I snorted. She took the piss so well you couldn't help but admire it.

Dad's quilt was one of those cheap thick numbers as stiff and bulky as an inflated airbed, and I nearly tripped coming down the stairs because I couldn't see over the bundle in my arms. Finally I staggered into the living room and dropped it onto an armchair. When I looked up Zoe was wriggling out of her jeans. Her long legs were smooth and pale and I glimpsed a lacy thong under the tail of her T-shirt. I found myself wondering if her bra would match but she looked up and caught me staring, and flicked the hem of her T-shirt down so it covered her bum. I scratched my forehead as if trying to think of other bedding to bring her but really to disguise the fact I didn't know where to look. It was a pretty crap disguise.

"I'll leave early," said Zoe. "That way I'll be home before my dad wakes up. I really don't need his shit right now."

She pulled her hair back with both hands into a ponytail, arching her back. I couldn't help noticing how the pose made her breasts stand out, and what truly fabulous breasts they were. She was doing it on purpose, I realized. It was like showing a quiz-show contestant the prize he could have won if he'd played his cards right. Now the objection from my trousers was so vigorous I could have pole-vaulted across the room. But the signals were all mixed up, and I liked her, and I didn't want to blow this.

"There's your quilt," I said redundantly.

"Night." She pulled it off the armchair, wrapped it around her and wriggled down into the sofa, punching a threadbare cushion into a pillow. That mound must be the curve of her hips . . .

Christ, I thought, and headed for the stairs. "Sleep well," I said. I switched the light off in the front room, left the light on over the stairs, and headed for the bathroom. I'll skip the details, but I wasn't in there long, and went to bed glad I hadn't taken her up on her offer, if she'd been making an offer. She would have been seriously short-changed.

That day I'd been for a run, visited my dad's body at the undertakers, followed Elsa Kendrick home and worked a seven-hour shift on my feet at the Iron Bridge, and still I couldn't sleep. Today two different women had pro-positioned me. Or sort of had. For the best part of a year I'd been wearing the beige polyester uniform of Max Snax, a passion-killer more effective than leprosy, and in that time no woman had even checked me out, that I'd noticed. Before that I'd never had a girlfriend for longer than six weeks. Boxing and running and working, I didn't get to meet many girls, and I didn't go out of my way to find any. Yeah, Trudy in the kitchen of Max Snax used to grab me when I walked past, but she was a round, cheerful woman of indeterminate age who would grope anything, including sacks of potatoes.

I'd lost my virginity at fourteen when I was high on something, or drink, or both, to a girl with long fair hair and a bored expression. I was the third of four guys in a queue. She was legal, just about, but it wasn't an experience I looked back on for inspiration. But I once heard some guy on the radio talking about how after his wife had died all these women descended on him to offer solace, usually physical. I couldn't remember if he'd taken any of them up on it—maybe he was too polite to say—but I found myself wondering if the same thing happened to guys who had lost their fathers. I wished I could talk to Dad about it, and then I remembered he'd gone, and I'd never be able to talk to him again about anything, unless you counted prayer. I wasn't sure if I did count prayer but I was damn sure he didn't. He used to call it "talking to your invisible friend." Even if I did try praying to him, and he could hear me wherever he was, he'd pretend not to, just to be proved right. That thought made me smile.

Dad, why are these women chucking themselves at me? I could imagine him snorting. Well then, why do I *think* they're chucking themselves at me? *They're like buses*, Dad would have said. *Nothing for ages and then three come along at once*. Typical of him, stupid gags and no answers. I thought about it some more, without referring it to my dad. Maybe they wanted something.

Maybe just a shoulder to cry on, or someone to listen to them. *That's what your mother used to say*, a voice that might have been Dad's piped up. *All any woman wants is for you to listen*. Maybe, I thought. But why do they want *me* to listen to them?

I didn't hear her leave; in the morning the quilt was neatly rolled—or as neatly as it could be rolled—and left on the sofa. She'd scribbled something on the back of one of the unopened bills with a red pen. Her hand-writing was so bad the letters wriggled and swapped places without my messed-up brain having anything to do with it. Eventually I worked the message out, though.

Thanx
C Ya
Z
x

eight

According to the movie *Raging Bull*—a favourite at Delroy's gym—Jake La Motta the boxer used to get his wife to work him up into a sexual frenzy before a fight and then pour ice down his shorts. The theory was that he'd work out his frustration in the ring. I finished my run so fast that morning I was back shortly before I left. I went into my press-ups and curls, trying to think about anything except Zoe wearing not much but a T-shirt, even if that meant worrying about money instead.

If this new job lasted I wouldn't have to worry, I thought. I'd never worked evenings before, apart from the few times I'd done a double shift at Max Snax and come home too wrecked and smelly to train properly. Evening shifts—especially ones that paid as well as last night—would suit me a lot better. After the boxing club had closed down I'd never known what to do with myself in the evenings anyway. Telly was mostly crap, going to the cinema cost money, and reading had never been my favourite pastime.

Then it occurred to me that the job couldn't last. If it didn't take me closer to the truth about who killed my dad, I'd just have been taking favours from McGovern. And although I'd saved his kid's life and all, it probably wasn't a good long-term strategy to be in any sort of relationship with McGovern, or even appear on his radar.

I was on my sixth set of curls, the burn blazing hard in my abs, when the doorbell buzzed. A brief hope flared it might be Zoe, but I smothered it immediately—I'd probably never see her again—and deliberately took my time opening the door.

DS Amobi stood there modelling the latest smart-casual look for the ambitious urban police officer. Another man stood at his shoulder in the standard-issue blue suit and beige mac TV detectives always wear and hardly anyone ever does in real life. His bland face was hard to place . . . Of course, it was Jenkins, the DC who'd attended the inquest.

"Mr. Maguire," said Amobi, "we wondered if you could spare a few moments?"

"Here, or down the nick?" I said.

"Here is fine," said Amobi. "It's just a routine call, a

progress report on the course of our investigation." Jenkins stood there like a shop-window mannequin sent to make up the numbers.

I looked down the path. "Where's Prendergast?"

"DI Prendergast has several other cases to supervise," said Amobi smoothly.

"Do you have any progress to report?" I said.

"Would it be possible for us to come in?" If he'd bowed Amobi couldn't have appeared more eager-to-please and amenable. He seemed to be the new breed of copper, well-versed in PR, devoid of the second-hand swagger younger cops unconsciously learn off the older hands. It made him that much more dangerous and hard to read.

I stood back and held the door open. They entered, Jenkins nearly colliding with Amobi's back when the senior officer stopped to wipe his feet. From the look of Amobi's shoes my mat probably left his soles dirtier than they were to begin with. Amobi moved inside and Jenkins wiped his feet in turn, but without much enthusiasm.

I grabbed the towel hanging over the bottom of the banister and gave it a sniff. It would do. I wiped the sweat from my face while Amobi glanced at the quilt still rolled up on the sofa and cautiously planted himself on the free cushion beside it. Jenkins perched in the armchair, looking uncomfortable, as though he'd rather be sitting beside his boss, or wandering round the room peering at the family photographs for clues the way plain-clothes cops did on TV shows.

"We've made extensive enquiries locally," said Amobi. "Door to door in this street and the neighbouring streets, over the course of several days and evenings, to try and make sure we spoke to everyone. We thought perhaps the intruder might have escaped from the rear of the property, but no one in the houses backing onto yours witnessed anything suspicious."

I nodded. This sounded worryingly like a prologue to getting my rights read.

But Amobi sounded sincere when he went on, "I'm sorry not to be able to offer you better news. We have spoken to many of your father's acquaintances locally, and tried to piece together his last known movements as best we can. So far we've found nothing that could be considered out of the ordinary. We wondered if perhaps you might have recalled some details that weren't in your original statement." *Here we go*, I thought. "You were in a state of shock at the time," Amobi explained, "and witnesses often find vital information pops into their mind some days after the incident."

"What about Hans?" I said. My nose was running. I wiped it on the towel, and noticing Jenkins' distaste,

I did it again, properly. Amobi didn't react either to what I did or what I'd said.

"Hans?" he asked.

"The guy in the pub the night before my dad was murdered. The night Dad's keys went missing. He said he was a reporter for a German newspaper, the *Suddeutsche* something... Surely you know all this." Amobi's dumb-acting had irritated me into shooting my mouth off, and I saw too late that this had been his precise intention. Must remember never to play poker with this guy, I thought.

"We are pursuing that lead, but the witness descriptions weren't very helpful," said Amobi. "There was rather a lot of alcohol consumed on the night in question."

Not by Hans, I thought. "But you've been in touch with the *Suddeutsche* Wotsit," I said. "I mean, you have people who speak German. Don't you?" Perhaps that was too much to ask. From what I'd seen at the inquest, DC Jenkins barely spoke English.

"Like I said, we are pursuing that lead. But I'm interested to know how you got to hear about this fellow Hans."

"Same way you did. I asked."

"Have you made any contacts that you think might be useful, or found any leads you'd like to share with us?" He was doing that father-confessor thing, where they try to get you to blurt out your sins, as if the point was to make yourself feel better.

"Not really."

"You mean you haven't learned anything, or you don't wish to share it?"

"Yes," I said. Amobi let that one pass. The silence curdled.

Jenkins nonchalantly dug his big-screen phone out of an inner pocket and checked his email. After a moment he sensed Amobi watching him, looked up into a hard, cold stare, flicked the phone off and put it away.

Did you know my dad had a girlfriend? I thought about asking Amobi. *Did you hear how her jealous husband came to the pub looking for him?* But I wanted to talk to Jonno Kendrick myself, before the cops got to him. Afterwards I'd leave him somewhere they could scrape him up easily.

"Mr. Maguire"—Amobi opened his hands, all innocence—"we want to find out who murdered your father. We know you do too, but there are risks involved. As policemen we are paid to take risks."

"Right," I said. Two could play dumb, I thought, although I wasn't acting. I really wasn't sure what Amobi was getting at.

He sighed. "You were seen a few days ago at an

address in Maida Vale. Posing as a gardener, you entered the residence of a known criminal."

Shit. The Guvnor's house was under surveillance. I should have known that—for years the Met police had dedicated a whole branch of the force to convicting big-time gangsters like McGovern, and it had got them precisely nowhere. Of course they were watching his house. The question was, how long had they been watching me?

"Can I ask what you were doing there?" said Amobi.

"You lot suspect me of killing my dad," I said. "I know I didn't, but I don't have fifteen thousand coppers to go knocking on doors for me, asking who did. So I thought I'd go right to the top."

"You walked into McGovern's house to ask him who killed your stepfather?"

"Yeah."

"What did he tell you?"

"Ask him yourself. You're the ones paid to take risks." That shot caught Amobi under the ribs, I noted smugly. His eyes widened and he was going to say something hasty, but stopped and looked at the floor briefly.

"Mr. Maguire . . ." He looked up at me. "Joseph McGovern is a very dangerous man. He is utterly ruthless. He has people maimed and blinded and killed, without compunction. Not just enemies—friends he has fallen out with. Employees he has no further use for. Children and loved ones of people who own an asset or control a business he wants. I think you are a brave man, and you think you have nothing to lose. But believe me, if you get mixed up with McGovern, you will regret it. He will find a way to make you suffer. He always finds a way."

I could have sworn the temperature in the room had dropped a degree or two. Amobi reminded me of a hellfire preacher, only more scary, because of his quiet, measured, matter-of-fact delivery and his perfect diction with its faint echo of Nigeria.

"I know all that," I said. "I looked him up. I know the Serious Crimes squad have been after him for years. And they haven't caught him, because he knows everything they do before they've even decided to do it. Maybe he's psychic." It was a lot more likely that McGovern had senior coppers on his payroll, but Amobi knew that just as well as I did. "If I had any dirt on McGovern, you'd be the first to hear about it. And McGovern would be the second. Well, maybe the fourth or fifth." The after-thought kind of spoiled my little speech, but I didn't want to sound like I was accusing Amobi of being bent. Then I wondered why I even gave a shit about how DS Amobi felt.

"We can help each other," said Amobi.

"Fine. You let me know who this guy Hans really was and bring him in for questioning, and I'll tell you what McGovern's garden looks like."

Amobi smiled. "Thank you for your help, Mr. Maguire," he said, as warmly as if I'd written out a full confession and drawn him diagrams. He rose to his feet, and Jenkins did the same. I wondered if Amobi tripped on the step going out whether Jenkins would stumble too.

"Thanks for coming by," I said.

Amobi flicked a card out of his breast pocket as smoothly as a conjuror. "If you change your mind, this is my personal number," he said.

I looked at the card, and took it, and thought about doing something rude with it. But it would have looked childish and Amobi was too cool, so I just slipped it into the back pocket of my tracksuit. McGovern's tracksuit, I remembered with a guilty twinge.

Amobi opened the door for himself, stepped out—without tripping—and gave me a wave. "Thanks again," he smiled. Damn, I wished I had teeth that good.

Jenkins smirked wanly as he pulled the door shut. "Thanks," he said.

I paid my dad a visit that afternoon, and sat there staring at the body in the coffin. I wanted to sit there until I felt something, but my head was full of the upcoming funeral and what I was going to say and the arrangements I'd made with the priest and whether anyone would turn up. And what I would tell people when they asked me what had happened. Or what I would tell myself. Was McGovern so paranoid and vicious he had some wannabe amateur screenwriter whacked? Did my dad offend the Guvnor's ego, or did he actually find out something important? If he had, what was it? Was it in those notes that went missing?

Or was it anything to do with McGovern at all? If the cops had talked to the old guys in the pub, they might well have heard that story too, about the jealous husband who came looking for my dad. Amobi wouldn't have missed that, like I did at first. But then, I knew that man was Jonno Kendrick, and chances were the cops didn't, not yet anyway. Which meant I still had a chance to get to him before they did.

It was no good. I was sitting there staring at a bad waxwork someone had swapped for my living, grumbling, snoring Dad. He wasn't here, and there was nothing for me to feel, so I left.

At the Iron Bridge that evening, the staff special was some minty-lamby-nutty concoction that melted in the mouth. It tasted so amazing I paused to savour it, which was a mistake, because in those few seconds Gordon added two greasy pans to the stack and nearly toppled the whole lot onto the floor. I caught them with my elbows, wrestled them in the direction of the sink and fought on. Eventually the tide of scummy steel receded and Eccles reappeared, taking out his wallet.

"I've spoken to Josie," he said. "Next week we'll start putting you through the books, so you need to pass her your bank details."

"I'd rather have cash," I said.

"You take home the same after tax and insurance," said Eccles. He clearly considered the conversation over and was moving away when I piped up.

"I need Monday night off, Chef."

"Is that what you're down for?"

"Not exactly," I said.

If I'd smacked him on the back of the head with a skillet he could not have looked at me with as much disgust at my betrayal.

"I know it's short notice, I'm sorry."

"Please don't mess me around, Finn. I really thought we understood each other."

He could have faced off against Prendergast, I thought. They were both scary enough. *I wouldn't put either of them up against McGovern*, a little voice added.

"My father died a few days ago. The funeral's on Monday."

Eccles stared at me. "You have got to be fucking kidding," he said.

"That's why I needed this job. But I've got to have Monday night off. In fact, I'm not really asking."

Eccles tapped the arm of his glasses on his teeth. "Fine," he said. "But if you don't turn up Tuesday, don't bother coming back."

"Thanks, Chef," I said.

Halfway to the swing doors he stopped and turned and walked back. "And Finn . . . I'm sorry about your dad," he said.

"Yeah, thanks, Chef." *You prick*, I added mentally as I wiped down the sink. As it happened, I could have come to work Monday evening. The funeral and the reception, or whatever it was called, would be over by six, and I wasn't planning to spend the evening shitfaced and wallowing in nostalgia.

nine

My soul was an old horse
Offered for sale in twenty fairs.

I'd memorized the poem so I wouldn't have to read it off a page. I hadn't known what it was called, only that my dad used to declaim it whenever he'd had too much to drink, which wasn't often enough for me to remember much of it. I'd managed to piece together a few phrases in my head, and went searching for them on the Net. Turned out it was called "Pegasus," by an Irish poet called Kavanagh, and it took some finding because there was an English poet with the same name and initials, and by the time I'd worked that out I was nearly cross-eyed with the effort of ploughing through endless verses online. I'd never really cared about poetry—why can't writers just say what they mean?—but when I finally managed to read it I knew it was what Dad would have wanted, and this would be my last chance to in-dulge him.

The poem was about an artist trying to find a proper job and being endlessly rejected. The symbolism was so obvious even a thicko like me could understand it.

. . . the buyers
Were little men who feared his unusual airs.

Yeah, Dad, that's why they stopped hiring you; you scared the bastards.

I'd been worried that the chapel was too big, and that on the day it would look pathetic and empty. But by a quarter to ten a few people had turned up, and then a few more, and then even more, and they had spread themselves along the pews in loose little knots, and by the time the service had started the place was respect-ably full. On my right, about halfway up, a few close neighbours sat politely listening. Dad used to stop at their gates occasionally to exchange local gossip and grumbles about over-development and muggings and house prices, and even the endless parking problems, though we'd never owned a car. Me, the neighbours would only nod at. More often I caught them looking at me sideways, clearly thinking I was bad news. The nods were their way of placating me so I wouldn't burgle their houses and pee in their tropical fish tanks.

On the left of the chapel, up near the front, were the luvvies—dad's old actor mates. You could tell them as soon as they arrived by the way even the blokes hugged and kissed each other, and by the loud hoots of laughter they theatrically stifled. Now they sat there solemnly, listening to my delivery, no doubt thinking my dad would have done it better, wondering whether there'd be anything to eat afterwards or just booze, and please God please let it be a free bar.

"No more haggling with the world . . ."

As I said these words he grew
Wings upon his back.

Still on the left but further towards the back sat Jack and Phil and Sunil the newsagent, from the Weaver's Arms. To the right, in the furthest pew at the back, sat DS Amobi. He hadn't brought Jenkins along, and I was grateful—that twat would have spent half the service playing with his phone. In the pew in front of Amobi was a tall guy with a bent spine and a lumpy woman in glasses, sitting quietly with their hands in their laps. I suddenly realized they were Jerry and Trudy from Max

Snax, and an unexpected lump filled my throat when I only had two lines to go.

> . . . *Now I may ride him*
> *Every land my imagination knew.*

I stumbled on the final words, and saw the sad sympathetic smiles of the actors in the front row. Did they think I was filled with emotion about losing my dad? Or did they know I was faking it, and the only sorrow I'd felt at that moment was for myself? I folded away the printout I had never glanced at, stepped away from the lectern and made my way back to my seat in the front row, aware of the squeaking of my scuffed black shoes on the tiled floor.

The young Polish priest, Father Januszek, stepped forward. He had a strange 1970s haircut that made his ears stick out and apple cheeks like a kid in a yogurt advert, but at least he didn't spout theatrical clichés about all the world being a stage or boom out fairy stories about Jesus receiving Dad in heaven. He talked about Dad's career, and the parts he had played, and the reviews he had got when he first started out, and managed to make it sound like he'd been the chairman of Dad's fan club. Of course I had supplied him with all the details, from an old CV I'd found among Dad's files on AnyDocs.

"In later years," Father Januszek was saying, "Noel had started to explore new aspects of his talent through writing. Sadly, he was taken from us before his project could come to fruition, a project we would all like to have seen." He sounded so full of regret for a moment even I was convinced, until I remembered that a few days ago Father Januszek had never heard of my dad. All the same, when he ended his address with a cheesy little joke about Dad taking his last bow before the final curtain, I found it in my heart to forgive him. The priest caught my eye and invited me back up front for the final part of the ceremony.

Dad's favourite band had been U2. I'd grown up with their distorted and layered guitars reverberating through the house, while Dad had sung along tunelessly. When I'd finally grown sick of the pious droning I'd made him wear headphones, but he still sang along tunelessly. Now as their guitars echoed, faint and plaintive, from the beamed chapel ceiling I knew it was time to let him go.

I pressed a single button on a beech wood box mounted on a plinth. With a discreet hum the short red curtains in the rear wall parted, and the coffin jerked into motion, rolling slowly backwards through the gap to where everyone knew the flames of the furnace waited, licking. The curtains closed again and the music faded. Father Januszek called down a bland, non-denominational blessing upon all present and pronounced the ceremony over.

The congregation sighed and shifted in their seats. The actors leaned over to each other and exchanged reviews, while the neighbours checked their watches, wondering if they really needed to stay and express their condolences. I remembered a motto from one of Dad's threadbare showbiz anecdotes: "As long as the audience outnumbers the performers, you have a show," he'd told me. If Dad and the priest and I were the cast, then a crowd this big was definitely a success.

A latecomer had slipped in and was sitting at the back, a slim woman all in black, big shades covering most of her upper face, her hair drawn up under a beret. Elsa Kendrick, I thought, and my gaze flicked to Amobi, who was at the other end of the pew from her. He saw me looking and nodded solemnly, then rose and headed towards the pale sunlight spilling through the chapel doors, without even a glance towards Elsa. That was Elsa, wasn't it?

"Finn, that was a lovely ceremony. Your dad would have been proud." A stocky man in his forties had taken my hand and was gripping it firmly. His face was vaguely familiar, but that's the trouble with actors—you know you've seen them in your living room, but were they really there or only on the telly?

"Sorry—Bill Winchester, I was in *Henby General* with your dad for a while, back in the 1990s, or possibly the 1890s . . ."

There were lots more conversations like that, as Dad's old mates introduced themselves and congratulated me—anyone would think I'd got married—and recited the bit of their CV that overlapped with Dad's. No one asked what exactly had happened to him, of course, not to my face. That conversation would be reserved for later, vague speculative gossip exchanged in hushed tones over port and brandy in the pub. I shook hands and thanked people for coming and gave out the directions to the Weaver's Arms so often I wished they'd been printed on the order of service with the hymns, all the time working my way towards the doors to catch Elsa Kendrick. But before I could get to her Jerry and Trudy stepped forward from their pew, blushing and embarrassed. Trudy babbled something about being so sorry, and Jerry nodded, and I thanked them for coming and really meant it. But by the time they moved off—Andy was probably docking their pay for the hours they missed—Elsa had vanished, if it had been Elsa. Maybe it was another of Dad's old showbiz friends. She'd certainly looked familiar.

I hurried out into the bright, damp air and looked

around, but saw only a few knots of mourners lighting up cigarettes in the shade of the gloomy evergreens that lined the drive to the crematorium. A voice called after me from the chapel doors, the thin high voice of a woman too old to catch up.

"Finn? Finn ..." So many strangers calling me by name. It was a brief sort of fame, I thought. Dad had longed for that, but I wasn't so keen on it.

I thought this woman was another of Dad's old acting cronies, but as she approached I noticed she was much older than most of them, with silver hair cut in a smart bob, some serious jewellery on her fingers and an old-fashioned fur stole that looked new and very expensive. Too well-off for an actor, I thought—if she'd made that much money from acting I'd probably have known her face. She was about eighty, maybe, though she wore a lot of make-up, impeccably applied, and her eyes had the mischievous sparkle of a woman far younger.

"Dorothy," she said, "Dorothy Rousseau." Reaching forward she grasped my shoulders and I leaned down to let her kiss me on both cheeks. "Noel never even mentioned me, did he? Ungrateful cad." She squeezed my upper arms with her bony fingers. "My God, you're built like Charles Atlas." She stood back and blatantly assessed me like a butcher judging a side of beef. "Not bad-looking, either. Did your father ever get you to do any modelling?"

"He bought me an Airfix kit for Christmas once."

She stared at me for a moment, then hooted with laughter and clapped her hands. I liked her laugh; it had a girl's giggle in it.

"God, you're so like him. I was Noel's agent, years ago, when he first started out. We argued, of course—he was such a prima donna, God! But he was a lovely man, and I was always fond of him, and so very sorry to hear about what happened."

"Thank you, Dorothy."

"And you were marvellous up there, darling—no, really, I mean it. And what a great turnout!"

"Yeah . . . I'm not actually sure how all these people heard about it."

"Oh, that was my doing, dear, sorry. I may have retired, but I still have the connections, and as soon as I heard the news I put the word around. Nothing worse than a funeral where nobody turns up to drink your booze and blacken your name with disgusting stories. They're not just here for the beer either—this lot really did love your dad, though no one even knew where he'd been for the last few years. And he could be such a pain in the backside, he was his own worst enemy . . . Oh

God, do you hate me for saying that?" She clutched my arm as if for reassurance. I wasn't surprised Dorothy had become an agent—she was way too over-the-top to be an actor. "There are plenty more who would have been here if it wasn't for the ridiculously short notice," she went on. I would have apologized for that, but she wasn't letting me get a word in edgeways. "Charles Egerton, for one. He always had a bit of a hard spot for your dad, if you know what I mean."

"Charles Egerton?"

"Oh God, I keep forgetting how young you are. And how old I am. Charles Egerton, he was in all those old Ealing Jeeves and Wooster films, darling, playing Jeeves. Of course he's getting on a bit now, retired to his castle in Spain years ago. Practically a recluse. He was so fond of your father, you could have had your very own gay grandad."

"I think I went there once. His castle in Spain." I'd almost forgotten, it was so long ago. A big tumble-down house surrounded by mountains . . . walking in the woods with Mum and Dad. The smell of hot earth and rosemary. Mum and Dad and me splashing in the pool together—I must have been . . . six? And a tanned old man with a long white beard and a cackling laugh I found a bit scary.

"Anyway, I really mustn't hog you, Finn darling, you

have guests to attend to." I bent down and she kissed me again, or kissed the air around me, chattering all the while. "I can't come to the pub, I'm afraid, I'm bad enough sober. I just have time to talk to your mother. Where has she gone?"

"My . . . sorry?"

"That was Lesley at the back of the church, wasn't it? In the shades and the beret? Such a shame about her and your dad, but I'm glad she came to the service, life's too short. Do you know where she's staying?"

"My mother hasn't come," I said. "That was someone else."

"Oh." She blinked and looked puzzled, then rolled her eyes like a dotty old aunt. "I am hopeless. Just ignore me. Alzheimer's probably. Billy, you creep—!"

She rushed off to embrace Dad's old mate from the hospital soap, and left me standing there with my head spinning.

That couldn't have been my mother . . . could it?

Christ, can actors drink. The pub had roped off the back of the lounge with its own little bit of bar, and now that corner at least was roaring like it was Saturday night rather than Monday afternoon, even with only a dozen or so mourners. But they weren't exactly mourning, and the actors were waving their arms about so much as they played the other characters in the stories they were telling, it felt like the room was packed. They were all tales about my dad, a lot of which I hadn't heard before, plus a few I had, but with newly added scabrous detail. The beer and the shorts and the port and brandy gushed like an oil strike, and McGovern's bounty behind the bar was burned up in less than half an hour. Without even pausing in his anecdote Bill Winchester slid his credit card along the counter and told the barman to keep it coming. Spot the actor with the steady job.

I sipped my drink slowly, trying to keep sober. Jack and Phil and Sunil kept buying me pints but I passed them over to the thesps, who sank them no questions asked. I wanted to keep my head clear, partly to re-member all these tales from when my dad actually had a career, but also to think about my conversation with Dorothy Rousseau.

Eventually I managed to catch Bill Winchester having a whiz in the gents,' a bleach-scented sanctuary from the racket and hooting next door.

"It's a shame Dorothy Rousseau couldn't come to the wake," I said. "I bet she had a few stories about my dad."

"Damn right," said Winchester. He wasn't slurring his words yet, but he was staring carefully at his knob in case it went astray and pissed all over his shoes.

"Dorothy has an infinite supply of the very finest dirt on the biggest names in British showbiz. Who was on coke when they met the Queen, who gave who a hand job backstage of some seventies West End musical that closed after three nights . . . That's why everyone says they love her—they're fucking terrified of her."

"Has she ever forgotten a face?"

"Dorothy? Oh no. Dotty by name, mind like a stainless-steel rat trap." That's what I'd been afraid of. It meant the woman in black really was my mother.

The world toppled slowly off its axis and rolled about inside my skull like a marble in a pudding bowl. *My mother.* I'd been staring right at her, and I hadn't even known. Why hadn't she come over and said something? Was she ashamed of herself, or ashamed of me? *You know why, and so does she.* Because I would have told her to piss off back to America. I'd had the whole conversation mapped out in my head since I was twelve years old.

I'd have another chance, I guessed. She'd pop up again, if only to reassure herself I wasn't a total fuck-up because of what she did. *Hate to disappoint you, Mum, but I am.* Lousy timing on her part, I thought, showing up when Dad was dead. He might have taken her back. I never would.

Dad's ashes were rattling around in a bland grey

vase inside a cardboard box under my chair in the pub. They were still there when I came back from the bogs, which surprised me, because the locals from the Griffin estate would nick anything, and I'd half-expected to be searching for Dad in every car boot sale in West London for the next few weeks. But of course back here in his little box he was surrounded by lots of drunken theatrical buddies, and the locals were probably afraid to gate-crash in case they got snogged by some old queen, or worse still had some Shakespeare recited at them.

A big platter of sandwiches was going round, watery ham and tragic lettuce between fat slices of white sliced loaf. The Weaver's kitchen wasn't going to worry Chris Eccles any time soon, but actors don't get to eat much, and alcohol makes everything taste better. The platter was bare before it got halfway round the room.

If that had been my mother sitting at the back, where was Elsa Kendrick? If she and Dad had been a couple, why hadn't she come to the service? Had something happened to her? I checked my phone; it was later than I'd thought, and I wouldn't have time to change out of Dad's suit. Maybe that was for the best—it would serve as set dressing. I'd just have to be careful not to get blood on it, particularly my own.

I picked Dad up off the floor—it wasn't the first

time—and headed for the door. I had all sorts of excuses prepared for leaving while I could still walk, but nobody even noticed me slip out into the dusk.

Canal Market Road ran parallel to the canal, but it didn't lead to a market, and hadn't for about a hundred years. Nowadays it petered out at a bus garage. The road had once been a sort of business park, and was lined with crumbling industrial units, a few of them with the shabby remnants of Art Deco detailing, if you cared about that sort of thing. Today most of the businesses were struggling to survive, like weeds sprouting through the cracks in a concrete car park just in time for a hard frost. I'd chosen a unit about three-quarters of the way up, until recently the premises of a firm that made flat-packed cardboard boxes. Appropriately, it had folded. There were still a few lights burning in the deserted building. Whoever had locked up for the last time clearly didn't give a toss about the electricity bill—it was no longer their problem. A fresh "To Let" sign had been nailed to the building's facade, high up. It didn't help the impression I was trying to create, but on the other hand there were so many "To Let" and "For Sale" signs around the eye stopped seeing them.

I lurked on the front step of the shut-up unit with a

cigarette cupped in my hand, trying to look like a minor executive having a crafty fag. I didn't take a drag from it—no need to go that far, the mark wasn't here yet. In fact, he was late. Not a way to make a good impression, if he wanted the job I'd detailed on the phone.

Three cigarettes past the appointed time the grinding of gears and whistle of a diesel engine told me an articulated lorry was approaching. When it appeared around the dogleg in the street I realized it was not an artic as such, but just the tractor. That figured, of course, as supposedly the job was to pick up a trailer. The tractor unit was a shiny, freshly-scrubbed crimson, with three air horns mounted above the windscreen, but no chrome flourishes or badges or fairy lights behind the windscreen—nothing whimsical or cute about it. It slowed as it approached and finally pulled up at the kerb. I could dimly see the figure up behind the wheel check a notepad and lean over to peer out at the unit I was standing outside.

I took a quick drag of my cigarette and wished I hadn't—I'd forgotten how much they made me want to puke. As it was I had to swallow a hacking cough. Maybe Jonno Kendrick thought it was the hack of a smoker who overdid it rather than a total amateur, because he ignored me totally as he swung himself down from his cab and walked up to the locked door, giving it a shove before looking around for a doorbell. Not finding one he turned to me, frowning.

"Anybody on reception, mate?"

"Nope." I tossed the cigarette away. He was a big man—not tall, but stocky, and half as heavy again as me. A lot of that was beer and pies, but he had forearms like Popeye, if Popeye had gone for Maori tattoos instead of anchors.

"Have I got the right address—Canal Market Road?"

"Yep."

"What the fuck's going on?" he muttered to himself, and he rattled the door again.

"They went out of business two weeks ago."

"Two weeks? Then who phoned me?"

"I did."

"You? Is this some kind of joke?"

"Yeah. The kind that's not funny."

"Fucking right it isn't. I've come all the way from Kensal Rise, you little prick. On a bloody wind-up?"

He took a step towards me. I stayed where I was. He was working himself up, which suited me. The jowls wobbled on his fleshy hairless face, and he sprayed spittle when he spoke.

"Not a total wind-up," I said. "I needed to talk to you."

"Fuck that, I came down here for a sodding job!"

"You know a pub near here, the Weaver's Arms?"

"What the fuck?" Indignant, baffled, getting angrier. Pale in the face rather than red. Danger sign.

"You called in there a few weeks ago, looking for my dad. Noel Maguire."

When he heard the name he hesitated, staring at me, breathing deep, his eyes bulging. I saw him measure me up, his eyes flicking over my shoulders. He raised a finger and poked it at my face.

"Listen, son, where I go and who I talk to is none of your *fucking business*."

I noticed the fob of the keys to his truck poking from between his chubby fingers. That was careless of him. I'd snatched them out of his fist before he even saw me move. He swiped for them clumsily.

"Give me my fucking keys."

"Don't want you rushing off, Mr. Kendrick."

"Give me my fucking *keys*!" he roared, and tried to snatch them back. I dodged, and he stumbled, and he turned, and came for me again, moving faster, and I ducked away. I needn't have worried about his weight; yes, he was big, but he was slow, and you could tell where he was headed before he'd even changed direction. I had to hang about and wait for him to come after me, mostly so he'd get himself all worked up and frustrated, clapped-out without me having to raise a finger.

But he wasn't as green as he looked, because he swung a backhand at me that I only just dodged, and I smelled the sweat off his knuckles as they whistled past my nose. He turned again more nimbly than I thought he could and threw all his weight with a low punch that would have bust my gut if it had connected. I diverted it, stepped inside his guard and landed a couple of quick jabs to his face. Light and fast, but he staggered back clutching his nose as if I'd whacked him with a wrench. When he pulled his hand away and saw blood he finally broke, roared like a bull and came charging at me. I sidestepped and smacked him square on the jaw. The blows barely made him flinch, so I made sure the third landed right on his ear. Not under it—I need-ed him to talk, which meant not breaking his jaw, not yet. He roared again and staggered away, and bent over, cursing and clutching his throbbing head, and I knew I had him.

"Fuck! *Fuck!* You little prick, what do you fucking want?"

"You went looking for my dad, didn't you? In the Weaver's Arms?"

"Yes! Yes, I did, so what? I never done nothing to him."

"No, you got someone else to do it for you, didn't you?"

"Fuck this, I think you've broken my nose—"

"Why did you go looking for him?"

"He'd been shagging my wife, that's why! Look at it!"

"It's not broken, not yet. You mean your ex-wife."

"I mean my *wife*. We're still married."

That threw me. *Dad!* I thought. *You didn't. You . . . berk.*

Kendrick straightened up, glanced down and saw the blood splattered down the chest of his grey hoodie. He groaned. He seemed more worried about his laundry than me.

"What were you going to do when you found him? My dad."

"Give him a warning, that's all. Tell him to stay away." He sniffed and coughed.

"Or what?"

"Or he'd be sorry. Fuck this . . ."

I'd promised myself I'd watch my temper, but I had to clench my fists to stop my arms shaking, and having clenched them I really wanted to hit something with them.

"Why would he be sorry? Were you planning to slap him around a bit, the way you slap her? Only you couldn't find him, so you hired some German scumbag?"

Kendrick stared at me as if I was mad, turned his head away and spat a long gob of bright red spit onto the pale concrete of the forecourt.

"Smacking my wife? You been speaking to Elsa? Fuck . . . ! Not you as well." He looked like he was trying to laugh. "You know I wanted to divorce her. Years ago. Said she'd top herself if I left. She's such a fucking liar."

"Bollocks," I said.

"I was going to warn your dad about *her*. She's a nutter. A pisshead. A whatsit, a fantasist. How old are you? Twenty?" I didn't answer. "Christ, you have no fucking clue." He spat blood again.

Elsa Kendrick a pisshead? Shit. The way she'd necked that chardonnay, that smell in her neat little living room—spilt wine gone sour. Not hard to get rid of, but she probably didn't even notice it. Jesus, that's why she'd been suspended from her job.

"I wasn't going to smack him. I was going to tell him to stay away. She's tried to poison me, pushed me down the stairs . . . afterwards she claims she can't remember any of it, that she has blackouts."

"Did you ever tell the cops about this?"

"Fuck, you're not even twenty, are you? More like twelve. Look at me, look at her. She claims it was self-defence—who do you think the cops believe? *You* fell for it. Jesus, even I fall for it sometimes. She rings me up and tells me she's sorry and she's going to get help. Then it starts all over again. Anyway, one way or another, your old man must have got the message." He glanced at me as if he was embarrassed to be confessing all this to a kid.

"What do you mean?"

"He dumped her, didn't he? Two weeks ago. I knew as soon as she rang me up, crying and saying she was sorry, that she wanted me back, could we start again. I knew he'd dumped her. You can tell him it's not me he has to worry about. Stupid sod."

"My dad's dead," I said. Kendrick had been about to spit again but the gob stayed in his mouth. "The service was this morning. Someone came into our house a few days ago, hit him over the head while he sat at his desk."

"Fuck," said Kendrick. "And what, she told you I must have done it?"

"It's your word against hers," I said.

He hesitated a moment, then pulled up his hoodie to reveal a rumpled T-shirt underneath, and started to yank that out from under his belt. For a moment I thought he was going to strip off and streak down the street to protest his innocence. But he merely hoisted up his T-shirt and top to reveal his pale, hairy pot belly, and even in the cold yellow light of a distant sodium streetlamp I could see the puckered scar that stretched diagonally from his waistband nearly to his ribcage, just missing his navel.

"Butcher's knife," he said. "She'd spent all weekend

sharpening it for when I came home, one Monday night." He tucked his shirt back in. "Sorry about your dad, yeah? You can believe me or not, I don't give a fuck. You can find out the hard way. Like he did."

I tossed him his keys. He snatched them out of the air, walked past me and climbed into his cab without another word. I stood there staring into the misty night as he fired up his engine, wheeled around, bumped over the pavements and sped back down Canal Market Road.

ten

I'd hidden Dad's ashes round the side of the industrial unit before Kendrick arrived. Now I retrieved the vase, still in its box, and headed home. It wasn't a long walk, and as I turned into our street my mind was still ping-ponging between Elsa Kendrick's version of events and her husband's. I didn't want to believe Jonno Kendrick, but he'd looked genuinely surprised when I'd told him Dad was dead. Elsa Kendrick had lied to me the first time we met, the day after Dad died, when she'd been so eager to know if my mother was about. And now my mother had come back. Was that a lucky guess on Elsa Kendrick's part, that my mother was back in town? Or had she known something I didn't?

Through the half-closed curtains of my front room a single side-light cast a homely glow into the night street. I didn't remember leaving a light on. I normally made a big deal about switching everything off when I left the house, but then today had hardly been a normal day. I put my key into the front door, turned it, and froze on the threshold.

There was someone here, I could feel it. The place was warm, for one thing, and there was a faint scent of soap, classier and subtler than the cheap crap Dad used to buy.

I stepped inside and shut the door, the hairs on the back of my neck standing up, my whole body tense. I hugged the box closer under my arm and entered the living room as quietly as I could.

My mother stepped out of the kitchen, clutching a mug of something. "Hello, Finn," she said, as if I'd just come home from school, and Dad's ashes were my Show and Tell project.

She sipped her tea. She was wearing the same coat she'd worn at the funeral that morning, and her delicate little hands were cupped around the chipped china mug; I remembered how she used to moan about this house always being cold, and how Dad would flinch and whoop when she stuck her hands under his shirt to warm them.

"How did you get in?" I said at last.

"I still have keys. Your dad never changed the locks. Maybe you ought to, after what happened."

"Yeah. I will now."

"Can I make you something? The kettle's just boiled."

"No thanks," I said. I stood there with my coat on, trying to decide whether I should walk out again. But she would just stay here and wait for me, and I'd have to come back at some point. I felt anger well up like lava in my heart. It's my bloody house! *Or maybe it's hers*, said a little voice.

"Hard to know where to start, isn't it?" said my mother. I didn't look at all like her; my eyes were blue, hers were brown. I was big and hulking, and she was tiny and birdlike, with the bones of her slender hands almost visible through her pale skin. She had a pixie's face with high cheekbones and delicate little ears. I didn't remember her hair being blonde, but maybe she was hiding the grey.

"Start what?" I said. I was going for nonchalant but it came out petulant.

"Catching up," she said. She moved into the room and sat down, her legs neatly folded to one side. It came back to me in a rush, how she always walked and sat as if she was modelling.

"You left, I quit school, Dad got murdered," I said. "There, we've caught up. Goodbye."

She didn't move. I hadn't thought she would.

"I'm sorry, Finn," she said. "It was never about you. It was me being selfish and insecure and . . . it's no fun growing old and having no money and no future."

"Tell me about it," I said, in a tone of voice that warned her not to try. My mind was tilted like a sinking cruise liner, the thoughts in my head running around in panic and colliding with each other while the carefully composed notes for the speech I'd been planning all these years were dropped and scattered and trampled underfoot. I placed Dad's ashes on the table, shrugged off my jacket and chucked it at the sofa. Opening the cardboard box I took out the urn and placed it on the middle of the tiled mantelpiece. It looked ridiculous and lumpen and ugly, advertising death like those decaying petrol-station bouquets that pile up near accident black spots.

"I can't stay," my mother said, before I could. "But there are a few things I wanted you to know, and you might need time to think about them, before you decide whether . . . if we should talk again."

I tried to focus on the urn. Maybe I could stick some flowers in it. Dad wouldn't have minded.

"Your father and I had been in touch. Before he died. We were talking about getting back together."

That made me turn and stare.

"I was so mixed up when I left." Her composure had slipped, I noticed with some satisfaction, and she was starting to babble. "I was in this weird place and my career was going nowhere and I'd got involved with this charity . . ." She paused, trying to slow down. "It sort of, took over. Maybe it was just another pathetic mid-life crisis, but I thought if I left, I could start over, with a clean slate."

"A clean slate?" I was trying to sound cool but even those three words betrayed the tremor in my voice.

"I know how bad that sounds, but I really believed—I somehow persuaded myself that I couldn't be any good for you if I was unhappy. And I was unhappy. I told myself that you needed stability, and your dad, and I needed . . . "

"To leave."

"I'm sorry. I don't know how often you want me to say it, I can't mean it any more than I do right now."

"Right," I said. "Is that it?"

"He was going to take me back. Noel. He said the hard part would be persuading you."

"He wasn't a complete idiot, then," I said. My mother sighed, put her mug down and stood, buttoning her coat up. She pulled the black beret from her coat pocket and pulled it on, tucking her hair up inside it.

She was still very pretty, I realized; somehow the faint lines of age suited her pale, fine features. She took a folded note from the other pocket and laid it down beside the cup. "My cellphone," she said. "If you want to talk again."

"Could you leave the house keys as well?"

She hesitated, and I glimpsed hurt in her eyes. But she fished a ring with two keys from the same pocket that had held the note and laid them down by the mug. She never carried a handbag, I remembered now. She hated them.

"You should change the locks anyway," she advised in a little voice.

I bristled. I didn't need her to tell me to do what I'd planned to do anyway, and I'd do it at a time that suited me, not her.

"Goodbye, Finn."

She turned and walked out, and I let her go. I heard the latch click and the gentle tinny rattle of the letterbox, and the clack of her heels as she walked away. Of course, now, all the things I'd meant to say for years were jostling in my head. *I don't want you back anyway. You ruined my life. You broke Dad's heart. Fuck off back to America.* I hadn't said any of them, and now I knew I never would. I picked up the folded note with her mobile number—cellphone number, she'd said, she even talked like a bloody Yank, why did she have to come back?—carried it into the kitchen, stepped on the pedal of the bin, ripped the note into pieces as small as I could manage, and I sprinkled them into the rubbish.

Dad and her had been talking? When was he going to tell me? How had they talked? I hadn't seen any letters. Maybe by email . . . I wasn't surprised Dad had never found the nerve to raise the subject. He knew how much I hated my mother, how I blamed her for everything that was wrong with my world. It was anger at what she'd done that drove me wild, anger at her running away like that, abandoning us.

Abandoning me.

It was too late now—Dad was gone, and even if he had fallen for her sob story, I wasn't going to. I wished I hadn't ripped up the note—I wanted to ring her, that instant, and tell her to stop wasting her time. You wanted a clean slate, you've got one. You didn't want me in your life then, I don't want you in mine now. We're quits, so long, goodbye.

The doorbell rang. She'd forgotten something. Accidentally on purpose, so she could come back and work on me some more. I stomped to the front door, fumbled with the latch in haste and finally jerked it open.

Zoe's nervous smile faded when she saw the look on my face, and she stepped back uncertainly.

"Hey!" I said. Under her parka she wore her shapeless brown school uniform, the frumpy look rounded off with a totally impractical shoulder bag bulging with books.

"I'm sorry," she said. "I should have called or something, but I don't have your number, so I just . . ." She shrugged.

"No, it's fine," I said.

"Is this a good time?" she said. "I know you had the funeral this morning. Maybe you want to be alone."

I said nothing, but pulled the door wide open, and she stepped inside. Her hair brushed my face as she passed me and I tried not to let her see me breathing in its scent.

"I told my dad I was going to do homework with my friend Phoebe. Are you any good at history?"

"I can't even remember what I had for breakfast," I said.

"English? Do you know any Spanish?"

"Zippo."

"Looks like I've come to the wrong place."

I grabbed her parka as she shrugged it off but a Velcro band on the sleeve snagged on her school cardigan. As I helped unsnag it my hand caught her right wrist, and lingered there a moment of its own accord. Gently Zoe pulled her right hand away and laid it on my cheek, and her left hand on the other. She kissed me on the mouth, softly and hesitantly, until I kissed her back, my arms slipping round her slender waist, pulling her close, her back arching as she pressed her mouth up against mine, her hands sliding up my face to run through my hair.

It felt like we'd been in bed the whole evening but it wasn't even ten when we finally fell back, panting and sweaty, limbs happily entangled. Her breasts were as wonderful as I thought they'd be and she, clearly proud of them, let me admire them from close up. When I kissed them she'd squirm and giggle, then the fire would catch again. I was sure I had some condoms somewhere, but she kept a handful hidden in her school bag, "just in case," she said. You could not help but admire a girl so fabulously equipped in every respect. Surprisingly, the faff and fumbling with the slippery packets was part of the fun, and although the first bout didn't go the distance, in the second we pretty much tied on points, and the third was a knockout.

My father had overcome his embarrassment of talking to me about sex by going into unnecessary detail, ignoring how I cringed with my fingers stuck in my ears singing la-la-la. He kept repeating loudly, *Please your partner or you'll end up pleasing yourself.* I knew what he meant now, and I was glad he'd persisted. Zoe seemed glad too, as she lay there glowing with perspiration and playing with her hair.

"Got any cigarettes?" she said.

"Do you ever bring your own stimulants, or do you just bum them off other people?"

"Excuse me, but after all that stimulation I think I've earned one cigarette."

"Your dad would smell them on your breath."

"I'll tell him it was Phoebe," she said.

"Would he believe you?"

"No," she sighed. "He doesn't believe anything I tell him. And I can't tell him the truth."

"Why not?"

"Lying's easier," she said.

"Would you lie to me?"

"Try me."

"What does your dad do?"

"He's a policeman."

"Shit." I sat up. She turned her head to look at me, and I tried not to notice how lovely she was.

"What's his name?" I said. "Your name, I mean."

"Prendergast."

"Shit." I practically leaped backwards out of the bed, and stood there starkers, my hands in my hair. "He's the one who told you about me—that I sold drugs when I was a kid—"

"He didn't tell me. He brings his work home, his files. I look through them, when I can't sleep. I don't sleep much."

"Holy crap . . . you must know everything about me."

"Of course I don't." She frowned, laughing. I found myself wishing I did have some cigarettes, and went to pull my jeans on—the corner shop would still be open. With a grunt of exasperation Zoe sat up, grabbed the T-shirt hanging over the foot of the bed and pulled it on. "Fuck's sake, Finn, what's the big deal?"

"What are you going to tell him about me?"

"What? Why are you being so paranoid? Nothing! I told you, he never listens to anything I say anyway."

I looked around for my T-shirt, and realized she was wearing it. She was leaning up against my headboard with her arms folded, looking at me through her fringe, and I felt the wave of anger break and recede, leaving nothing but froth and confusion.

"When were you going to tell me?"

"I just told you."

"He thinks I killed my dad."

"So what? You didn't."

"Yeah, but thanks to him the cops aren't looking for anyone else, and I'm having to do all their bloody work."

"What work?"

"Finding out who did. Whether it really was some burglar, or that crazy girlfriend, or that fucking nutcase McGovern—"

"McGovern?" she said.

"Never mind," I said.

"McGovern the gangster?"

"You've heard of him?"

"I've seen his file."

"Holy shit. Could you get hold of it for me?"

"No. Are you insane?"

"No. Right. Sorry," I said.

She leaned forward, with a look of real concern. "Finn . . . why are you doing this? Asking about who killed your dad. What do you think you'll achieve?"

"I just have to know the truth," I said. "He was my dad. I owe him that much."

Zoe shook her head. "You can't go after McGovern," she said. "The guy's like a war criminal or something. If he had your dad murdered . . ."

"What?"

"You'll never be able to prove it. He's killed loads of people, it's like his hobby. Finn—leave it, please. Let SOCA handle it."

"SOCA?"

"Serious Organized Crime. My dad's the local liaison."

"OK, if you can't bring me McGovern's file, could you just read it and tell me what's in it?"

She looked away. "I have to go."

Pulling the bedclothes back she clambered off the bed, pushed past me, pulled off my T-shirt, flung it at me and ran naked down the stairs. By the time I got to the living room she was already half-dressed and cursing the zip of her uniform skirt. Her blouse had ended up draped around Dad's urn, somehow, and I apologized silently to him as I carefully pulled it free. *To hell with that*, he said. *Don't blow it now.*

I handed Zoe her blouse. She shrugged it on and quickly fastened the buttons I'd so carefully undone a few hours earlier.

"Forget it," I said. "Forget I asked, I'm sorry. Do you have to go?"

"Of course I have to go, you pillock," she said. But I could hear a laugh in her voice. Her brown cardigan crackled with static as she tugged it on and flipped her hair free of her collar. When I grabbed her hips and pulled her towards me she looked surprised and not displeased.

"That was amazing," I said. "You're amazing."

I bent down to kiss her, and she kissed me back, and when she heard my breathing deepening she pushed me away again and turned and grabbed her coat and bag.

"Yeah, that was fun," she said. "We must do it again sometime."

"Sorry about the homework," I said as I saw her to the door.

She paused on the step outside. "Seriously, Finn . . . stay away from the Guvnor. He's like a disease. Everything, everyone he touches . . ." Her voice tailed off to nothing. Without another word she turned and walked away, her head down, and with that little skip in her step girls use when they're trying to hurry without actually running. I watched her till she vanished round the corner, then stepped back inside and shut the door.

There was no answer at Elsa Kendrick's flat. I knocked and rang for a few minutes, then stood back, looking up at the windows. It looked like she wasn't in. I cursed at having come all that way for nothing. When I'd phoned Jonno Kendrick that morning to get her mobile number, he'd said, "Hold on a minute" and put the phone down. After five minutes of listening to 1970s cock-rock playing on what sounded like his cab radio, I got the message and rang off. In spite of the wasted effort, part of me was relieved. I hadn't known what I was going to say to Elsa. The only thing I knew for sure about her was that she was an exceptional liar, which meant she was hardly going to burst into tears and blurt out a confession as soon as she saw me. I didn't have any new evidence to confront her with, apart from my conversation with her ex-husband, or husband, or whatever he was. Though it would still have been interesting to watch her reaction when I told her what he had told me.

There was no answer from the upstairs flat either. I could hardly wait around all day for Elsa to return. I didn't have a car, so I couldn't stake the house out, and like most suburban London streets there was nowhere to park anyway. I had a bicycle at home, but sitting on a bike was hardly a discreet way to stake out someone's house. Short of breaking into the place opposite and twitching their net curtains, there was no way I could keep an eye on Elsa Kendrick's flat, without some nervous neighbour taking me for a criminal and calling the cops to frogmarch me away. I glanced at my phone. It was nearly time to go to work anyway. I'd have to think of some other way to reach Elsa, maybe a message relayed through her old workplace, something designed to pique her curiosity. Of course I'd tried that before, when I claimed Dad had written about her, and she'd seen right through me that time. She was a slicker liar than I was. But I'd think of something.

199

When I arrived at the Iron Bridge I was greeted like an old friend by the waiters and kitchen staff already on duty. I'd discovered there was a real camaraderie in the place, clearly born from a mutual terror of Chris Eccles. Working for him was meant to be a baptism of fire—or maybe a baptism of boiling goose fat—and a successful apprenticeship could get you a job skivvying in any restaurant in Europe. Maybe the trainees mistook me for a fellow dreamer starting at the bottom by scrubbing pans. I hadn't tried to explain to any of them that my idea of haute cuisine was taking a sandwich up to my bedroom. But it was nice to be welcomed, and it was with a twinge of shame that I remembered I was only there to pick up information. If there was none to be found, I wasn't going to stay . . . was I?

But why shouldn't I? I needed a job, and this was a job. Yeah, it was thanks to McGovern I'd got it, but maybe I could have got it for myself if I'd walked in and asked for it. Eccles didn't scare me. In fact, I quite liked the guy.

Like Zoe said, I hadn't a hope in hell of proving anything against McGovern, even if he had ordered my dad killed. And if he hadn't, what was wrong with staying here? Apart from anything else, the food was the best I'd ever tasted, and I was in serious danger of getting a belly. Maybe even I could learn to cook like that, if I set my mind to it. There wasn't much reading involved—you didn't see the chefs flicking through cookery books. I could run a kitchen. I might have my own restaurant someday. Zoe could do front of house, and when the last customer had left we'd fuck like bunnies, on a different table every night.

All this was running through my head—and other places—as I went outside to empty the scrap bins from the lunch-time rush. Eccles was very keen on recycling, and all the food waste had to be set aside for composting, and the other garbage sorted into glass and cardboard and plastic. After carefully flattening some fruit boxes with my size ten trainers I piled them into the massive aluminium hopper under the window of Eccles's office. As I dropped the lid and dusted my hands I heard a voice I couldn't place at first, with a high-pitched laugh that sounded more like a sneer, from inside the office. It came to me at last: McGovern's fixer, James. A hand reached out to shut the window, and when I saw the sleeve of a chef's jacket and the chunky Rolex on his wrist I knew Eccles was in there too. It was a warm day but clearly he didn't want his conversation with James to be overheard.

Eccles's office window was about two metres from

the top of the steps that led from the back yard up to the rear doors, and its sill was about the same distance from the ground. But in the corner nearest the steps an extractor fan was mounted in the window, to vent the little kitchen fitted into this end of Eccles' office. I skipped up the steps, clambered over the handrail, gripped the rail with my right hand and stretched my left foot out to rest on a waste pipe emerging from the wall just below, currently dribbling hot water into the drain. I grabbed the sill of the office window with my left hand, pressed my back against the brick and held my breath to listen to the voices coming through the extractor vent.

". . . mostly it stays up north, visiting the Normandy and Brittany markets for local produce and game. Twice a week in the summer."

"Is the van marked?" That was James's voice again.

"It has the logo of the restaurant on it, if that's what you mean."

"Customs must give you a hard time about bringing in all that booze and dodgy meat."

"We don't buy booze and the meat's not dodgy. And we're part of the European Community anyway, so . . ."

"So your van doesn't get stopped?"

Eccles's voice faded away. He seemed to have finally realized what James was getting at. Bit slow of him, I'd thought. "Not often, no."

"How often?"

There was another pause. I could imagine Eccles tapping the arm of his specs on his perfectly straight white teeth.

"Once a fortnight, maybe. I'd have to ask Christophe, my buyer."

"That'll be fine," said James. His words implied a shrug, as if he suspected Eccles of dragging his feet. The same van did the same run every week filled with smelly pâté and runny cheese, and Customs waved it through. I was beginning to see how investing in an up-market restaurant might appeal to the Guvnor.

The waste pipe under my foot started to bend. It was only plastic, and the hot water running through it had softened it. I clutched the window ledge harder and tried to take some of the weight off my left foot.

"When's the next trip?" said James.

"Not for a fortnight. Christophe's on holiday, and we have enough fresh produce laid up." Now Eccles was obviously lying, and in danger of getting a slap. Or worse.

"That's perfect," said James. "Let us have the keys and let us know where it's parked, and you'll have it back by the end of the week."

"What does Mr. McGovern want it for?" There was another brief pause.

"You didn't really just ask me that, did you?" The smirk was gone from James's voice.

The waste pipe under my foot snapped and my foot flailed, kicking the aluminium hopper so hard it rang like a gong. My left hand didn't have enough grip on the windowsill and it slipped free. I nearly wrenched my right arm out of its socket hauling myself back to the handrail, but eventually I grabbed it with both hands and stilled and stood there, my heart racing, bent over the rail. I was trying to hear if my presence had been registered, if James had heard me kick the hopper or the loud hollow *ponk* when the waste pipe snapped off. Where it had broken, the steaming water now gushed and tinkled noisily, like an incontinent baby. But nobody came to the window, and the door to the kitchen didn't open. I swung myself back under the handrail, tripped down the steps and retrieved the slops bin I had come out with. I was worried about Eccles; if he'd been dumb enough to invent any more reasons why James couldn't do whatever he liked with Eccles's van, James might decide to stop asking nicely. I could always blunder into Eccles's office, like I'd got lost on my way to the toilets. It might put them off their stride . . . or James might decide it was one accidental appearance too many. Fuck it, I thought, and opened the door that led to the office corridor.

Eccles was coming back down from the public area as if he'd just shown his visitors out. His face was empty and neutral, until he saw me standing there. He frowned. I donned my best gormless potwasher's grin.

"Everything all right, Chef?"

"You can't come through here in your overalls, Finn," he said.

"Right, Chef. Sorry." I had to stop myself from tugging my forelock as I backed out.

When I emerged James was standing in the yard. Shit, I thought, how did he get back here so quick? And what was he looking for?

"All right?" he said. His wide toothy grin made my skin crawl. "How's the job working out?"

"Great," I said.

"Money OK?"

"Great. Thanks." I wished I could stop saying *great*, I sounded like a moron. Although maybe that wasn't such a bad idea. "Tell the Guvnor I'm really grateful," I added.

James gave me a look. Either he didn't like being asked to run errands or he didn't like being reminded that he had a boss to answer to. He looked at the broken waste pipe, the down section leaning away from the wall, the water steaming and gurgling from the broken lip. "How long's it been like that?"

I shrugged.

James nodded up at Eccles's window. "He needs to watch out. Looks like a health and safety hazard to me." He smiled, then turned and walked out of the yard, whistling.

Back home that night I chucked my coat onto the sofa, took my phone out and checked it again. It looked like Zoe wasn't the sort of girl to text every thought that went through her head, or a stream of smileys and LOLs. She knew how to play it cool. So did I—I hadn't checked my phone more than a hundred times that evening. At about seven she'd sent: *Cant cu tonite. Sorry. x*

Pity, I'd texted back. *X*

Nothing since. Now I was worried that the capital X had been coming on too strong. Then I decided to stop worrying. I plugged the phone in to recharge, slogged up the stairs, scrubbed my teeth, checked for zits and collapsed into bed.

I woke around two. I'd heard the front door softly close—Dad coming in from the pub, I'd thought sleepily.

That's what woke me up properly. I remembered that Dad was dead, and that whoever killed him had taken his keys . . . and I still hadn't got round to chang-ing the locks. So who had opened the door? Or had I dreamed it?

I held my breath and lay there and listened. And heard nothing. A ticking from somewhere—probably the battery-powered clock on the wall by the front door—and a police siren distorting as it sped along the raised section of the motorway three streets away to the north. The deep rumble of a goods train, or a late-night landing at Heathrow.

I pulled the sheets back, dropped my feet to the floor, lifting them at the last minute so they made no sound as they touched the rug. I stood, and the ancient floorboard under the rug creaked, as I should have known it would. I stood still. And heard nothing. It was bloody cold. Now I was up I wanted to piss.

I headed for the bathroom and pulled the string. The clack of the ceiling switch resounded through the house like a pistol shot, and the light flickered on sullenly. I hated those economy bulbs Dad had fitted—they never seemed to get bright enough. I finished, shook, tucked it away and flushed the bog. The gushing echoed through the house, and mixed in with the echo down below was a sort of scuffle, as if someone had tripped on some-thing. I reached for the string and pulled it, and the bathroom light flicked off, and I stood there motionless for thirty seconds while my eyes re-adjusted to the dark. Silence again. There was a cricket bat in the cupboard under the stairs, I remembered. Right now that seemed like a really stupid place to keep it.

eleven

I started down the stairs, this time placing my feet carefully, trying to remember where each step creaked and to avoid that part. I made it to the bottom almost without making a sound, and stood there by the front door, feeling the slight draught of cool night air on my bare feet. I was holding my breath and listening, and I could still hear nothing, and I wondered if the sound of the front door closing had after all been part of a dream. Or maybe it was the reality, and all·the rest had been a dream. Maybe Dad had come home and woken me up, and everything I thought had happened in the last week had never happened.

But the living room was empty, and the table was bare, apart from the unread bills still scattered on it. No crappy old laptop, no pile of notes, no Dad. The movement behind me was so stealthy it might have been a spider's scuttle but I heard it all the same and turned and registered the hand rising under my jaw and slapped it away, and whatever it was that hand had been holding flew across the pitch-black room and hit the wall, and at the same time a sledgehammer hit me in the solar plexus, driving all the breath from my body. Instinctively I raised my arms to block, just in time to catch a smashing blow to my curled fists, aimed at where my cheekbone would have been if I'd doubled over like I was meant to. The figure in front of me was slight and lithe and fast and he pressed forward while I retreated, desperately trying to catch my breath. He was whacking me above and below, trying everything to get me to drop my guard. A jolt of pain from my right kneecap nearly made my leg buckle—he'd stamped on my knee, but his aim had been off in the dark, or I'd have been on the floor screaming by now. I registered a bigger movement and realized he was aiming a roundhouse kick at my head.

I stepped forward so the toe of his boot went behind my head and his shin cracked my ear. Lifting my arm, I grabbed his raised leg and held it, pushing him off balance while I drove my free fist into his balls. I heard him grunt through gritted teeth, and with a twisting wriggle wrench himself free. In that instant I knew I was really in trouble; anyone who could take a punch like that to the nuts and not go down puking had had serious training.

He was a shadow in the dark now, both feet planted on the floor, in a slight crouch with one leg behind him, his knees bent and his arms loosely raised in a karate stance. His hands were black shapes, like he was wearing leather gloves. We were both in the dark, but it was my living room, not his, and when I stepped to the left and feinted he stepped to the right and collided with the corner of the table. In that instant I closed in, landed a jab to his solar plexus that made him gasp and followed through with a left to his jaw, but he pulled his head back just enough to stay clear, grabbed my arm as it went past and pulled it into a lock.

I hadn't learned all my fighting at Delroy's and I knew what was coming next, so before he could break my arm at the elbow I drove my weight further forward, pushing both of us off balance, so the table cut into the backs of his thighs and tilted him back. I pulled free and stepped back, but he closed in, and as I looked up I saw the shape of his head pulling back, and instantly lowered mine. His head butt didn't connect with my face but our foreheads collided, and my head seemed to ring like an anvil, and stars whirled in the darkness.

I managed to break free but he recovered quicker. Before I could raise my block again his foot flashed up into my chest in another hammer blow, then flicked down and came up again, connecting directly with my chin and rattling the teeth in my head as I stumbled against the fireplace. I saw his hand reach out to grab the urn with Dad's ashes, and I knew he was going to smash it over my head, and the sheer bloody cheek of it made me yell and dive in and grab him close.

The vase went flying somewhere, our legs tangled and we fell to the floor in a grunting writhing heap. I tried to use my weight to pin him down but it was like wrestling with a wiry psychotic octopus on coke. He switched from karate to close combat, palm-heeling me on the nose, and I didn't know a blow to the kidneys from a range of ten centimetres could hurt so much. Somehow he writhed from under me to behind me, both of us on our knees, and his arm snaked round my throat and started to squeeze, and the blood thumped in my head and those bloody stars reappeared, white bursts against orange. I clawed backwards at his arm and his face, hoping to rip a nostril, but he pulled his head back. His other arm was pushing my head down and forward. Bite him, I thought, but there was nothing to bite, and I could feel myself weakening, consciousness slipping away. I dropped my hand to the floor to push myself up and felt something cylindrical and plastic under my fingers. When I scrabbled to grab it my fingers touched a cold hard wire, and nearly bent it before I recognized what it was—what I'd knocked from his hand.

Lifting the syringe, I drove it deep into his forearm and pushed home the plunger.

"*Scheisse!*" he yelled—more in indignation than in pain—released me, and leaped to his feet, plucking the empty syringe from his arm and flinging it aside. I saw his hand slip round to the small of his back and I scrambled to my feet, desperately trying to scrape together the last dregs of my energy as he brought his fist back round. The blade of a long, broad knife gleamed faintly like a ghost in the dark, and my left hand grabbed the wrist of the hand that held it, and my right hand punched him in the throat with all the strength I had left. I felt the gristle of his windpipe collapse under my knuckles, and the iron tendons in his arm flex and flinch and sag; he dropped to his knees, choking and wheezing, and fell forward, his jaw slamming into my bare toes.

It hurt like hell, but I barely felt it. I clutched at one of the dining chairs, dragged it out, and collapsed onto it, and sat there, bent over, my elbows on my knees, shaking with adrenaline, for what felt like days.

The silence had re-gathered. The clock was ticking nonchalantly on the wall, a distant roar announced a motorbike doing a ton on the motorway, and the only breathing in the room was mine. The attacker lay face down on the stained threadbare rug; I could just see the whites of his eyes staring across the floor, peering under the sofa as if looking for odd dropped coins, like my dad used to do.

Once more the street was a blue disco of police vehicles crackling with RT gossip, with neighbours flocked behind a cordon looking on in morbid fascination, wondering if this was going to become a regular occurrence. At least this time I didn't have to change out of my clothes. I had tried not to touch anything; I'd just switched on the light, grabbed my phone from the table where it had been charging, called the cops and went to sit at the foot of the stairs. I was still in my pyjama bottoms when they knocked at the door, and I stayed sitting on the stairs until the Scene of Crime people brought me my regulation white paper suit and trainers. As I followed the uniforms out into the street and down towards the car that would take me to the station, I noticed the onlookers in their dressing gowns and hastily-tugged-on jeans nudge each other and nod, *Him again*. By the time I got back from the nick there'd probably be a petition going round to have me evicted.

If I got back from the nick. When the door of the interview room opened and Prendergast entered with Amobi, the sad, bitter smirk on the older man's face suggested that if he hadn't got me for the last one he'd get me for this. I felt like smirking too when I looked at him. *Do you know what sort of noises your daughter makes in bed?* But I kept that to myself, for now.

Amobi was carrying a supermarket carrier bag, one of those "lifetime" ones with the pious ecological slogans printed on the side. It was nearly empty; I wondered what it was for. Was he planning to go shopping after this interview? Amobi left the bag on the floor, and he and Prendergast pulled back their chairs and sat down.

"OK, Mr. Maguire," said Prendergast with weary resignation, "why don't you tell us what happened? This time."

This time. As if my last statement had been a fairy tale and this was just going to be the sequel.

"A guy came into my house and tried to kill me," I said.

"Why did he do that?"

I shrugged. "Ask him."

"Do you know who this man was?"

"Nope. But he seemed highly-trained. Like a professional."

"A hit man, you mean?" asked Prendergast. From his look you'd think I'd claimed the guy was a werewolf.

"Maybe."

"But you fought him off."

"I got lucky."

"So how did this . . . *hit man* get into your house? Did he break in?"

215

"I think he had keys, and he let himself in. Same as last time, when he killed my dad."

"What makes you think this was the same man?" said Amobi. Prendergast probably couldn't bring himself to admit the possibility that it wasn't me who'd murdered my father.

"The old guys at the Weaver's Arms mentioned a man who called himself Hans. He said he was a journalist and he bought them drinks all night. He got my dad pissed and nicked his keys. This guy matched their description, plus he spoke German."

"You spoke to him?" asked Prendergast.

"He said 'scheisse' when I stabbed him with that syringe," I said. "It's German for *police officer*."

Prendergast took a deep breath. Amobi cut in quickly, "We'll show those witnesses his photograph and see if they agree he was the same man," said Amobi.

"In the meantime," said Prendergast, "why would a hit man come after you and your dad?"

"No idea," I said.

"We know you've been making enquiries of your own," said Amobi. "Did you talk to anyone, make anyone suspicious?"

"Like who?" I said.

"Stop acting like a twat, Maguire," rumbled Prendergast.

"I've talked to lots of people," I said. For a minute it occurred to me to mention Elsa Kendrick. The cops could track her down far more easily than I could. But what would be the point? If her husband had been telling the truth, she might have had a motive, yeah. But it was Hans who'd killed my dad, and judging by Elsa's poky flat she would never have been able to afford a professional killer's services.

"Might it have anything to do with your visit to McGovern?" asked Amobi.

"I didn't do anything to piss him off," I answered truthfully. And then I remembered what I'd heard at the window of Eccles's office. Amobi seemed to notice the thought occur to me and was about to follow up when Prendergast spoke again, with an elaborately casual air that suggested he was about to wallop me with something.

"You do know, Mr. Maguire, that if you find an intruder in your house you're only entitled to use reasonable force to eject him? You killed this man. You crushed his larynx."

"I wasn't trying to kill him," I pointed out. "I was trying to stop him killing me."

"How do you know he wanted to kill you? Did he threaten you?"

"He came at me with a knife." Was Prendergast going

to suggest that the twenty-centimetre combat blade with the blood gutter was mine? And the guy was wearing a scabbard for decoration? Prendergast glanced at Amobi, who bent down, reached into the supermarket bag and drew out a clear plastic evidence bag wrapped around an X-shaped metallic object. Now I saw the point of the carrier bag—they'd wanted a "ta-dah" moment, when they'd confront me with a vital piece of evidence that would force me to change my story and dissolve in a sobbing heap of contradictions. Of course it didn't work that way, because I had no idea what was in the evidence bag until Amobi unrolled it.

"Are these yours, Mr. Maguire?" said Prendergast.

I looked more closely. It was a pair of secateurs, brand-new, judging from the state of the blades. The handles were wrapped in black tape, Teflon plumber's tape maybe. They were unlocked and lying open, the black blades gleaming nastily under the harsh strip light of the interrogation room.

"No," I said. "We don't have any plants to prune."

"These aren't for pruning," said Prendergast. "Well, not plants, anyway. These were found in your kitchen and if they're not yours, we have to assume the intruder brought them with him. What exactly did he say to you?"

"He didn't say anything. He came at me with a

syringe, we fought, I grabbed the syringe and stuck him with it. It slowed him down enough for me to hit him before he stabbed me."

"I don't think that's quite accurate," said Prendergast. "If that guy had wanted to kill you, he would have just stabbed you and left. I think he was going to knock you out with the stuff in that syringe, and when you were out cold, he was going to cut one of your fingers off. Maybe more. Maybe your thumbs. But he wasn't out to kill you—he was out to frighten you."

I said nothing. I was staring at the secateurs in the bag, feeling a bit sick.

"So you see," said Prendergast, "killing him wasn't reasonable force."

"You're fucking kidding," I said. "The guy wants to knock me out and cut my fingers off, and killing him isn't reasonable force? Then what is? How was I supposed to know what he was planning? And why don't you have that huge bloody commando knife in an evidence bag, the one that was still in his hand when the plods arrived?"

"Look, Maguire," hissed Prendergast, leaning his pockmarked, grizzled face close to mine, "you think we're just going to let you walk out of here when you've witnessed two murders in ten days? Even if you're as innocent as you make out, which I doubt, you're a fucking idiot." The sarcasm had gone—he was deadly serious, spitting out his words. "You're sitting here making smartarse remarks when someone out there wants you mutilated or dead. You've been lucky so far—how long do you think you'll last out there on your own? You think because you managed to stop this one, whoever sent him is going to give up? We know you've been wandering around stirring up shit and asking stupid questions. Tell us who you've been talking to, what they said and what you've heard. And then we'll charge you with suspected manslaughter and get you remanded in custody so you're out of harm's way while we round up the fuckers who killed your dad. Once we've done that, all the charges will be dropped and you can fuck off back to your burger bar."

I looked at him, trying in vain to spot a trace of Zoe in the face of the furious, frustrated old man facing me. Christ, did he take all this home with him?

"Do it," I said. "Put me up in front of a judge and see how far you get. I've told you everything I know. Charge me with aggravated self-defence in my own house, or let me go the fuck home."

Dawn had broken when I finally emerged from the nick, and the morning rush hour was just starting. The baggy white overalls and cheap trainers the Scene of

Crime people had given me made me look like a home-less house painter, but they were slightly warmer than walking home in bare feet and pyjama bottoms, and this being London nobody looked at me twice anyway. Amobi had taken a statement, his tone and his manner studiedly neutral. I was told I would have to testify at an inquest, again, but for now I was free to go. He even offered me a lift, if I didn't mind waiting an hour for a patrol car to become free. Or he could get someone to call me a cab. But I didn't want to sit around in that nick a moment longer than I had to, I didn't want another ride in a police car, and I didn't want to waste money on a cab. I told him I'd walk home.

In fact, I ran. The trainers weren't bad for running in, and the overalls flapped and rustled, but they didn't restrict my movement and I figured when I got home I could just bin them. This gave me a business idea—disposable running wear—and I had just franchised the concept across three continents and made my first billion when I turned the corner into my street and saw a slight figure in a black coat sitting on the low wall of the house opposite mine, her hands buried in her pockets, her elegantly booted legs crossed at the knee to keep warm. When my mother looked up and saw me slow to a jog she smiled and stood, and the look on her face was easy to read: happiness and deep relief.

"Finn . . . I called the station as soon as I heard. They said you'd already left."

"How did you find out?" I said.

"I still have Donald's number." She nodded at the house she'd been sitting outside. Donald was our neighbour opposite, a white-haired old bloke who was always up at six, for no reason I'd ever been able to fathom. "I called him to find out when you were most likely to be around, and he told me about last night. What exactly happened?"

"I'm knackered, and I really need a shower," I said.

"Please, Finn. We need to talk."

"No, I mean—yeah. We should." For a brief moment when I first saw her, my heart had lifted too, and I'd forgotten to be angry. Maybe it was a side-effect of nearly being murdered, but suddenly all the sulking and the tantrums seemed pointless somehow. I fished in the pocket of my overalls and found the keys I'd remembered to grab from their hook before the cops had taken me away a few hours earlier. The same keys I'd made my mother give back, the day of Dad's funeral. "It's just, I'd like to put some clothes on." I opened the door.

"Oh, right, OK, sorry, I thought . . ."

"You can put the kettle on if you want," I said. "Though there isn't much to eat."

"Why don't I buy us both breakfast somewhere?"

"Yeah, OK." Neutral territory, I thought, good idea.

"Where's good around here these days?"

"Nowhere," I said. I stood in the living room and looked around. It was hard to see any sign of a fight, or of the room being swept for evidence by the cops; at least this time there had been no blood to mop up. Dad's urn was lying on the floor against the sofa, where the intruder had dropped it. I picked it up and checked it for cracks, but it seemed intact.

"Donald said someone broke in and attacked you," said my mother.

"Yeah," I said. "The same guy who killed Dad."

"Why? What did he want?"

"I don't know." *Not yet*, I thought.

"Oh God, Finn, I was so frightened when I heard. Are you sure you're all right?"

"You can say it," I said. "*I told you so.*" She looked at me, puzzled. "You told me to change the locks," I said.

"I should have told you not to," she replied. "Then you would have done it, just to spite me." I thought about that. She was right.

"Let me go and change," I said.

I wasn't being funny, but there really was nowhere decent to eat locally at that time in the morning, except for the identikit hotels along the motorway crammed with identikit businessmen. That's how my mother and I ended up in Max Snax with our order being taken by my replacement—a guy in his early twenties whose face was a mosaic of acne and whose mouth hung slightly open, revealing spectacularly crooked teeth. Mum studiously avoided looking at him and focused on searching the menu for something edible. She finally settled on a vegetarian special that I knew wasn't very special, and was only vegetarian in the sense that it didn't have any meat in it. It didn't have many vegetables either, unless you counted spuds and soya. I ordered an orange juice and toast, figuring that if Jerry in the kitchen gobbed on the toast it would be easy to spot. He wouldn't have done it out of malice—it would have been his idea of a joke. I really didn't miss this place, I realized.

"Are you a regular here?" asked my mum as we took our seats. Jerry had shouted my name and waved from the kitchen, and Trudy had given me a myopic smile when they noticed us at the counter.

"I used to work here," I said.

"What, for pocket money?"

"Didn't Dad tell you?"

"He told me that you'd joined a boxing club and you showed real promise. That you ran ten kilometres a day. That you'd left school early but hadn't worked out what you wanted to do yet." Peering into her sandwich she didn't notice my look of bemused contempt. "You always were unconventional, very single-minded. I knew you wouldn't end up stacking shelves in a supermarket."

"I used to work here full-time," I said. "I used to dream of stacking shelves in a supermarket, but they wouldn't have me, because I still can't read."

"You're dyslexic, Finn. That doesn't mean you're stupid."

"No, it just means I'm not qualified to do anything, except maybe sell drugs, and I tried that and it didn't work out too well."

And I told her what I'd got up to since she'd left. The stabbings I'd witnessed, the gang bangs I'd taken part in, the shoplifting raids I'd led, all that stuff, in no particular order. I was trying my best to shock her. I wanted her to cry, knowing I would despise her if she did, because it would have been out of pity for me and sorrow for herself. But she stared at me, unflinching, not interrupting, not hiding her face or turning away, while I laid on every grisly detail I could think of. As I talked I realized that this list of sins was not just an accusation, it was a confession: it was her fault for abandoning me, true, but the choices I'd made were still my own. I couldn't take any credit for straightening myself out if I didn't take some of the blame for being bent.

By the time I'd run out of dirt my mother's coffee had

gone cold and her vegetarian special had congealed into a cheesy lump. I sipped my vaguely-orange juice. Jerry had been over-diluting it again.

My mother sat there for a while, saying nothing. I guessed what was coming next—hand-wringing, apologies, pleas for forgiveness. I wasn't sure if I was going to be able to listen.

"When you had just turned eleven," said my mother, "they cancelled *Medics*. The daytime soap about a city doctors' practice ... I played the receptionist." I looked blank, and she shook her head. "It doesn't matter. It was a crap job, but the money kept us afloat, and I could say I was working. But after it ended I couldn't find anything else—radio, commercials, theatre ... I looked too young to play mums and too old to play girlfriends, and they were ninety per cent of the parts for women, and they still are ... Anyway, Noel and I didn't tell you, because we didn't want you to worry about money, and there was no need to—I could have just signed on, or done something else. Except I'd never wanted to do anything else." She looked at me. "It's weird talking to you like this. The last conversation we had was about your favourite cartoon on TV."

I said nothing; that had been another life, and I didn't remember it.

My mother looked at her coffee. "I'd got involved with this charity—nothing to do with acting—that wrote to condemned prisoners in America. Typical bleeding-heart-liberal do-gooding nonsense, but it made me feel better about myself. I ended up writing to this chap called Enrique Romero. He'd been sentenced to death by lethal injection for a double homicide, and was in his third year on Death Row. He told me he was innocent—that didn't mean much, they all said that—but the thing about Enrique was his paintings. He was the most amazing artist. You might have seen his one of Gabriel? 'The Flaming Sword'? Dividing the saved and the damned?" Her eyes had been flitting about, and now they landed on me, searching for a reaction. I just shrugged, waiting for her to go on. "He sent me pictures of his paintings, and I found them . . . extraordinary, so moving. I think I was the first person to tell him that. Anyway, a year after we had started to correspond, he was pardoned. Someone else confessed to the crime he'd been accused of, and that was it, he was free.

"I thought . . . I was in love with him. I'd persuaded myself I was in love with him, I couldn't stop thinking about him, and your dad knew what was going on, and there was nothing either of us could do about it. And when Enrique got out of prison he wrote to me, and he told me I was the first person who'd ever believed in him, and that he loved me too, and that I should join him . . ."

She blinked rapidly, though I saw no tears.

"I think it was the single stupidest, most selfish thing I've ever done," she said. "But at the time, it felt like I didn't even have a choice."

"Did it work out?"

She snorted, at her own naivety, I assumed. "For a while, yes. I was obsessed, like a teenager again, and his paintings began to sell on the back of the publicity. It was just like I dreamed it would be. For a while."

"What happened?"

She shrugged, and smiled bitterly. "He'd been in prison so long, he found it hard to adjust. And it's one thing writing letters; living together takes a lot more effort. I should have known that, I'd lived with Noel for long enough. And the guilt didn't help."

"I thought you said he was innocent?"

"Not his. Mine. I'd left my only child to follow a daydream halfway round the world." She looked out the window, unable to meet my gaze. "Enrique and I started to argue, and soon it seemed there were more arguments than conversations. We managed to agree it wasn't working out, and it would be better if we split. So we split."

"When was this?"

"Two, three years ago? I tried for some acting jobs, but got nowhere. Then I had a go at selling cars—not those huge American monstrosities, imported Mercedes—and the hideous thing was, I was really good at it. The English accent helped, of course. Plus I didn't have a family, so I could work all hours. For the first time in my life, I was doing really well, and making money, but what was the point? There was no one I could share it with. And then," she sighed, "I was browsing the Net one day and I came across Noel's name, and it all came flooding back to me. I remembered I'd had a life once, and a family, and I'd been so . . . cherished, and I'd thrown it all away, like a total idiot." She sniffed, wiped her nose on a napkin and grimaced. I knew why—Max Snax napkins were made of paper so cheap and shiny they might as well have been plastic. In fact, Andy would have preferred that—he would have washed and reused them.

My mother cleared her throat. "I got hold of your dad's email address, and I emailed him, and he emailed me back, and we corresponded for a while, and eventually . . . I told him I was sorry, and I wanted to come home, if he'd have me, and he said he would. He just wanted some time, so he could find a way to tell you."

Funny, I thought. That's the same thing Elsa

Kendrick said. Anyone would think my dad had been scared of how I'd react. *Maybe he was,* said a small voice.

"Where's Enrique now?" I said.

"I don't know," she said. "That whole experience feels like some sort of schizoid episode. At the time it seems more than real, and afterwards . . . you can't even begin to understand it."

"Do you remember Spain?" I said. She looked mystified, and shook her head.

"Me and you and Dad, years ago, we visited that friend of his, the one who had that old castle with the pool. It came back to me the other day, at the funeral. It was more like a dream than a memory . . . I just remembered being really happy, all of us together."

She hesitated, then slid her hand across the table and laid it on mine. The weight of it, its warmth, and the firm bones beneath her soft palm, felt completely familiar, as if she touched me every day.

"I'm not going to apologize any more," she said. "But I've come home, and I'm here for good. You might decide you never want to see me again, and that's fine. But I'll always be your mother. There's nothing you can do about that, I'm sorry."

"Wasn't that an apology?" I said.

"Oh shit—yes, it was. Sorry. Damn—!"

I laughed. "Where are you staying?"

Her smile vanished, as if we'd bumped back to earth. "A hotel near Covent Garden, until I can find a flat."

You don't want your house back, then? I thought.

"You should call me," she said. "I'll take you out for a decent meal."

"I lost your number," I said.

My mother produced a sleek smartphone from an inside pocket and unlocked it. "I'll give it to you now," she said. "You can put it straight into your own phone."

"Sure," I said. Squinting at her screen she recited her number, and I punched it into Dad's old mobile. "I suppose you'd like mine," I said.

"I'll wait till you call me," she said.

"Morning, Finn, and how are you today?" I hadn't noticed Andy sidling up to our table. He must have scuttled across the floor, doing his imitation of a hermit crab at low tide.

"Fine thanks, Andy," I said.

"I trust you're enjoying your meal?" He addressed both of us, rubbing his hands together unctuously. I knew that was as close as he ever got to washing them.

"We were," said my mother.

"Good, good. I just wanted you to know, Finn, that if you wanted to reapply for your position here, your submission would be favourably received."

"I thought you'd found someone." I nodded at the

guy behind the counter, picking his teeth with his fingernail.

Andy grinned apologetically. "Dennis doesn't project the right Max Snax image," he explained.

"Did you notice before you came over here that we were in the middle of a conversation?" My mother smiled. Uh-oh, I thought.

"Finn was one of our finest team members," said Andy.

"He was," said my mother. "He's not any more. He's a paying customer who's entitled to some privacy. And I'd rather he got a job skinning baby seals alive than went to work for an ill-mannered oik, serving deep-fried vomit to the desperate cretins who come in here. Now kindly leave us alone."

Andy swallowed and grinned and bobbed. "Enjoy your meal," he said.

My mother watched him slither away in the direction of his office, then turned back to me. "Oops," she said. "You didn't *want* your old job back, did you?"

"Not really."

"Thank God for that. Let's get out of here."

twelve

As I rode the Tube to work I stared at my phone. At first I'd liked it that Zoe hardly ever texted me, that she wasn't the sort of girl who needed constant attention and reassurance. Now I was beginning to suspect that maybe I was that sort of boy. For years I'd got by without any close friends, and now I had one—I was pretty sure she counted as one—I wanted to tell her everything, about last night and this morning when my mum turned up, so I could start to figure out what I thought of it.

But by Hammersmith station she hadn't texted me and I still hadn't texted her. I didn't want her to know how much I was starting to need her, in case it freaked her out or frightened her off. I didn't even want to know it myself. And another, selfish part of me was curious to see if she needed me more—or enough, anyway, to make the first move. But Baron's Court came and went, and the tube train rocked and lunged into the underground tunnel, and still my phone lay in my hand, blank and silent. I tucked it into my pocket.

When I emerged from Pimlico station I felt it vibrate and whipped it out quicker than a gunfighter. No message . . . I'd imagined it.

"Get a bloody grip," I told myself, and set off for the Iron Bridge.

Of course, my glorious career as a pot scrubber would have been cut off in its prime if Hans or whatever his name was had taken those secateurs to my thumbs. Maybe that was the idea—not just to frighten me, but to make sure those rubber gloves didn't fit any more, and keep me away from Eccles's restaurant. Like Prendergast said, whoever sent Hans was unlikely to give up, and since Hans wasn't around to get paid they'd still have the money to hire someone else. How long that would take, I had no idea, but I had to act quickly if I was going to find out what the Guvnor wanted Eccles's van for. Even if it had nothing to do with Dad, the knowledge might give me some leverage.

Eccles wasn't at the Iron Bridge that evening. He'd disappear every so often to do TV work and commercials, not come back for days sometimes. Then again, sometimes he'd pretend to disappear, only to pop up unannounced in the Iron Bridge to see how well it was run in his absence. It helped to keep his staff in a constant state of fear and uncertainty. Let's hope he didn't do that tonight, or I'd be stuffed.

It was early in the week so business was slack and the pans were only piling up at half the normal rate. I worked my way through the stack at top speed to clear the backlog, pulled off my overalls and draped them over the counter the way I did when I was going to the loo, but I didn't head for the loo. I headed straight for the back door, and though I was nearly one of the lads now none of the apprentice chefs took any notice. From the rear I doubled back into the building, up the moody corridor to Eccles's office, and tried the handle. Locked, of course. Not a big deal—it just gave me that much less time. I took out my phone, punched a few buttons to withhold my own number, and dialled.

"The Iron Bridge, good evening," said Georgio. He had a lovely voice, like hot treacle, which was one reason Eccles made him maître d', I supposed. I pushed open the door into the main restaurant just enough to see Georgio on the phone at his station near the front door.

"Hello, this is Peter Finlay, from Francisco Associates? I think I may have left my wallet in the restaurant last night."

"I'll have a look. What sort of wallet is it?"

Francisco was one of the restaurant's biggest clients, a big firm of brokers a few streets away. I'd heard the waiters boasting about the huge tips they left—the Iron Bridge was practically the firm's staff canteen. "Dolce and Gabbana," I said, then wondered if D&G even made wallets. But as I watched, Georgio glided across to the bar where lost property was usually stowed. When he ducked behind the counter I nipped over to his station, flipped open the cabinet below—Georgio rarely locked it, silly boy—and grabbed the key to Eccles's office.

"I'm afraid I can't find it," said Georgio on my phone. "Are you sure it was left here?"

"Oh, wait a minute," I said. "It's here, on my desk. Sorry about that, hell of a day. Thanks all the same, goodbye."

I hung up, slipped my phone into my pocket and doubled back for the kitchens. Georgio was still behind the bar, but Lori the Chinese waitress noticed me, and frowned; I didn't belong in the staff area. But when I gave her my biggest grin, as if I belonged there, she smiled back at me and carried on.

I threw the keys on Eccles's desk, sat in his chair and wondered where to start. There was a pile of invoices from suppliers, but even if I'd had half the night to read through them I doubted they'd be any use. I should start by searching the desk, I thought—but all the drawers were locked, and if Eccles left those keys hanging about I didn't know where. OK, I was trying to find out about the van, so I needed documents relating to it—there'd be a file with insurance details, or a servicing agreement, or something to tell me where it was kept. I dragged over his in-tray and flicked through the papers stacked in it, but for all the sense I could make of them they might as well have been a heap of spaghetti. I tried looking for the logo of a petrol station or a breakdown service. Nothing. I shoved the in-tray back across the desk.

The computer screen leaped into life, dazzling me momentarily. The desktop was an amazingly vivid image of Tower Bridge at dusk, all glowing lights and reflections off the river. I must have jogged the mouse with the in-tray and woken the PC up from standby, but there was no lock screen, no password, nothing. I knew Eccles hated technology and liked preparing everything by hand, but this seemed like overdoing it. I wondered how often he even used this computer. The keyboard was spotless, practically brand-new, and the icons on the screen seemed the standard ones you see on every new PC—rubbish bin, browser, a shortcut to the maker's website . . . and *RTTracker*? I looked more closely at that.

Its icon was a cartoon of a lorry in a crosshair. When I double-clicked on it a log-in dialogue appeared, both fields automatically prefilled: *User: ECCLES_IRONBRIDGE, Password:* a row of dots. I clicked the *Log-in* button.

Almost instantly the screen filled with squiggly yellow lines on a beige background, centred on a flashing red dot with a white label. Thicker orange lines crossed diagonally from the top left to the bottom right of the screen, where they met a wobbly orange circle. There were lots of labels and words and numbers, but none of them made any sense to me. I clicked on a picture of a magnifying glass with a dash in it, and the image zoomed out. Of course—it was a map. The different coloured lines were roads. But a map of where? I zoomed out again. The yellow roads vanished, and green roads appeared, snaking around the shrinking orange circle. And in the middle of the wobbly orange circle a single word appeared bigger than all the others: *Paris.*

It was France, where Eccles's van went every week. And that flashing red dot, heading for Paris, was his van. It must have been fitted with a tracking device, so Eccles could find out exactly where it was any time he liked.

Shit, I thought, does the Guvnor know about this?

I checked my phone. I'd been away from my post for

ten minutes. The kitchen would run low on pans soon, and I'd be missed. Putting the office keys back would not be a problem—I figured I could just leave them around for Georgio to find, and he'd be too worried about his own job to report it. I exited the tracker program and opened it again. When the log-in dialogue reappeared I clicked on *Forgot your password?* Then I switched to email and clicked on *Send and receive.*

And waited.

Twelve minutes. I clicked "Send and Receive" again.

Ping.

I opened up the reminder email, grabbed a pen and a bit of paper and painstakingly copied down the text. My tongue had crawled out of the corner of my mouth again, but I let it. I had just deleted the email when my dad's phone beeped and rattled on the desk. I nearly jumped out of my skin—I'd set the volume to max because the kitchen was so noisy, and I'd forgotten to silence it. I stood to go, snatching the phone up, and checked the screen.

Need 2 c u 2nite—xx

It was from Zoe, and it had two x's. I counted them a few times, just to be sure.

"Finn?"

Georgio was standing in the doorway. I'd been so gobsmacked to hear from Zoe I hadn't even heard him approach—and he did not look happy. I tried to keep the idiot grin on my face.

"What are you doing? And how did you get in here?"

"The door was open. I was hoping to see the boss about getting a day off."

"Mr. Eccles is not here. You are not supposed to be in his office, and the door was not open." He plucked the keys from the desk and stared at me.

I shrugged. "Oh, right," I said. I hoped he would believe he was an idiot. I sure as hell felt like one.

"You're needed in the kitchen," said Georgio. He opened the door wide and stood back to usher me out. I'd seen him do that before, late at night, with a politician almost too drunk to walk. His absolute self-assurance was like a gravity field that pulled you towards the door and slung you through it. I crash-landed at the sink, where the pots had piled up into a massive, greasy, teetering pyramid, and got stuck in. Maybe I should have worried about what I was getting into, but all I could think of was Zoe, and I couldn't help whistling.

"Sweet Thames, flow softly . . ."

"Serious Organized Crime wants to give you a medal," said Zoe. "My dad nearly blew a gasket." We were lying in my bed and she was resting her chin on my belly, looking at the bruise Hans's heel had made on my sternum. She seemed fascinated by the marks he had left on me, and while we'd been making out she'd somehow managed to nudge every one of them hard enough to make me yell. I wasn't sure if me nearly getting killed made a difference to her, but it made a difference to me; when she'd walked in I'd gone for her like a randy bear, without the finesse. I hadn't slowed down till she'd kicked me in the kneecap Hans had stamped on.

"They've been after that guy for years. He was the number one suspect in half the Camorra killings last year."

"The Camorra?"

"The Naples Mafia."

"Jesus. There's no reward, is there? That'd be a lot more use than a medal."

"His name was Hans Ostwald."

"No shit. He really was called Hans?"

"Good liars stick as close to the truth as possible." She pressed her chin into my bruised sternum till I yelped, then grinned in satisfaction and wriggled up to slide her arms round my neck.

"Does Serious Crime know who sent him?" I said.

"Of course not. But whoever did must be seriously connected. And there'd be nothing in writing, no emails, not even phone calls."

"Great. Maybe I should try to catch the next one alive."

Zoe sat up, suddenly grim, and folded her arms across her breasts. "What do you mean, the next one?"

"Until I find out why my dad was murdered, they're going to keep coming after me," I said.

"You don't know that."

"No, but it'd be sensible to assume that."

"But you said all your dad's notes had gone, that there weren't any clues."

"I want to show you something," I said.

She sat beside me in the bed as I called up the *RT-Tracker* site on my laptop, praying the battery would last long enough to let me log in. It did, and I entered Chris Eccles's ID and password, and the map appeared: now the red dot with the white label was on the east of the city, flashing at three o'clock inside the orange circle of motorways that ringed Paris.

Zoe peered at the label. "That looks like a number plate."

"It's the registration of a van belonging to Chris Eccles, the chef. The Guvnor's borrowed it. Well, not the Guvnor himself, his sidekick James."

"Shit, and you're tracking it?"

"I think it's bringing something back from Paris. And when it does, I'm going to go take a look."

Zoe was horrified. "Finn, please don't. I've told you about McGovern, everyone has."

"If he had my dad killed, I want to know why."

"But what if this has nothing to do with your dad?"

I shrugged. "It's all I've got."

"God, you're so bloody pig-headed!"

"Yeah, that's what my dad used to say."

The PC wheezed and rattled, then popped up a warning message as the battery ran out. I shut the lid and slid the laptop onto the floor.

"Will you do something for me?" said Zoe.

I looked at her.

"Will you ask your mother about this?"

"Not just yet," I said.

"You don't trust her?"

"She'd tell me not to get involved. That I should inform the police, let them handle it."

"I like her already," said Zoe.

"I don't trust the police."

"Do you trust me?" she said.

"Sure."

"Then please don't do this." And she kissed me, and this time I didn't go for her like a bear, and she didn't poke my bruises, much. But I never answered her.

* * *

When Zoe woke me with a kiss the next morning she was already in her school uniform, smelling of soap. "Your shower is rubbish," she said. I made a grab for her, but she dodged and headed for the door. On the threshold she turned. "What are you doing today?"

"Going back to sleep."

"Are you going to tell the police about that van?"

"I miss you when you're not here," I said. It was a crude attempt to avoid the question, and it didn't work. She looked at me as if I'd slapped her, and turned away, blinking. "Wait," I said. I leaped out of bed, grabbed my trousers and followed her bollock-naked down the stairs, getting to the door just as she turned the latch, and holding it shut with my hand. She looked at me with such anger and disappointment I could barely meet her eye. I fumbled in the pockets of my jeans.

"I changed the locks yesterday," I said. "Bit late, I know, but . . ." I pulled the keyring out of my pocket. The keys on it were shiny and new; I offered them to her. "They came with three sets of keys," I said.

She looked at the keys, and then at me, and she was thinking really hard about something. I didn't ask why this was such a big deal because I didn't want to know. I didn't think I'd ever understand her—one minute so funny and sussed, the next so vulnerable and bitter she radiated pain.

"Thanks," she said, in a small voice. She took the key-ring and slipped it into her pocket, so it barely jingled.

"Will I see you tonight?" I said.

"I don't know," she said.

She turned the latch and tugged the door open, and I hopped backwards so it wouldn't catch my toes when it opened. It was raining slightly and she tugged up the collar of her school blazer, as if that was going to make a difference, and she scurried away without another word or one glance back.

thirteen

I never asked Zoe about her mother, I realized later that morning, as I went through my workout. I was so preoccupied by my own it didn't occur to me. Was her mother around? Was she dead, or separated from her dad? Prendergast wore a wedding ring, I remembered, but that didn't mean anything. Maybe he was the sentimental type, though that didn't seem likely. Didn't it ever bother him when she stayed out all night? I wondered what Prendergast had done, or hadn't done, to make her hate him so much. I wondered if either of them even knew.

I cursed. I'd lost count of how many press-ups I'd done. Fine, I'd just keep going till I couldn't do any more. But before I could start again my mobile rang, and that gave me an excuse to knock off. I was out of breath when I answered and my palms were so sweaty I nearly dropped the handset.

"Yeah, hello?"

"Who am I speaking to, please?"

"Finn Maguire," I said, before I remembered that it was them who had called me, so they ought to know. It was probably some phone spammer, I decided, and I tried to think of a good way to wind them up.

"This is Nicola Hale, from the law firm Hale and Vora." Yeah, right. Her name was probably Seema Singh, calling from Huckster & Huckster in Mumbai. "Could you confirm your date of birth, please?"

"Why don't you confirm it?" I said. How dumb did she think I was?

"I'm sorry, I need to be sure I'm talking to Finn Maguire."

"You are talking to him. But I don't know who he's talking to."

"Um—sorry—Mr. Maguire, you may have received a letter from us?"

That threw me. I glanced through the bills and junk mail that had been piling up on the table. Under a wrinkled menu from a pizza delivery joint was a thick, cream-coloured envelope with *Hale & Vora, Something* printed in the corner. *Solicitors*, that was it. Addressed to me. How long had it been there?

"Eh, yeah. I haven't opened it yet."

"We do need to speak to you, and we were hoping you might be able to come to our office."

"What's this about?"

"I'm afraid I can't discuss that without establishing your identity."

Shit, I thought, it's the house. The bank must know my dad's dead and they've stopped paying the mortgage.

"Is this about my dad?" I sounded like a lost orphan, I realized.

"Are you free around four today? We're at 391 Lincoln's Inn Fields."

"Sure," I said, my heart sinking.

"And you will need to bring some ID."

Lincoln's Inn Fields was right on the border between the West End and the City, so there weren't many fields, just a little park hemmed in by a square of massive Georgian townhouses. The gleaming brass plates beside every door announced the entire square was occupied by law firms, and judging by the Jags and BMWs parked on the off-street forecourts, law firms that made a lot of money. I'd opened the letter—nearly cutting my finger on the rigid flap of the envelope—but even though I'd read it a few times, I still didn't know what this was about. It simply asked me to contact Kamlesh Vora or Nicola Hale at their offices. If the bank was going to evict me, I thought, it was pretty bloody mean to make me schlep all the way into the City to let me know. But then banks weren't exactly known for their people skills, in spite of all their cheesy adverts.

The glass door of 391 was locked. I rattled it and saw the receptionist give me a good look-over before she buzzed me in. You could see her wondering if I was a rough sleeper trying to bum a cup of tea. My battered fibre suitcase didn't help, and I found myself wishing I'd washed or changed my jeans since splattering garlic butter over them the night before at work. But she clearly decided to live dangerously and pushed the button. I heaved open the plate-glass door and approached her huge wooden counter clutching my little suitcase to my chest like Paddington Bear.

"Eh—I'm here to see Nicola Hale?"

"Have you brought some ID?"

When I slid the suitcase across the beech wood desk Nicola Hale raised one perfectly plucked eyebrow. She was slim, neat and efficient, with blue eyes and long blonde hair, in her late twenties, I supposed. She looked at the case as if it might be full of laundry.

"It's all in there," I said. She was a lawyer, she was paid to read, and if they wanted to evict me I wasn't going to make life any easier for them. Or admit that I couldn't make head nor tail of most of the stuff in there.

"Allow me to express our condolences on the death

of your stepfather," said the bloke I presumed was her boss, who had introduced himself as Kamlesh Vora. He was an old Indian guy, bald on top apart from a neat fringe of white hair, and sporting a silk tie that probably cost more than everything I was wearing.

"Thanks," I said. We were sitting in a conference room lined with books so thick you could have built a bomb shelter out of them. Hale had the case open now and was sifting through the piles of documents and the envelopes full of printouts from the mortgage people. She pulled out a bundle of old passports, opened one and glanced across at me: I felt my face starting to burn. I could have brought my old passport and instead I brought an entire bloody suitcase full of bumpf. Why didn't I just get a friendly passer-by to write "I CAN'T READ" on my forehead? Of course, they might have written "WANKER," but I wouldn't have known, would I?

Hale offered the passport to Vora, who slipped on a pair of glasses to look at it, and nodded to Hale. She slipped the passport back inside the case while he put his glasses away.

"We act for the estate of Mr. Charles Egerton," he said.

"Who?"

"He was a friend of your father's. A distinguished

actor in his time. We handled his business affairs here in the UK after he retired to Spain."

Oh, *that* Charles Egerton. The one Dorothy Rousseau had mentioned at the funeral, the old man with the beard I could only just remember.

"Right," I said. "I met him once, a long time ago. How's he doing?"

"Mr. Egerton passed away two months ago," said Vora. "As I said, we act for his estate."

"His estate? You mean the place in Spain?"

"His entire estate," explained Hale. "We're the executors of Mr. Egerton's will." She was still browsing through the contents of the suitcase, which I considered rather nosy, now we'd established who I was.

"He stipulated that his entire estate should pass to Noel Maguire, your stepfather," said Vora.

"My father's dead," I said.

"Yes," said Vora. "We had been trying to trace him, but without success, until his death was reported last week in *The Stage*."

"Yeah," I said. "He'd sort of given up, dropped off the radar."

"Do you know what your father's wishes were?" said Vora. "Did he make a will?"

"Yes," said Hale. She was holding up a letter she'd

taken from an unsealed envelope. She glanced through it. "It's a standard form, from a newsagent, but it's been properly signed and witnessed."

"When did he do that?" I said.

She checked the date. "Four years ago. It was very sensible of him," she said. "Every parent should do it." Her eyes flicked down the page. "He leaves everything to his adopted son Finn Maguire."

"Ah," Vora said.

"Oh," I said. "Does that mean . . . ?"

"That Mr. Egerton's estate passes to you? Yes, it does," said Vora.

"Sorry, when you say his estate . . ."

"Savings, shares and assets valued at roughly eight hundred thousand euros," said Vora. "Plus the property itself, of course."

"Although there will be death duties to pay," added Hale.

My mind was racing. I owned a house in Spain? With a shitload of money attached? Then something else occurred to me. "Who else knew about this?" I said. "Apart from you two?"

Vora opened his hands in supplication. "To the best of our knowledge, no one," he said. "Mr. Egerton was pretty much a recluse, who had almost no contact with the outside world."

I sat there for an hour or two, taking it in. "Holy crap," I said eventually.

"Yes," smiled Vora. "We're very happy to be the bearers of such glad tidings."

"Could we get your bank details?" said Hale, flicking open a notebook and clicking an expensive ballpoint pen.

"I don't have any," I said. "Actually, since my dad died, it's all been a bit of a mess."

I saw Hale look at the paperwork tossed and jumbled in the suitcase, and at me, and decided I'd spare her the trouble of finding a delicate way to phrase her question.

"I have reading difficulties," I said.

She nodded. "Would you like our firm to help you sort everything out?" she said, as if she was offering to do my laundry. Which in a way I suppose she was.

"How much do you cost?" I said.

"Not as much as trying to do it yourself," said Hale. "We'll save you more than we cost, put it that way."

"Sounds good," I said. I took out my phone and glanced at it. "I have to go to work."

Both Vora and Hale looked a little taken aback as I stood up. "Where do you work?" asked Hale.

"At the Iron Bridge," I said. "You know, the restaurant."

"You're a chef?" said Vora.

"I wash saucepans," I said. "Can I leave that case with you?"

"Mr. Maguire," said Hale, "you've just inherited half a million pounds. You don't need to wash dishes for a living."

"I know, but I said I'd be there, and now I'm late," I said. I opened the conference-room door.

Hale hurried after me. "Please, take my card," she said.

I didn't bother trying to read it, I just stuffed it in the back pocket of my jeans. "Thanks," I said. "I really have to go."

The baggy overalls I wore at work were usually taken away to be laundered—or incinerated, maybe—and a fresh set left on a shelf in the locker room. But when I arrived at the restaurant, ten minutes late, I found the shelf was bare. Tall, skinny Gordon was wearing them at the sink, scraping away at a stubborn lump of pastry. "Hey, Gordon," I said, "thanks for filling in. I'll take over." He looked at me mournfully like a freshly whipped blood-hound, but didn't say anything. His eyes flicked over my shoulder.

"Finn," said Georgio, behind me, "Mr. Eccles would like to see you."

I caught the pitying glances of the apprentice chefs as I trailed after Georgio towards Eccles's office. I had the feeling they'd seen this before: another failed candidate about to be gutted, roasted, sliced thin and eaten rare.

Eccles carried on working on his invoices as I stood in front of his desk. I recognized that technique. The head-master of the first school to expel me had let me stand there for ten minutes before he had finally got round to expressing his disappointment: I hadn't let him down, he told me, or let the school down, I'd let myself down. He was even more disappointed that evening when he found that someone had slashed his tyres. It would have been funnier just to let them down, of course, but that would have taken too long.

"Georgio tells me he found you in this office yesterday," said Eccles. "What were you looking for?"

"You," I said.

He put the last invoice aside. "Here I am," he said. "What did you want?"

"Some time off," I said.

"How did you get in?"

I took a deep breath. This schtick was starting to bore me. I knew where this was going, and I wanted to tell him he could shove his job, because I didn't need it any more—I owned a sodding castle in Spain,

255

apparently. But I realized I liked Eccles, and I didn't want to let him down.

"What's the problem?" I said. "Is anything missing?"

"No," said Eccles. "But that's not really the point."

"Georgio doesn't look after your keys very well," I said.

Eccles put his pen down and scratched his forehead. He was trying to figure out how he could ask how much I knew without giving away how much he knew. I didn't envy him.

"Have you been in touch with your friend Mr. McGovern?" he asked.

"No," I said. "And I told you, he's not a friend."

Now Eccles looked right at me, and saw how much I meant it. "Do you have any idea what you might be getting into?" he said.

"Not so far," I said. "Do you?"

Eccles tapped his teeth with his specs for a moment. "Tell you what," he said, pulling out his wallet, "take as much time as you need." He flicked out a wad of twenties and offered them to me. "Your services are no longer required."

Damn it, I thought. Now he's fired me, I can't tell him to shove his job. It wouldn't sound half as good.

"Keep it." I was going to add, "*You need it more than I do*," but it would have been hot air—even now Eccles had far more money than I did. But walking out of his office leaving him holding a wad of cash would rattle him more than anything I could have said. So that's what I did.

As I grabbed my coat from the staffroom and left I felt a bit sorry for Eccles—having lent the Guvnor that van, he was in far deeper shit than me—but that was the second time in a fortnight I'd been fired, and even if they were rubbish jobs, it still stung. I'd honestly performed them to the best of my ability, done the work as well as I could—better than most—and I'd still got canned. Earlier that morning I had worried about how what I planned to do might affect Eccles, but now I was too pissed off to give a toss. There was an Internet café near the tube station. I went in and paid for a two-hour session, a cup of weak tea and a red apple that tasted of nothing whatsoever. Taking a seat in a dim little cubicle in front of a bulky old-fashioned monitor, I fired up the browser, logged into the *RTTracker* website and dug in my back pocket for the bit of paper that I'd written Eccles's log-in details on.

fourteen

It had taken me ninety minutes to get there, the last twenty on foot from a deserted, dirty tube station, and I wondered if I'd come to the right place.

In the Internet café I'd sat sipping tea and watching the red blip of the van's tracking device circle London on the motorway until it was directly north of the city, then turn south and slow down as it hit the city streets. Zooming in, I'd followed it down past Hendon to a spot just inside the North Circular, where it turned off a dual carriageway into a blank area marked "Goods Yard," and finally halted in the north-eastern corner next to a railway line.

Now I'd got there the "goods yard" turned out to be an industrial estate so new it hadn't been detailed on the maps. Massive units of yellow brick with tall roller doors rose from a sea of rippled concrete floodlit with sodium arc-lights, and as I entered through the main gates and headed east I felt as exposed and vulnerable as a rat on a skating rink. Huge articulated trucks rumbled past as I headed for the eastern perimeter, where a four-metre fence capped with razor wire discouraged suicidal strollers from exploring the railway, and turned north. I tried to creep along in the little shadow I could find, wondering if I was being observed on CCTV, and if I was, whether that was good or bad. None of the passing truck drivers had appeared to notice my presence, and if I disappeared tonight, no one would ever know what had happened to me, apart from the people who made it happen. And I longed to show Zoe this castle in Spain. See her act all cool and offhand then.

At the north-east corner of the estate stood a unit identical to all the rest. There was no sign that it had ever been leased out to a business. There were no cars on the forecourt, and the customer reception area to the right of the main door was unfurnished, apart from its virginal white service counter. No mail on the desk or the doormat, no lights from inside. I couldn't slide under that roller door without losing some serious weight, and I wouldn't get through the reception door without a sledgehammer. I went round the side instead, along the side of the unit that faced the razor-wire fence, and peeked around the corner at the end. Even here it wasn't dark—the yellow light of the sodium lamps bled everywhere like dye from a cheap T-shirt. Right on the corner, next to me, was a fire exit door—a slab of wood with no handle, just the usual "Keep Clear" sign. I looked more closely; the door wasn't properly closed. The edge protruded from its jamb about the length of a fingertip. I'd come all this way, I thought I might as well give it a try. The door rattled when I pulled at it, but refused to open. I pushed it shut in frustration and it popped out again—this time a little further. There was obviously something wrong with the latch. I pulled and pushed and pulled and pushed, and the door opened enough for me to just reach the push-down bar on the inside. Stretching my fingers to their utmost I managed to touch it, and get just enough leverage to push it down.

The door popped open.

There was a bad smell from somewhere, like cheap bleach, that caught in the back of the throat. The fire door opened onto a narrow breeze-block corridor, and now I could see a light—a faint yellow glow from where the loading bay must be, spilling from a door that hung ajar at the end of the corridor. I tiptoed up to the far door and held my breath as I pulled it open, but it was still new and freshly oiled, and barely made a sound.

There were two vehicles parked in the loading bay. One was a big four-wheel-drive, the other a high-sided white van with a refrigeration unit mounted on top and *The Iron Bridge, Pimlico* in blue lettering on the side panels. I looked around, but the rest of the loading bay was empty and bare, apart from what looked like a wooden lockup in the corner. The smell seemed to be coming from the van itself, and under the stink of cheap bleach I picked up the sharp tang of urine. The rear doors were locked, but checking the ignition I found the keys still hanging there. I took them round to the back, unlocked the van's rear door, took a deep breath and turned the handle.

The rear interior light had been left on, I noticed; wouldn't that drain the battery? When I looked down and saw a pair of wide, frightened eyes staring at me I forgot about the battery.

The floor was covered with crumpled, stained news-paper and piled haphazardly with cheap sleeping bags. When I looked more closely I saw that each bag held a huddled child, and some held two. There were about ten altogether, all girls as far as I could see, and the old-est must have been twelve. They all stared at me, faces grubby, eyes wide, too fatigued and frightened to speak or even cry. There were chewed heels of bread scattered about, and discarded skins of coarse sausage; I caught the faint whiff of garlic but it was overwhelmed by the stink from a chemical toilet in the far corner that must have been slopping and splashing all the way from

261

Dover. I had just opened my mouth to tell them, "It's OK," when my head slammed into what felt like a manhole cover and I sank to my knees, stunned.

I stayed conscious long enough to realize my head hadn't slammed into anything—something had slammed into it. But now more blows were raining down and I could feel boots hammering the small of my back. It was all I could do to curl up into a foetal position, and pull my forearms up to guard my face before they started laying into me with kicks and lumps of wood and what must have been a bike chain. I could hear high-pitched screeching and thought it must be me. Then I realized the little girls were screaming because they were watching a man being beaten to death. Someone must have got fed up with the noise because the last thing I heard before I passed out was the van doors being slammed shut.

Zoe was sitting up in my bed, her arms folded. She was smoking. Smoking in bed's very dangerous, I tried to tell her, but she couldn't hear me over the pounding dubstep, and my mouth was full of blood, where I lay across the foot of the bed. She leaned forward and she looked at me like I was a slug on her pizza and she screwed her cigarette out on my face.

The pain of it woke me up. Blood was running from a

cut to my cheek. I was curled up in a moving metal and plastic box and I could smell petrol and cigarette smoke. The lid of the box was a rippling grey plastic sheet and around the edges yellow light flickered and pulsed. My ears were filled with the roaring of tyres on a road, mingled with a teeth-rattling thump of drum'n'bass played at maximum volume on a top-of-the-range car sound system.

I was in the rear of the four-wheel-drive and the plastic sheet stretched over it was just a roller-blind affair to stop people peeking into the boot. I could have pushed through it, I supposed, and got a fist in the face from one of the guys I could hear and feel inches away from me in the back seat, hooting and laughing and boasting about kicking someone's teeth out. I checked mine with my tongue. A few had moved about, and two were chipped, but they were still all there. Maybe that treat was yet to come.

The music was pounding out so loudly, either because the passengers liked that sort of thing, or to cover the sound of me screaming and kicking the sides of the car when it stopped at lights. Not that I could have kicked very hard—I could barely move for the pain. It felt like every inch of my skin, every bone in my body, and every internal organ had been flayed, battered and mashed. My hands were tied in front of me but my feet were free.

I wondered why they'd left them that way. Maybe they wanted me to walk somewhere and it would save them the bother of lugging me.

Could I kick my way out of this, or just seize a moment and run for it? My feet and legs hurt like hell, but I didn't think anything was actually broken, and if it came to running adrenaline would take care of the pain. They might not bother chasing me—they might just shoot me. But if they had a gun wouldn't they have shot me already? Whys and hows and what-ifs crowded into my mind and I tried to push them down, to breathe deep and think clearly. They'd known I was coming, that much was obvious. The faulty fire door and the keys in the ignition had all been part of a setup, and I'd walked right into it like a chicken pecking feed off a chopping block. That prick Eccles must have panicked. He could have gone to the cops and reported his van stolen, but obviously he was more scared of the Guvnor, and he'd tipped McGovern off. Lying in the back of that four-wheel-drive, swallowing mouthfuls of spit mixed with blood, I couldn't blame him.

The rumble of the tyres on tarmac faded and I felt the car turn sharply to the left. Now it was bouncing and rocking on its springs and I could hear the tyres splashing through mud and puddles. The jolting went on and on, every impact jarring my bruises and sending fresh jolts of pain shooting up my spine and down my legs. At long last the car slowed and stopped, the driver killed the engine, and the thumping music was silenced. I felt the car's suspension rise a little as the passengers got out and slammed their doors. Three of them, not four as I'd thought. A diesel engine chugged idly somewhere nearby—an excavator, maybe?

The tailgate opened with a hiss and I squinted out at the three figures standing there. At the back was James, lighting another roll-up. The other two were lumps of rough I'd never seen before, in leather jackets and jeans. The one who'd opened the tailgate had long greasy hair. He leaned over and slapped my face, not that hard, just enough to wake me up. "You get out," he grunted. Was that a Polish accent?

I crawled and shuffled towards the lip of the boot, sat up and lowered my feet to the ground. It was a sea of oily mud, dotted with black puddles, and around us were walls of wrecked cars. A breaker's yard, I thought. A big one. Greasy Hair took my arm and dragged me towards James, who had just opened the boot of an ancient battered Jaguar saloon with no wheels.

"I knew you were a fucking pain in the prick, Maguire," he said. "From the moment you turned up. I told the Guvnor you probably pushed his kid into the pool yourself, but he wouldn't listen. So I sent someone to find out what you were really after." He picked a shred of tobacco off his tongue and smiled. "She's lovely, isn't she, Zoe? Amazing tits. Mind you, I wouldn't, not any more. That girl's had more cock than a chicken farmer. Hope you wore a condom."

Zoe? Zoe had shopped me?

I hesitated, and that's what gave me away. James saw he had driven a skewer into my belly, and he grinned.

"You're a fucking liar," I said.

He just grinned some more. "You know it's true. I can see it in your face. You're crying inside. You're crushed. Well, not crushed exactly. Not yet."

He wiggled his eyebrows like a cheap Groucho Marx impersonator, and his two chimpanzees sniggered, and I wondered if even with my hands bound I could finish strangling him before they split my head open. I didn't even see James's fist move before it hit me in the mouth, and I felt my upper lip split against my teeth.

"Don't," he said. "Don't look at me like that. You're done. You screwed up. You're fucked."

I gobbed blood that splashed into a puddle and floated as black foam, and tried not to think about Zoe being the one who'd shopped me. "Did you kill my dad?" I said.

James grinned and nodded at the gaping trunk of the Jag. "Get in," he said.

I looked around. What I had thought was another wall of cars was a vast steel crusher, and the ticking diesel engine was its power plant. Looming over them all was a crane with a grabber hook, four steel talons clenched, like one of those funfair games no one ever wins.

James slapped me in the face, making sure to hit the open wound. "The sooner you get in," he said, "the sooner this will all be over." When I turned to run he kicked my legs from under me and I tumbled into the rancid mud, rolling till I was caked in it.

"Put him in there," James snapped at his minders. They hauled me to my feet, dragged me back and heaved me face first into the boot of the Jag. "I *was* thinking of cutting your throat before you went in the crusher," said James. "But you've pissed me off now, so I'm not going to bother. Cheer up, this is going to be fun. You know, like a theme-park ride. Keep your hands and legs inside the car at all times. I'll tell Benny to go extra slow, so you can really enjoy it."

And he slammed the boot lid shut.

I lay there in the darkness, trying to think fast, trying desperately not to focus on Zoe and what she'd done to me. But if James had kicked me in the nuts before throwing me in here I couldn't have felt sicker or more winded. Of course, that's what he wanted—me to die in pain, knowing I'd been betrayed, still unsure who'd sent Hans to kill my dad and why. I heard a mobile phone ring and James answering it. I lay still and tried to listen.

"Yeah," he said. "Yeah, no problem. Twenty minutes."

That was all I heard before the Jag I was locked into shuddered, rocked and sank, rattling me about so my head cracked off the metalwork. The sound of breaking glass and screaming steel was deafening, but underneath the roar I could just make out the diesel engine revving up. I could guess the grabber hook had seized the Jag, shattering the windows and crumpling the roof, pushing it down into the mud under its weight; now it rose and jolted the Jag free of the mud's suck, and I felt the car rise into the air and wheel slowly round, rocking like a pendulum.

I squirmed round to face the front and fumbled in the darkness ahead, trying to feel what was there. I stubbed my fingers on pressed steel struts running vertically and diagonally between the boot and the passenger compartment. Between the struts were panels of rough fibre, plastic or hardboard maybe. I scrabbled at them with my fingernails as the Jag rocked and swung.

Abruptly the car dropped, and I rose into the air a fraction before being slammed into the floor again as it landed. Ignoring the pain, I swivelled my body backwards, pulled up my knees and kicked at the fibre panels, trying to avoid the unyielding metal braces that framed them. I felt one panel bulge and burst outwards.

Now the car was rising into the air again, swaying, but not so wildly this time. Whoever was controlling the crane must have been lining the car up with the crusher's jaws. I pulled my foot back, squirmed round and dived towards the hole I'd kicked. Writhing and twisting, I pushed my bound fists forward through the gap until they touched spring and wire and damp foam padding. I shoved hard, snaking my body round and forward and praying my shoulders would fit through the gap between the braces.

I felt weightless again for an instant, then the car landed again, hard, and my nose slammed into smooth metal, making my eyes water. The Jag must have been dropped right into the maw of the crusher. I braced my feet behind me and pushed, towards the sound of rending of metal and tinkling of glass, as ahead of me in the passenger compartment the grabber claws opened to release the Jag's roof. I could hear the whine of the motor hauling it free and clear as inside the car's shell I wrenched my right shoulder, then my left, through the cobweb of metal struts, pushing the rear passenger seat cushion forward. Now I could feel cool night air on my face, though it stank of diesel fumes and machine oil, but through the shattered windows, left and right, ahead and behind, I could see nothing but smooth, rust-coloured steel slabs. As I fought my way through, my head now level with the rear windows, there was a shuddering bang and the steel jaws to the right and left started to move in. My hips snagged on the diagonal brace, and I must have cursed aloud, but I could hear nothing over the scream of the crusher's engines and the hideous wrinkling noise as the moving slabs touched the Jag's doors and kept going. I writhed and flexed free of the struts, driving myself forward, not knowing where I was hoping to end up, just heading on and upwards, kicking my legs and feet free of the boot at last, as I felt and heard the car's metal skeleton grow rigid, then scream and fight back hopelessly against the pressure. Twisting round I scrabbled at the padded ceiling, dragging myself backwards over the passenger seats, until one hand grabbed empty air. The sunroof was a gaping hole, its glass panel long since gone.

The rusting metal bit into my palms as I gripped the rim of the sunroof with both hands and made one last desperate heave, and around and under me the car imploded, screeching and spitting shards of metal like shrapnel and showering me with crumbs of glass. Even as I scrambled through the shrinking gap and scrabbled for a foothold on the lip of the sunroof the whole car

roof bent upward, and my foot fell back into the boiling, screeching maelstrom of tortured metal and plastic
and leather. It landed on what felt like a headrest that
trembled and bulged and burst just as I pushed off as
hard as I could, up into the night and the dark and the
clouds of diesel fumes, hopping up to teeter on the lip of
the jaws as they closed to only a shoulder width apart,
my ears filled with the crusher engine's roar, the dying
grind of the Jaguar's chassis, and the sad tinkle of glass
fragments falling like tears. The jaws stopped moving,
but the engine roared on.

Greasy Hair was sitting in the cab that controlled
the crusher, and he was staring right at me, and he
looked really pissed off. I didn't know where the other
two were, but I guessed I'd find out soon enough. I
ran straight at him along the long bar of crusher's jaw,
and saw him scrabble at the handle of the cab door. He
opened it slightly too late, because I got to it in time to
kick it shut against his face. It's hard to punch someone
with your hands bound, I discovered, but if their hair's
long enough you can grab it and bounce their face off
your knee a few times. The third time I felt Greasy
Hair's nose go, and dropped him. He tumbled out of
the cab and off the platform, landing on his head, to end
up lying in the mud with his neck ominously twisted. I
leaped down after him and slithered as I landed, ending

up on my arse, and was relieved to see a knife in his limp hand. He had pulled it on me but never got to use it. It was a bloody sharp one too, judging by the way it went through the twine around my wrists as I held it in place with my foot. I looked up just in time to see Greasy Hair's mate running at me with a length of steel pipe, and my hands came free just as he swung it at my head. I ducked and came up again and hit him on the hinge of his jaw with my left. I think I broke it, but to his credit he came back, and kept on coming until I cracked one of his ribs, twisted the pole out of his grasp, and laid him out with it.

I stood there panting. There was no sign of James, or the four-wheel-drive. I tossed the pole aside, pulled out my mobile phone, staggered across and sat down on a nearby cable reel, propped on top of a heap of rubber trim. The name I wanted was at the top of my phone list, alphabetically, which was handy, because I barely had the strength left to press "call" or lift the phone to my ear.

The phone at the other end rang and rang. What time of night was it anyway?

"Dominic Amobi." He sounded sleepy.

"This is Finn Maguire," I said. That seemed to wake him up.

"What can I do for you, Finn?"

"There's a van full of kids parked in a warehouse in North London," I said. "Trafficked from Europe. You need to send someone quick, I don't know how long they'll be there."

By the time I made it to the entrance of the breaker's yard my trainers were two lumps of mud on the end of my legs. The gate was lying open; I stepped out and looked up and down the long, empty stretch of dual carriageway. No road signs, no tube stations, nothing. The sky was clouded over, so I couldn't work out which way was north, even if I'd been able to see the stars beyond the sodium glare. Just inside the front gate was an office, a prefab shed raised up on cement block stilts, and now I went back to take a look. It was empty, and locked, but a rock through the window soon sorted that. The owners wouldn't worry about a broken window— they'd count themselves lucky I hadn't burned the office down. It did occur to me, but I couldn't find a lighter. It was very unlikely that James had chosen this place at random to get rid of me—I bet a lot of his problems had vanished into that crusher.

I found the number of a cab firm, and used the office phone to get someone to pick me up. Then I went outside to wait at the gates, filthy, exhausted and aching. The cab driver who eventually turned up hesitated

273

when he saw the state of my clothes, but when I offered him a huge wad of cash just to drop me at the nearest tube station he let me get in, although not before he'd taken an old fleece blanket out of his boot and spread it over the back seat for me to sit on. I didn't mind the expense of the cab—Greasy Hair and his mate were paying. I'd cleaned out their wallets before I left.

Pale cold dawn was starting to glow in the charcoal sky when I got home, and I was so tired I felt barely there, like a ghost haunting my own house. Dragging my feet up each stair, I finally staggered into the bathroom and set the bath running. It always took hours to fill, and I wasn't sure I could stay awake that long. As I headed for my bedroom I started to pull my shirt off, and winced. Every move I made seemed to open a wound or wrench a twisted muscle or add a new bruise onto an old one.

Zoe was asleep on my bed, fully dressed, as if she'd dropped off while waiting for me. My pillow lay lengthways beside her, and she'd thrown her arm over it, like she never did when we lay together. She looked so peaceful and innocent as she slept; her full lips were slightly parted and each breath was like a sigh. I wanted to grab her by the hair and drag her out into the street, but I didn't have the strength left.

She opened her eyes, and I could see her wondering

where she was. Then she noticed me, and tensed, and sat up blinking, and her eyes focused on my face.

"Oh my God—"

"Why did you take the keys?" I said. "Yesterday morning. You thought you'd never see me again. Were you planning to move in or something? Squat here?"

Her eyes were brimming as she looked at me. Christ, that girl could turn it on when she wanted to.

"No, of course," I said. "You had to take them. You had to pretend you didn't know what was waiting for me."

"I'm sorry, Finn. I asked you not to go."

"What are you doing here?"

"I hoped you'd be all right somehow."

"If you'd warned me, you wouldn't have had to hope," I said. "Was it all an act? Was any of it real? Are you even Prendergast's daughter?"

She pulled a plastic CD case from under the pillow behind her and held it out to me. I didn't move. She gave up and tossed it at me, and I let it fall at the foot of my bed.

"My mum died when I was twelve," Zoe said. "Overdose. After that it was just me and my dad, and he didn't have a clue. When I started to grow up, it was like he resented it. If I put make-up on he'd tell me I looked like a whore. And just to spite him I started acting like one, and the more he shouted at me and took my phone away and grounded me and bullied me the further I'd push it. I'd go with anyone, get out of my head every chance I got.

"Then this guy I knew—thought I knew—invited me to a party at his parents' place, their country getaway. But it wasn't really his parents' place, and it wasn't really a party. I was the only girl there. His name was James."

I looked down at the DVD in the plastic case. I could guess where this was going. Zoe was staring at the wall, her jaw set, determined to get through her story without sobbing or feeling sorry for herself.

"It started as soon as I got there. There was a guy with a video camera following us everywhere. And when James started pawing at me, the cameraman made sure he got a close-up. I'd had a few glasses of champagne by then. And when James offered me some pills . . ."

"He drugged you?"

"He didn't force me to take them. He didn't have to. I wanted to try everything, and I wanted not to care. And for a few days I did try everything. Two guys at once. Three. Spit roasting, footballers call it. They even got me to—"

"Enough," I said. "I'm not interested."

"I told myself it was a laugh, I didn't care who saw the video. But I did, really. They sent me that"—she nodded at the DVD, and now her voice caught—"and then I knew I did care, that I'd been totally stupid, but it was too late. They said they'd put it on the Net. Show it to my dad. I couldn't let them do that. It would end him, I know it would, and even after everything . . . I couldn't do that to him. I begged them not to. Told them I'd do anything."

"Anything being me," I said.

"I'm really sorry, Finn. I did—I do like you. You're really sweet, and you've been good to me."

"Go home," I said.

"Please don't send me away."

I took the DVD out of its case and bent it until it snapped in two. I tossed the pieces back to her.

"You know what they were doing with that van?" I said. "Smuggling kids, little girls from Europe. Christ knows what would have become of them. And when I walked in there James and his mates worked me over, really well. Then they drove me out to the East End and tried to fit me into the glove compartment of a Jag. You want me to feel sorry for you because you let yourself get shagged on camera and didn't fancy your dad finding out? When you fucking hate the prick and he hates me? You know what—stay or go, I don't give a shit. I need a bath."

I headed for the bathroom, peeled off my stinking

trousers and shorts, and stepped into the tub. The water was so hot it nearly took my skin off. As I eased myself into it, feeling my bruises and scars tingle in the scalding water, I heard Zoe stumble down the stairs. She paused briefly at the foot of the staircase and I heard keys drop on the floor. Then the front door slammed.

I sighed as I lay back, enveloped in the steam that had condensed in the cold air of the bathroom. I wondered how much of Zoe's story had been true. Maybe she had come to care about me, a little. I heard farmers grow fond of their pigs sometimes, and get a lump in their throat when they send them for slaughter. I could imagine how funny James found it, filming a girl for a porn video, knowing she was the daughter of a detective inspector. Passing the video round at his chimpanzees' tea party so they could all have a laugh and a wank. Or maybe he'd kept it for his personal collection. After all, if the word got out that it even existed, DI Prendergast would have become a joke. He'd have had to quit the force. And what a waste that would be, when the Guvnor could have had a DI in his pocket.

Shit. Prendergast *did* know about it. He had to. Why would the Guvnor go to all that effort to blackmail a schoolgirl like Zoe, when he could blackmail her dad? I remembered what Amobi had said—*McGovern will find a way to get to you, whatever it takes.*

Prendergast was the chief liaison officer with the Serious Crimes squad, Zoe had told me. That meant he'd be briefed on every move they planned against the Guvnor. That's how McGovern always knew what the cops were planning before they knew themselves—Prendergast was feeding him info from inside.

And what had Prendergast told the Guvnor about me? What was he telling him now? Amobi would have reported to him that I'd found the van with the kids in and called the cops, and now Prendergast would report that to the Guvnor.

And I'd found the van because it was fitted with a tracking device, and Eccles had known that, but he hadn't told James when James "borrowed" it. The Guvnor was going to be seriously pissed off when he found out. I'd be ready for his heavies if and when they came for me again, but they'd come for Eccles too, unless someone warned him. They'd feed him feet first into his own meat grinder.

I didn't owe Eccles anything.

Dammit.

I clambered out of the bath, dripping.

fifteen

Of course Eccles wasn't answering his phone, the pillock. I left a voice message, but I had no idea if he'd get it before the Guvnor got to him. That's how I found myself riding the Tube east again to Pimlico, when it was still so early half the carriages were empty. I stood all the way to make sure I didn't fall asleep and wake up in Cockfosters. I felt like I was sleepwalking, but I had to tell Eccles to talk to the cops before McGovern came to talk to him.

I knew the celebrity chef had a classy flat with a view of the river, but that lay on the other side of the restaurant from the tube station, so I tried the restaurant first. The rear gates lay open, and Eccles's flashy high-wheelbase estate car had been backed into the yard, but there was no sign of the man himself. I knew he did a lot of his own shopping in the London produce markets, getting up at four and lugging crates of fresh fish and meat and veg into the restaurant's walk-in fridge at the crack of dawn by himself.

I climbed the steps quietly and pulled at the door that led to the kitchens; it was open. The cooking area was deserted, and something told me not to call out. I could hear a scuffling and rattling, like a trapped rat, but louder . . . someone thumping a wall in frustration and fear. On one of the steel counters near the walk-in fridge I noticed a polystyrene box overflowing with glistening fresh fish, packed in ice that was slowly melting. The door of the fridge was shut, and a knife-sharpening steel had been shoved into the lock hole on the handle. The scuffling and banging was coming from inside. Whoever was trapped in there wouldn't starve, or freeze to death—it wasn't that cold—but they'd run out of air before too long. I reached for the handle of the steel.

"Leave that."

For a huge man, Terry, the Guvnor's gorilla, didn't make a lot of noise. I couldn't figure out where he had been hiding, but he was here now, standing between me and the back door, blocking out the light like that asteroid that killed off the dinosaurs. I could have tried to take him, or I could have pulled the steel out and hit myself over the head with it a few times. It would have been the same in the end.

"He'll suffocate in there," I said. Terry just nodded towards the restaurant. I took the hint.

"You asked me for a meet," McGovern was saying, "and now you come in here giving me fucking orders."

"I'm not," said Prendergast. He looked up as I entered, with Terry filling the doorway behind me. "Oh Christ," he said, and his head drooped, as if he hadn't thought his day could get any worse. They were seated at a table at the back of the restaurant, among a sea of spotless empty place settings. McGovern had had his back towards me, and now he turned, and when he recognized me his face lit up with surprise and amusement. To his left sat James, in the same dapper outfit I'd seen in the breaker's yard. I wondered vaguely how he'd managed to keep his clothes so clean. James looked as surprised as the Guvnor, but not as pleased, and he made to get up, but when the Guvnor twitched a finger on his left hand James sank back down into his chair.

"Maguire," said McGovern. "You get about, don't you? Wherever you're least wanted."

"Hey, Mr. McGovern."

"Come to do some scrubbing? That's handy. There's going to be some teeth on the carpet in a minute."

"I'll go fetch a dustpan and brush."

McGovern grinned at me, a big ice-cold grin.

"Nah, you stay there, wait your turn," he said. He turned back to Prendergast. "Go on."

Prendergast looked at me, shame and hate in his eyes, then back to the Guvnor. "I'm not telling you what to do. I'm saying if this is what you're going to do, I don't want to be involved."

"Thing is, Inspector, who gives a fuck what you want?" said McGovern.

"Not kids, not little girls," said Prendergast. "Drugs, guns, fine, I don't give a fuck. But I'm not turning a blind eye while your people start supplying paedos. I'll fucking give myself in, you can do what you like with that video."

"Now you're threatening me," said McGovern. "I'll tell you straight, I fucking hate that, it makes my blood boil, so don't do that, really don't. My business is my business, it's none of your business. What I bring into the country and how I bring it in is nothing to do with you. Giving me fucking orders—I didn't come all the way down here for a lecture about ethics and responsible fucking parenting. From you of all people."

"I'm not going to do it any more," said Prendergast. "I'm not going to be a part of this." He'd dropped his hands from the table onto his knees, and was rubbing his thighs, as if he was thinking of getting up and walking out. He can't be that stupid, I thought, he won't make it halfway to the door.

"What I'm wondering," said McGovern, "is why you're sitting here talking about it. If this upsets you so much, if this oversteps the boundaries of common decency, if this breaks some unwritten fucking law, why don't you just go ahead and shop me? Trying to change my mind, is that it? Make me see the error of my ways?"

"You're not pond-life," said Prendergast. "You're a successful businessman, a family man, respected. You don't need to do this, is all I'm saying." He glanced at me again, and it was like he wanted me to do something for him, but knew there was no point in asking because I'd be dead soon too.

"Duly noted," said McGovern. "Now climb back in your car and fuck off. And next time, don't call us, we'll call you."

Prendergast nodded in defeat, and his whole body sagged forward almost as if he was going to rest his face on the table. When he got up he moved quickly, and his chair started to fall back, but James moved even quicker. He was on his feet with a pistol in his hand, and he shot Prendergast twice in the chest, sending him sprawling backwards over his chair, the gun in Prendergast's hand firing one shot wild. The policeman's head hit the table behind him as he went down, dragging the tablecloth with him, toppling wineglasses that rolled and fell onto him with a cascade of tinkling cutlery. McGovern hadn't moved. He hadn't even flinched as the shots rang out, though the deafening bangs had made me instinctively duck, and I sensed even big Terry behind me twitching.

Then all was quiet again. One wineglass was still rocking against a spoon, clinking faintly, while blue smoke drifted upwards, creating cones of light under the recessed halogens. Prendergast groaned and tried to speak, but blood trickled from his mouth, and his head fell back. James tucked his gun away and sat back down, the old familiar smirk creeping back onto his lips.

"Stupid prick," said McGovern. "Coming in here with a shooter down his sock. What did he take me for, a fucking amateur?" He pushed his chair back and stepped forward to stand over Prendergast's body. I thought for a moment he was going to spit on it, but instead he bent down, pulled the revolver from Prendergast's limp fingers and examined it.

"Give a you a tip, Maguire," he said. "You want to shoot somebody, don't mess about, don't make fucking speeches. Just do it." He turned to James, barely raising the revolver, and shot him in the face. James blinked and gasped, and blood ran from a bloody hole where his left eye had been. Then his head fell forward, and he sagged, still upright, in his chair. "Like that," said the Guvnor.

I swallowed, waiting for my turn. Maybe Terry would shoot me in the back of the head. I wondered if I'd even

285

know what had happened before my face hit the carpet. I tried not to look round. I tried not to move.

"I really liked this place," McGovern was saying. "It was classy, you know. Proper classy, not just shitloads of velvet and gold leaf and poncey leather menus. And discreet as well, you could bring a girl here, or a contact, no one said a word. You didn't need to threaten anyone or pay anyone off. The staff were professional. Best investment I ever made. Now look at it." He gestured listlessly with Prendergast's gun at the wrecked tables and the broken corpses, as if they were someone else's fault. "Fucking blood and bodies everywhere. This joint is finished—it'll be packed with reporters and tourists and fucking ghouls, and no celeb's going to come within a mile of the place." He bent down and shouted into James's unhearing ear. "*And Eccles is going to need a new fucking van, isn't he? Since the last one got filled with shit.*" He seemed pissed off that James didn't react and didn't cower. Straightening up, McGovern turned to me.

"I don't need lectures from pricks like Prendergast. I've got kids of my own. I'd never, *ever* get mixed up in that paedo crap. Get my name dragged in the mud, every dosser in the street calling me a nonce. But James here thought he knew better. Went behind my back. *Used my fucking name, didn't you?*" This to James. "Cheeky sod."

Recalling something, McGovern smiled to himself

and turned back to me. "Remember when I said we should send you to this place? And James tried to answer back? Should have known then he was up to something." He thought for a minute. "I try not to mix personal stuff with business as a rule, but you saved my little boy's life," he said. He lifted Prendergast's gun and pointed it at the centre of my forehead. The range was too far for me to jump him, even if Terry didn't already have me covered. "What did you see here, Maguire?" he said.

"James came here to kill me because I told the cops about the van," I said. "Prendergast appeared. They shot each other. I called the cops."

"Naw," said McGovern. "That's not right." And he cocked the hammer of the gun.

"I didn't see anything," I said. "I was never here."

McGovern smiled that cold smile of his. "You know who you remind me of?" he said. "Me. When I was your age." He released the hammer of the gun with his thumb and lowered it. "Big mouth, big balls, nose for trouble. But I learned fast and I could think on my feet." He took out a handkerchief, rubbed the gun down and stooped to put it back in Prendergast's limp hand.

"You weren't here, and neither was I," he said. "In fact, I left the country a few days ago. I'll be back when the fuss has died down. But I'll be keeping tabs. And if

I hear you've changed your mind, I'll give you a reason to change it back again, all right?"

"Got it," I said.

"Now we're proper quits," he said. "Piss off." But I didn't move.

"I'm sorry, Mr. McGovern," I said. When he looked at me again his cold smile had cracked, like ice over a deep, freezing black torrent. "I need to know," I said. "Who sent that guy Hans to kill my dad, and me? You or James?"

"Who the fuck was your dad?" said McGovern.

"Noel Maguire," I said.

"Never fucking heard of him."

"He used to be an actor. He was writing a script for TV."

"Why would I give a fuck about TV?" said McGovern. "It's all bullshit. And if I wanted you dead, you'd be dead."

"It was about a gangster's deputy who tried to take over from his boss," I persisted. "Christ—that was it. Dad must have found out about James's plan to go into business for himself, and James had to shut him up."

"Sounds like your old man should have stuck to acting," said McGovern. "Now piss off. I'm not going to ask you again."

* * *

I pissed off, the way I came, and I was pretty sure no-body saw me go. An hour later Skinny Gordon turned up for the lunch-time shift, as I'd known he would, and he called the cops, and they let Eccles out of his fridge before he suffocated. He'd caught a stinker of a cold though, and the kitchen had to throw the fish away.

I went home to bed and slept for twenty-four hours.

sixteen

"Records show an emergency call made on your mobile phone near Leytonstone, four fifty-five a.m.," said Amobi. "About twenty minutes after you called me."

"I didn't tell you where I was because I didn't know where I was," I said. "I had to ask the cab driver. Soon as he told me I told the local cops so they could find those two guys before someone disappeared them, the same way they tried to disappear me."

"These two men tried to crush you in a car?"

"They caught me looking into that van full of kids. I don't think they were pleased."

"They're currently both in hospital. One fractured skull, one broken neck."

"I wasn't very pleased either." I saw Jenkins stifle a smile, but Amobi was too professional.

"How exactly did you find the van with the kids in?" he said.

"Well, I was out for a run, and I saw it go past, and I knew it was Eccles's van, and I wondered what it was doing up in that neck of the woods, so I followed it and had a look."

"You were out for a run twenty miles away, along the North Circular?"

"I run all over the place."

Amobi nodded. "The two men detained have previous convictions, and the children we found identified them as the traffickers."

"So you don't really need my statement, do you?"

"Were they the only two men you saw?" asked Amobi.

Good liars stick close to the truth, Zoe said. She'd have known.

"There was a third guy giving orders."

"Can you describe him?" Amobi clicked his pen and waited, poised to write. *Short. Slim. Had my dad murdered. Oh, and last time I saw him he had an extra hole in his head.*

"I was in the boot of a car most of the time," I said. "And I didn't hear them use his name."

Amobi took a photo out of a folder in the desk between us and slid it over to me. It was a police mugshot of James, about ten years ago. His hair was longer and he was wearing little round glasses that made him look a bit like a chemistry teacher, but the sneer was unmistakable.

"That's him," I said. "Have you caught him?"

Amobi took the photo back and slipped it into the folder. He clicked his pen shut and slid it into the inner pocket of his jacket. *No more notes?* I thought. Amobi leaned forward with an intent expression and his fingers intertwined. Jenkins adopted a similar glower, though I doubted he had any idea what Amobi was going to say.

"His name was James Gravett and he was killed yesterday in an exchange of fire with a police officer," said Amobi. "At the restaurant where you've been working recently. The officer involved died of gunshot wounds at the scene."

"Shit, seriously?" I said. I was impressed by how sincere I sounded.

"You haven't heard about this?"

"Eccles fired me a few days ago," I said. "No notice or anything. Is he allowed to do that?"

"You didn't hear about the shooting on the news?"

I shrugged. "Never listen to the news," I said.

"The officer involved was DI Prendergast," said Amobi.

"Prendergast? The guy I met, your boss? Jesus, that's awful," I said. "I mean, we didn't exactly get on, but . . ."

Amobi's look made me shut up, and I realized my acting abilities were in fact on a par with my singing voice, and the less noise I made the better.

"So you're saying you know nothing about this incident, and you weren't there that day?"

"That's pretty much it, yeah."

Amobi nodded, and again he didn't push it. He wanted to let that particularly smelly sleeping dog lie. He's just another copper after all, I thought—if they think the truth won't suit them, they don't go looking for it.

"Thank you very much for your assistance, Mr. Maguire." Amobi picked up the folder, and Jenkins sprang to his feet. Must have been his feeding time. "The CPS may be in touch if this goes to trial," Amobi added.

"You're welcome," I said. "In fact, I was wondering if you could do me a favour in return. You know, as a reward for saving those kids?"

Amobi put the folder back down on the table. Jenkins hovered uncomfortably, unsure whether to sit down again. He looked at Amobi for a clue, but Amobi was looking hard at me, and waiting. I took out my mobile phone.

"If I wanted to find out where a mobile phone number was based, how would I go about it?" I said.

"You mean, find out where the phone is being used?"

"I mean, find out where it is most of the time, even when it's not being used. The handset has to be logged into the network to get calls, doesn't it? And you can find out where it goes by what phone masts it's nearest to."

"It's called triangulation," said Amobi, "and yes, under certain circumstances the police can request that information from the phone networks."

I scrolled through the mobile's directory to one number and handed the phone over to him. He looked at the number coolly for a moment, as if admiring its mathematical qualities, then passed the handset back to me.

"I'm sorry," he said, standing up, "but as DC Jenkins will tell you, we cannot request that information unless it's part of an active investigation. And if we did access it, we would not be able to share it with any member of the public."

"That's right." Jenkins nodded authoritatively.

"Fine," I said. "That's what I thought. Guess I'll just have to call the network myself, see how far I get."

Amobi opened the door of the interview room and stood back to let me go first.

The text popped up on my phone a few hours later. The sender field was blank, and the time stamp was for an hour in the future, so I guessed Amobi had used some anonymizer system to cover his tracks. But now I had the information, I wasn't sure I wanted it. I'd felt wary of trusting anything anybody told me, since Zoe had sold me out. My mum had already betrayed me once, when I was a kid, so why was I so surprised that she'd been lying to me again?

Her phone was mostly operating from an address in Shepherd's Bush. Nowhere near Covent Garden, where she'd said her hotel was. What the hell was that about? I could have just called her, or thrown her number away and tried to forget about her. But I couldn't do either of those—I was too angry. It was only a small thing, but as I thought about it I filled up with so much rage I could barely think straight, like one of those kids you see in supermarkets sometimes, writhing on the floor and kicking their heels on the lino, screaming until they can't breathe. All Mum owed me was the truth, that's all. Just once.

The address itself was in a back street ten minutes' walk from Shepherd's Bush Green, a shabby narrow townhouse four floors high. The ground floor was a kebab shop, and the building backed onto a tube line. Maybe it was the vibrations from passing trains that had shaken half the rendering off the facade and dislodged all those roof tiles. From outside the building looked as if it had been chopped up into bedsits with a hodge-podge of inhabitants. A few windows had neat white net curtains, and one even had a potted chrysanthemum on the sill, but in most windows the curtains looked like they hadn't been opened in years. Some didn't have any curtains at all, just blankets wedged into the top of the sash window frames.

My mother was striding down the street in her black coat and long boots, looking too classy for this neighbourhood, where old men in greasy parkas squatted on benches clutching tins of strong lager, and drawn-looking women with peroxide blonde hair pushed buggies over-laden with supermarket bags and snot-stained kids. Just as at the funeral, my mother's face was hidden behind big sunglasses, but I could see she looked pale, tense and preoccupied. She didn't notice me standing at the bus stop across the road, or maybe she did, and after all this time didn't recognize me. I watched her pause outside the kebab shop, pull a bunch of keys from her pocket and open the street door that led to the flats upstairs. I was about to dash across when a bus pulled up at the stop, and by the time I made it to the far side of the road the tenement door had already shut.

Then it opened again, and a big pear-shaped woman in too much make-up emerged, wearing a short leather skirt and wedges way too tall and way too young for her. I smiled and tried to enter the hallway as she left, but she blocked my path.

"Looking for someone, love?" she said. I fished for an alibi but my mind had gone blank. "Twenty quid for twenty minutes? Half strip and blowjob?" she went on. She hadn't said "someone," I realized—she'd said, "some fun."

"Another time, thanks," I said, and smiled as though I'd been flattered by her offer. She forgot about me and walked on, wobbling on her heels, while I hurried in and up the stairs, taking them two at a time. The first landing had three doors leading off it, one to the rear, one to the front, one to the side. I paused, wondering if I should just pick a door and knock, when I heard footsteps ascending the stairs overhead—someone light on their feet, but tired after slogging all the way to the top. I took the next two flights stealthily, trying to walk on my toes and not make the floorboards creak under the threadbare nylon carpet. But as I ascended the last flight I heard drum'n'bass music thumping from somewhere on the top floor, and realized that racket would hide any noise I might make.

Somehow I'd expected the top landing to be lighter than the landings below, but the lonely bare light bulb dangling from the ceiling had blown. The landlord must have been relying on the pane of glass set high into the roof above for illumination, but the skylight was so caked in bird shit and green slime it was like trying to swim under canal water, and the doors to each flat were pale oblongs in the gloom. The deafening drum'n'bass was coming from the door at the rear, so I knocked on the one in the middle. It opened almost immediately, and whoever was inside left it ajar and walked away.

"I thought Mercedes would get their top saleswoman a better flat," I said as I entered. My mother turned from the battered wooden wardrobe where she'd just been hanging up her coat and turned to me, amazed and afraid. "Who were you expecting?" I said. "Room service?"

The small room had, impossibly, been divided into two even smaller rooms, and through a sagging concertina door in the thin partition I glimpsed a double bed in the room beyond. At the far end of this one, by the window, a stunted sofa faced an ancient TV, while the corner behind me had been converted to a kitchen— if you could call a tiny sink, a picnic table, two chairs and an oven-toaster on top of a cupboard a kitchen. The only sign of food was an empty bottle of Jack Daniel's.

"Finn," my mother said at last, "how did you find me? What are you . . . ?"

"Why?" I said. "Why did you spin that stupid yarn about staying in a hotel in the West End?"

"Oh God," she said, and hid her face with her hand. "I didn't want you to feel sorry for me." When she looked up she seemed angry at herself. "I was worried you'd think you had to invite me to stay at our—your house, and—it would have meant taking everything too fast. I wanted to get to know you again, but that's going to take time, and . . . it had to be your decision. And because you wanted to know me, not because you pitied me. I'm really sorry, I know how it must look."

"What about the rest of it?" I said. "All the things you told me, how much of that was true?"

"All of it," she said. "Except for the part about me being good at selling cars. They fired me after two days. I was really broke, and I was lonely, and I knew I'd been stupid. I told your dad I was sorry, and he said I should come home. Look—" She returned to the wardrobe and dug her coat out again. "There's a cafe across the road, let's go there and talk. This place is such a dump, and we can barely hear each other over that racket." She nodded at the rear wall. The music from the back room wasn't as loud in here as it had been on the landing, but the toaster-oven was rattling faintly in time to the thump of the bass.

"What is there to talk about?" I said.

"Well, we could talk about you," she said. "Not all that horrible stuff you've been through, but where you're going, what you really want to do with your life. Whether you've got a girlfriend. All that mother-son

299

stuff. Besides, this cafe has got the most amazing muffins—we could split one." She patted her pockets and checked for the jingle of keys.

There was something so bright and cheery and fake about her tone that I held back.

"Why are you in such a big hurry to leave?" I said.

"Sorry, what?" she said. "This music drives me insane—the landlord does nothing about it, but it's only on during the day, thank God—"

Jesus, how could I have missed it? When I turned to check out the kitchen again I saw two glasses sat draining in the dish-rack. Looking again through the folding door into the poky bedroom, I noticed one suitcase sitting open on a chair, and another protruding from under the rumpled double bed.

"Mum?" I asked at last. She smiled at me, feigning confusion, badly. "Who did you think I was when you opened the door?"

I hadn't heard him climbing the stairs under the pulsing din, and was only aware of his footsteps a moment before he appeared in the open doorway. He looked a few years younger than my mother, wiry and lean, with old blue tattoos bubbling up from under the neck of his T-shirt. He had dark skin, and a fine fuzz of black hair was appearing on his shaven skull under a woollen beanie. A silver ring glinted in his right ear.

When his brown eyes lighted on me he grinned, revealing fine, even white teeth, though two of them were broken.

"Hey, we got company," he said. "Finn, right?" There was an American or Canadian twang to his voice and he didn't offer to shake hands, maybe because his own were full. One held a square bottle of spirits wrapped in a brown paper bag—more Jack Daniel's, I guessed—the other a half-full plastic carrier bag, the sort that usually splits ten minutes after you leave the corner shop.

"Finn, this is Enrique," said my mother, in a small voice. Enrique grinned at me, shut the door behind him with his heel and moved over to the picnic table to dump his shopping.

"Enrique Romero, right?" I said. "The painter?" My mind was racing. *The guy my mother left us for?*

"That's me," said Enrique. "Want a drink? We only got two glasses—you'll have to share with your mom."

"Pass," I said.

"Something to eat maybe? I just got some more cheese and crackers."

"How was this going to work out?" I said to my mother. "You and him and Dad. Was it going to be like a threesome, or were you planning a rota?"

"Finn, please don't," she said.

"Why did you tell Dad you wanted to get back

301

together, if you were still shacked up with your pen pal?"

"Yo, what the fuck," said Romero. "Lighten up, kid, OK?"

I glared at Romero, rage and indignation boiling up inside me, and I knew I had to get out of there before I blew out the windows. My mother had shut her eyes, in shame or pain or embarrassment at getting caught, I didn't know which, and I didn't care. "I should go," I said.

"Hey, hey—what's your hurry?" said Romero. He looked pained. "Look, I know this is kind of awkward, but we got things to discuss."

"We really don't," I said.

He pushed his hand against the door so I couldn't open it. I took a deep breath, trying to stay calm, trying to think straight, but my mind was clouded with choking black fumes of anger and confusion and disappointment. Romero's bomber jacket hung open; from the flex of the muscles under his shirt I could see the guy was seriously ripped. You don't get a torso like that from hefting a paintbrush. He twisted his neck and flexed his fingers, as if limbering up, and I could smell his aggression smouldering.

"Goddammit," he muttered to my mother. The way she shrank from him when he spoke that way made me tense too. "I told you," he went on, "didn't I tell you? The motherfucker's been having us tailed." He jerked his chin at me. "Bitch with red hair, she with you?"

"You want to step away from the door?" I said.

He just leaned on it with his elbow, tilted his head as if to weigh me up, and finally wiped his face with his free hand. "OK, kid, here's the deal," he said. "Fifty–fifty and we walk away, you never hear from us again. Unless you want to. She'll send you a postcard every Thanksgiving if it makes you happy."

"Fifty per cent of what?" I said.

He rubbed his nose and tried to grin as he fought to keep his temper. "Hey, we're all here in one room, no more bullshit, OK? You're smart, I'm smart, let's not break each other's balls. Fifty per cent of what the old guy left your dad. It should have been half hers anyway."

I turned to my mother. "You knew about the money?" I said.

"I visited Charles Egerton to ask him for a loan," she said. "He sent me away. Said he could never forgive me for abandoning you and your father, that he was leaving everything to Noel."

"Holy crap," I said. "Dad wasn't going to take you back, was he? That's why you hired Hans to kill him." My mother's face was drawn, and she couldn't look at me. "He took Dad's laptop and his notes just to mislead the cops."

"You only just getting this?" said Romero. He turned to my mother and snorted, "Kid's not that smart after all."

I ignored him and looked at her. "And you sent him back to kill me. So you could inherit, as my next of kin."

"Of course I didn't," my mother insisted. "It was just—when we couldn't pay Hans the rest of his money, he said he was going to start charging interest."

Jesus. Those secateurs . . . "Interest being one of my fingers," I said.

"I never wanted to hire that asshole in the first place," said Romero. "But no, she wants to get a professional, do it properly. That worked out great. Tell you what, the twenty grand we would have paid him, we'll take that out of our cut, how's that?"

"You don't get a cut," I said. My voice was calmer than I felt. "Open the door."

"Finn—" my mother said.

"We're not walking away from this empty-handed, kid," said Romero. "I spent a goddamn fortune getting over here, hiring that guy, renting this shithole. We get fifty per cent, or you get to be in pieces in my suitcase, and she gets all of it."

"Finn, please, just a third," said my mother.

"Who the fuck is talking to you, bitch?" said Romero.

"A few people have tried to kill me this week," I told him. "It didn't really work out that way."

"Please, Finn, don't do this," said my mother.

"I'm not going to shop you," I told her. "Even if I tried, I couldn't prove anything. I'm just going to let you walk away, because that's what Dad was going to do."

"No deal," said Romero.

"Step away from the door," I said.

He chuckled. "You think you're tough, all those muscles and shit?" said Romero. "You know what we call guys like you in prison? Dessert."

And he launched himself at me.

He was fast, hard and wiry, and we both went flying. I landed on the TV and felt it slide off its wooden stand onto the floor, the hard edge of the unit cutting into my back. Romero's right hand was round my throat clutching my windpipe while he punched me hard in the face with his left and I felt the skin of my cheekbone split under his knuckles. As I tumbled off the TV unit and onto the floor he lost his grip, scrambled to his feet and aimed a kick to my belly, but I grabbed the leg he stood on as I rose, throwing him off balance, forcing him to hop backward, arms flailing, till he collided with the door jamb of the bedroom, bursting the concertina door out of its rickety frame and making the whole flimsy wall creak and groan.

All the while my mother was shrieking, but whether she was actually saying anything I couldn't tell, because the guy next door had turned up the music to drown out the screaming and the racket of two men trying to kill each other. I pinned Romero to the door jamb with my left forearm while I pounded his belly with my right, trying to drive right through to his backbone, feeling the muscle there tense and give under my fist as he clawed at my wrist, his eyes bulging. Then his right hand snaked out and I saw too late the glint of the empty Jack Daniel's bottle as he swung it.

The first blow bounced off my head and I pushed harder with my forearm against his windpipe, but on the second swing the bottle smashed, and through the pain I felt shards of bourbon-scented glass scattering down my hair and shoulders. I had to loose my hold and grab instead at his right arm that clutched the broken stub. While he twisted and turned his right to break my hold he pounded my gut again and again on the same spot with his left fist. I've never been kicked by a mule but I'm pretty sure the sensation came close, and I twisted my torso to avoid his blows before he ruptured something, held his right wrist with my left hand and hit him as hard as I could in the face with my right elbow. I felt one of those lovely white teeth go loose, and I swear he grinned, like he was getting off on the pain, and I hit him again, and we staggered back, and suddenly my mother was crying out, trapped between him and the folding table. The whole rickety heap of fibreboard and cheap chrome struts was bending and buckling, and I realized I was pushing the broken bottle in his fist towards her eyes.

My instant of hesitation was all Romero needed. I felt my legs tangle in his and a hard shove brought me slamming down hard on the floor, driving most of the wind from my body. He was on me faster than a rat and his right hand pulled back to drive the broken shard into my throat, when suddenly his head jolted forward and downward, and my mother raised her arms again, and I pushed my right hand into Romero's face and held his head up steady while she brought the full bottle of bourbon down for a second time, with all her force, onto the back of his skull.

This time the bottle shattered, soaking us both in booze, and Romero's stab flailed and went wild, nicking my left ear. I grabbed his arm, wrenched it round and squirmed from under him till I was on his back. The raw bourbon was burning my eyes and a fragment of broken glass bit into my knee, but I pressed his face harder into the sodden purple carpet glinting with shards, reached out to where the TV lay screen-down on the floor, grabbed the flex where it entered the set, and wrenched it out. Yanking Romero's other arm back I lashed both his wrists together while he grunted and cursed and spat through his clenched and bloody teeth, and my mother sank onto the sofa with her hands over her mouth, saying over and over, "Please don't hurt him, please don't hurt him."

I didn't know which of us she was talking to, and I didn't ask.

seventeen

"Nicola Hale."

"Ms. Hale, it's Finn Maguire."

"Finn, good morning. I've been trying to reach you. We have a financial adviser we think you should meet."

"That's great, but right now I need a criminal lawyer, and I was wondering if you could recommend one."

"I trained in criminal law. What's happened?"

"I'm being questioned at Shepherd's Bush police station."

"Fine. Say nothing until I get there. Forty-five minutes, OK?"

I wasn't actually the one who was in trouble. Since it was me who had phoned the cops, they'd heard my side of the story first, and that's usually the one cops go with. Romero didn't help his case by calling everyone in sight a dumb British motherfucker. For a guy who'd done prison time this showed poor judgement, because thanks to me he already had plenty of cuts and bruises before the cops took him in, which meant that in the half-hour before the duty doctor turned up at the nick they could give him plenty more without getting into trouble. When the doctor eventually did appear they sent me to the surgery to be patched up first, allowing themselves extra playtime with Romero.

The fresh stitches in my cheek and scalp were just starting to throb when Nicola Hale was shown into my interrogation room. I started with that morning's events and worked backwards, leaving out everything about McGovern and James Gravett. They'd had nothing to do with my dad's death, and I didn't want Hale thinking she might have to spend the rest of her career bailing me out of police stations. She had got the gist of the story when there was a gentle knock on the door.

The man who entered was a big scruffy Glaswegian with unruly fair hair who introduced himself as DI Jones. He seemed cheerful and relaxed as he took a seat in the regulation-issue office chair on the other side of the desk, while a uniformed policewoman took a seat in the corner.

"We've checked out your story, Mr. Maguire," said Jones. "And I spoke to my colleague DS Amobi, from your local nick. He didn't exactly vouch for your sterling character, but he thinks you're one of the good guys."

"He doesn't know me that well," I said.

"I'm inclined to give you the benefit of the doubt myself," said Jones. "I just got off the phone to the FBI. Your friend—I mean, your mother's friend—Romero is wanted on a fresh charge of murder in the States. After he got out of prison he made a load of money from those paintings of his, but blew most of it on gambling and crack. Seems he fell out with his agent over his commission, stabbed him through the eye with a paintbrush and did a runner."

"How did Romero get into the UK?" asked Hale.

"We're looking into that," said Jones. "But it seems he should never have been freed in the first place. The FBI can't prove anything, but they think he used the money from the sale of his first painting to buy himself an alibi. He paid another criminal to confess to the crime he was jailed for. That's how he got off Death Row."

"He hired a man to kill my father too," I said.

"So I understand," said Jones. "Your mother has indicated she's willing to make a full statement."

"No," I said. "It wasn't her fault. She was being coerced by Romero. That's why Ms. Hale's here—I want her to represent my mother."

Jones frowned. "Your mother already has legal representation," he said.

"Not one of those useless duty hacks," I said. "Someone who knows what they're doing. I'll pay."

"Sorry, Mr. Maguire—" Jones looked genuinely confused. "The solicitor you hired is already here. They're in conference now."

"I haven't hired anyone," I said.

As we sat looking at each other, a bell rang outside in the corridor, and went on ringing. Moments later we heard running feet and shouting. Jones registered the racket at the same time as I did, and in a moment he was out of his chair, through the door and running down the corridor, with me right on his heels. At the far end of the passageway was another interview room, and a uniform cop with scarlet hands burst out of the doorway, shouting for the medic.

Beyond Jones, in the interview room, stood Elsa Kendrick, cornered by two officers in stab vests. In her fist she held a long, gleaming butcher's knife running with blood. Her face and her arms were splashed with it, and she was smiling like she was in a blissful dream. When one of the officers reached out she offered him the knife as if he was going to cut her a slice of cake.

Kendrick's big leather satchel lay open on the interview table, and the chair beyond it was lying on its side on the floor, and beside it lay my mother, twitching in a massive pool of blood that was slowly spreading, fed by the deep gashes in her face and her hands and her throat.

I heard the suck of my shoes in her blood as I knelt beside her, and felt its warm sticky wetness on my hands as I took her in my arms and hugged her and lifted her head. The fear and confusion on her face seemed to vanish when she looked at me. She raised her delicate hand to touch my face, and two of its fingers were missing, but she caressed my cheek, and there was no pain in her eyes, just an infinite sadness.

"Finn," she mouthed, and blood spilled down her chin. Her lips went on moving, but she had no breath left.

"Please, Mum, don't talk, don't say anything," I said. "Just hang on. Please don't leave me. Please, Mum. Please."

She smiled at me, and coughed, and her hand fell from my cheek, and her eyes were empty.

eighteen

There were two grey funeral urns on my mantelpiece now, and they bugged me. I had tried standing them at opposite ends, but it looked like my mum and dad were ignoring each other, and when I stood them together they looked like targets in a coconut shy. I didn't know why I was displaying them anyway—they weren't pretty, and they weren't exactly conversation pieces. On the other hand I couldn't just stick them in the attic. I was going to have the house redecorated, and it did occur to me to have them painted white, like the walls, so they would be there, but invisible. And then I could grow old and die here and be placed in a white pot between them, and we'd be a family again, until someone bought the house and threw us all into a skip.

It was an early Sunday morning in late May. The sun

was shining and innocent fluffy clouds were tumbling slowly across the bright blue London sky when I slipped both urns into a backpack, stepped out of the house and pulled the door shut behind me. I was getting ready to run when I noticed her coming down the street towards me, in a short skirt that would have flaunted her thighs if they weren't clad in black leggings. Her hands were fisted in the pockets of her denim jacket and her head was bowed.

When Zoe heard my door close she looked up, and paused, and I could see she'd been trying to think of what she might say to me, and hadn't come up with anything, and now it was too late.

"Hey," she said instead.

"Hey," I said. I hoiked my bag up my shoulder and strode past her.

"Can I walk with you?" she called after me.

"It's a free country," I said. "Mostly." I couldn't start running now. I didn't want her thinking I was afraid of her or trying to avoid her. I didn't particularly want to talk to her, but then I couldn't stop her talking to me.

"How have you been?" she said.

I shrugged.

"I heard about your mum," she said. "I'm sorry."

"What did you hear?" I said.

"That she was the woman killed in a police station by some loony with a machete," said Zoe.

"It was a butcher's knife," I said.

"If I'd known about the funeral I would have come, but I didn't know about it, so I . . ." She sighed, aware she'd started blethering. I was glad. Maybe if she got bored or embarrassed enough she'd go away and I wouldn't have to tell her to piss off. "That's if you'd wanted me to come," she added.

"It's a free country. Mostly," I said, and cursed inwardly. Now she had me repeating myself. I walked a bit faster but she didn't even seem to notice, tailing after me like a bad smell.

"I know how you feel, Finn," she said. I snorted at that, but she ignored me. "There were hundreds of people at my dad's funeral, most of them cops, and they all wanted to shake my hand and tell me what a wonderful man my dad was and how proud I must be."

"No one came to my mother's funeral, except me," I said. "Stop pretending you know how I feel."

"I'm sorry," Zoe said.

"Yeah. You said."

"I wished no one had come to my dad's funeral, if they were all going to spout bullshit," said Zoe. "He didn't die a hero in a shoot-out with some child-trafficker after an anonymous tip-off."

"How do you know?" I said.

"I just do," she said.

"Who have you been talking to?"

"Sergeant Amobi."

I stopped and turned. "And what did Amobi tell you exactly?"

"He said I should talk to you."

"Sounds like he was trying to get rid of you," I said.

I walked on down towards the main road that runs alongside the river, and paused at the junction outside Max Snax. It had just opened for breakfast and I noticed the spherical customer was back again, squeezed into the corner table filling his face with a triple-decker, while my replacement at the counter picked at a zit on his chin. As I waited on the kerb for a lorry to pass Zoe re-appeared at my elbow. She didn't look like she was going to give up any time soon.

I ignored her, crossing the road and turning right, and she followed, though I could tell she was wondering if I was actually heading somewhere or just trying to shake her off. In fact it was both. She slowed and stopped, and I thought she'd given up at last, until she called after me.

"You were there when my dad was killed, weren't you?"

That halted me in my tracks. I'd just stepped off the main road into the new waterside park from · where a shiny glass and steel footbridge arched over to an island in the river. The council had only just finished laying the park turf, but it was already dotted with petals from the cherry saplings, and the breeze off the water sent more drifting around me like shining snowflakes.

Zoe caught up with me. "Dad was working for McGovern, wasn't he?" she said. "They'd been blackmailing him with that video, and once that got out he was no use to them any more, so they killed him."

"I've no idea," I said. "I wasn't there." Her face fell. "But I'll tell you what I think happened," I said. "I think your dad was ashamed of himself, and what he'd done. I think he went there to kill McGovern but he wasn't fast enough."

"You think he knew about the video of me?" Her voice was harsh, as if she was trying to torture herself.

"Yeah. But your dad never told you, because then you wouldn't have been his little girl any more. I think he wanted to protect you, because he was your dad, and in his own way he loved you, in spite of everything. And that was the only way left he could show it."

She shut her eyes and shuddered in pain, but forced herself to go on. "Why didn't you tell the cops all that? Are you scared of the Guvnor?"

"Not particularly," I said.

"Scared of what he might do to you, or to someone you care about?" She'd opened her eyes now and was looking straight at me, but I knew a leading question when I heard one.

"There's nobody left I care about," I said. I turned and walked on towards the bridge.

"Then why not tell the truth?" she called after me.

I paused on the bridge and turned again, irritated. "You're right, I am scared of the Guvnor," I said. "Now will you piss off and leave me alone?"

"Or what? That's an island you're heading to, Finn. What are you going to do, swim for it?"

"If I have to," I said.

She came close and looked at me under her lashes. I wasn't going to fall for that again.

"I think I know why," she said. "If you had told the cops all that, it would all have come out, about my dad, and me, and the video. And the tabloids and the bloggers and the Internet would have gone mad, and that footage would have been everywhere, and the whole world would have seen me doing those things, and known it was me, and I'd never ever have been allowed to forget it."

"Just think," I said. "You could have had your own reality TV series." She actually laughed. "Look, don't kid yourself," I said. "It's probably all over the Net already."

"Yeah, but there's millions of dirty videos out there, mine's just one more, and if no one knows it's me, no one's going to care. That's why you kept it quiet. To protect me."

"If that's what you want to believe, go ahead," I said. "Now I was kind of hoping for some privacy, so will you get lost?"

The island had been derelict and overgrown until last year, when the footbridge had been built. Since then its old boatyard had been tidied up and its sheds repainted, the wild butterfly bushes hacked back, and wooden benches—as yet uncarved with any declarations of love for a football team—planted facing south and east along the river. At low tide the benches overlooked a pungent greeny-black expanse of Thames mud strewn with flotsam, but at high tide, like now, they looked out over silvery grey water that lapped and swirled eastwards to the City, under London's bridges and out to the sea.

The early-morning mist was still rising off the river like a cloud, fading into the blue sky, as I slipped the bag from my shoulder at the water's edge and took out the two urns. I hadn't figured out in advance how to take the lids off, but they were only thin metal, and a coin worked under one rim lifted enough of the tin for me to get a hold on the lip and bend the lid back in half. I did the same with the other, and stood there for a while, wondering if I should say a few words, or if there were any words to say.

For a few years, when I was little, my mother and father had been happy together. I knew that because I had lived with them, and there were a thousand moments that now only I remembered—the three of us together in Spain, here in the local playground, in their bed where they used to pin me between them and kiss me, chanting, "Finny sandwich!" That's how I wanted to remember them, and that's how I wanted them to be—together always, back where they'd first found each other, back when they'd loved each other. The song my dad used to sing to my mother echoed in my head, and I thought if I tried that as I poured their ashes, maybe they wouldn't mind that I couldn't sing a note. Maybe if I hummed it. Just the last verse.

Creeping fog is on the river, flow sweet river flow
Sun and moon and stars gone with her, sweet Thames
*   flow softly*
Swift the Thames runs to the sea, flow sweet river flow
Bearing ships and part of me, sweet Thames flow
*   softly . . .*

I tipped the urns upside down and the dust poured out, caught and mingled in the breeze, blew east and spread out across the water, mingled and swirled and sank into the dark depths, swept away downriver.

I didn't make it to the end of the verse. All the numbness I'd felt after I'd found Dad murdered, the numbness I'd clenched onto so hard when my mother died in my arms—in that moment, all of it crumbled and was swept away, dissolving like dust on the river, and I couldn't breathe. I wept, not caring if I was feeling sorry for them or sorry for myself or sorry for this whole mess I'd helped to make; but now Zoe was beside me, wrapping her arms around my neck and pulling me close, and I let her hold me until I could breathe again.

"I asked you to leave me alone," I said.

"You're welcome," she said.

"We're not getting back together," I said.

"I know that," she said. We stood there a minute.

"Have you had any breakfast?" she said.

"Give me a second," I said. I hated people dumping stuff in the river, but right at that moment it felt kind of traditional. I took each urn in turn and hurled it out into the deepest water I could reach.

"All done," I said to Zoe. "Let's go."

Acknowledgements

My heartfelt thanks to my agent Val Hoskins
for her infinite patience and faith;

To my sons, brothers, sisters and friends for indulging
my endless grumbles about the screenwriting trade;

To my parents for showing me how to work hard,
love and be happy;

And above all to my beloved wife Erika for her
boundless love, loyalty, humour,
encouragement and inspiration.